WHAT'S BEST FOR YOU

A MAINE OCTOBER WINSTON Joint

CEDRIC QUINCY

Also by Cedric Quincy

Faith Fiction
King of Kings (w/Isaiah David Paul)
Ain't Worried About Nothin' (w/Isaiah David Paul)
Style & Grayce (w/Isaiah David Paul)

The Misunderstanding of Don Ho
Blackberry Molasses
Free Your Mind
Where I Wanna Be

Rockstarz
Where The Playas Dwell

Urban Erotic Thrillers
KING (w/Donte Sweat)
Definition of a Bad Girl (under the name Mi'Chaune)

Hope Passion Love Soap Operas
Hope Passion Love

I also write the following:
Jarold Imes - Young Adult Fiction & Nonfiction
Isaiah David Paul - Faith Fiction
Donte Sweat - Erotic Suspense & Soap Operas
Jaz Punchard - Miscellaneous Genres

WHAT'S
BEST
FOR YOU

A MAINE OCTOBER WINSTON Joint

CEDRIC QUINCY

10's Lee Phelps

www.writesingwork.com

a literary entertainment company

Winston-Salem ■ Atlanta ■ Denver

10'sLee Phelps titles are published by

Write Sing Work, Inc., 4182 Clemmons Road #125, Clemmons , North Carolina 27012

Book Credits
Cover Designer: Jarold Imes

Model: Tripp Ali

Photographer: Trever Green

Characters Co-Created by Jaxon Grant, Tyson Anthony & Carter J. Banks

Editors: Tyson Anthony & JD Morrison

This book initially appeared on BGCLive the Cedric Quincy Facebook Page as Touch Me, Tease Me from September 30, 2016 - November 30, 2016
First Published by Tinsley Phelps, LLC June 2018 2021
First Write Sing Work Trade Paperback Printing March 2021

10 9 8 7 6 5 4 3 2 1

ISBN 13: 978-934195-49-9 / ISBN 10: 1-934195-49-9 (Print)

ISBN 13: 978-1-934195-18-5 / ISBN 10: 1-934195-18-9 (eBook)

Publishers Note:

A lot of changes has taken place since the original publication of this book. Write Sing Work, Incorporated has acquired the assets of Tinsley Phelps, LLC. We are also taking steps to diversify the literary catalog and introduce you to new genres while continuing our output from your favorite authors.

We are proud to present *What's Best For You* by Cedric Quincy as our debut Tinsley Phelps/Write Sing Work title. Originally published on BGCLive & Cedric Quincy Facebook page as *Touch Me, Tease Me,* we are bringing a highly coveted fan fiction piece to life. We know you enjoyed this story just as much as you enjoyed the novel it was inspired by. All of our appropriate sample clearances are as follows:

There is no Chapter 39—that was intentional.

This page was intentionally left blank.

1

Find Your Own Way

Maine's head turned quickly after he heard the girl in his bed roll off on the floor.

"What the fuck was that?" Chelle rolled her eyes and crossed her arms as she stood next to Maine.

"Cordell's annoying little brother acting like a pest," Maine grunted as he made his way to help Yonna off the floor, "you okay babe?"

Maine's concern for Yonna was genuine, and so was his attraction as his stiffness found a few inches of freedom out of slit of his boxers. Yonna grabbed his hand and used Maine to pick herself off the floor. She shook her head and looked up at the man that easily had a foot over her five foot three frame. "Did a gun go off?" Her words slurred and as she spoke, Maine could smell the ruminants of rum and Coke on her breath.

"Naw, Maine slammed the door in Corey's face when he asked for a ride back to campus." Chelle scolded as she found her way to the edge of the bed. "That was kind of fucked up, Maine."

"He shouldn't have followed us up here," Maine kept up his façade. Truth is, Maine was plotting on a way to get Cordell out of the house long enough so he could bring Corey to his room. He still had "tap that ass" on his bucket list and knowing Corey hadn't been topped made the conquest that much more appealing.

"You should go take him back to his dorm real quick," Yonna suggested as she stumbled back on the bed. "Give us time to freshen up. Maybe go another round."

Maine liked the sound of that. Last night was spectacular with Yonna riding him every way but sideways and Chelle's ass bouncing back against his washboard abs as her head buried between Yonna's legs. He quickly scanned the open drawer of his night stand. Counted four Magnum condoms, four strawberry-flavored condoms and half a bottle of Wet.

He scanned the floor until he found his cargo-styled, black and white fatigue shorts. Chelle was sitting on his black fishnet shirt. "You sitting on my shirt, Ma."

Chelle lifted her legs, pulled Maine's shirt from under her ass and tossed it at him. Maine caught it the air and put it on quickly. He rushed into his shorts, slipped into his Sketchers and ran out the door. He could hear the bed knocking against the wall coming from Cordell's room, so he knew his friend was occupied. In the living room, he could see one of Cordell's friends sliding in and out of some chick on his couch.

Damn he gotta phatty, Maine took a moment to indulge in the solid movement of ol'boy's heart-shaped ass. The girl's leg was shaking on top of his waist and he smiled at the free freak show. Maine caught the keys hanging on the key hook next to the door and he steadfastly made his way out to avoid interrupting their session. He stepped over three more bodies before grabbing the keys and opening the door.

The fresh air hit him and so did the sun. He made his way to the old, off-white 1989 Buick Regal he and Cordell shared to get around town. How the car made it around Greensboro and back and forth to the A was beyond him. He glanced at the backseat, remembering the action he got at the car wash last week by some DL brother who wanted to suck and ride his dick.

Best. Nut. Ever.

After the car cranked up, he left the apartment complex and headed down Yanceyville Road to make his way to NC Tech. He was at least five miles from the school and he was sure he'd catch up to Corey. "Touch Me, Tease Me" by Case, Foxy Brown and Mary J. Blige bumped through his radio. Maine was reminded of the way Corey's nut tasted in his mouth, and how his dome skills got better over the summer. He adjusted himself in his shorts and got confused at how a brown skinned boy in light blue overalls and a bubble butt could elude him so fast. Then he remembered there were multiple ways to get to NC Tech from his apartment complex.

He pulled over into the Mrs. Winner's Chicken & Biscuits about three blocks away. He reached into his pocket to pull out his Cingular cellphone. He dialed Corey's number and got his voicemail, twice.

I bet that nigga phone dead, he thought to himself. He started to enter the drive-thru, but realized he didn't have enough money to feed the rest of the folks at his apartment, let alone the two girls waiting in his room. As "Same Ol' G" by Ginuwine eased out of the speakers, he turned it up to hear the Timbaland bass knock. Maine sang to himself. Low key, he could sing, but he always played with it. He never took it serious.

"Yo Tremaine!" He heard and saw Elgin wave him down. Maine smiled. He always thought the political science and accounting double major was sexy as shit. Elgin had crazy zig-zag cornrows that Yonna twisted every ten days in the makeshift beauty salon in her dorm on campus. His smooth face was a nice toffee color. And his five foot nine wide receiver-shaped frame made haste to the passenger side of his ride. "Oh my bad, Maine."3

Maine turned the music down. "Sup man," he greeted as Elgin opened the door. He ignored the fact that Elgin put his government out there. He knew the man wanted a ride back to the apartment complex.

"Thank you," Elgin exhaled as he caught his breath. He put on the seatbelt and reclined in the seat.

"No problem," Maine turned the car around and headed back to the apartment. "I was on my way back. I got some company in my room."

"Your party still going down?" Elgin got excited. "Got any drink left over?"

Next to Cordell, Maine didn't mind sharing food, drinks or other things with Elgin. The man he was giving a ride to helped keep gas in the car and paid for oil changes. That was a fair exchange for someone who barely drove the car. "I hope so."

Getting rid of Elgin was going to be Maine's new problem. He didn't know if ol'boy was finish waxing that ass on the couch yet or if Cordell was through with the girl in his room. And he didn't want to share Chelle and Yonna with him.

As they got in front of his apartment, he could see Cordell's friend and the girl he was smashing on the couch making an exit. He parked the car and waited until Elgin got out of the car to lock up.

"Aye man, who all still in the living room?" Maine asked as he made his way to the front door.

"Cordell got some freak in his room knocking on the walls, screaming and shit," ol'boy volunteered. "Some girl still laying on the sofa. And I think there's someone taking a shower."

Maine smiled. "Cool."

"Aight man, I'll catch you at the next party," the man gave him dap. As he reached to give the man a hug, he saw his girl licking her lips at him. Maine winked at her.

"Yeah man, next party." Maine replied and walked past them. He turned around and stole a look at the girl's ass.

"That girl was looking at you man," Elgin's tone was so low, you could barely hear him.

"I know man," Maine smiled.

"I'd stay away from her if I were you. 'Keem is certifiable and he do more than football and dabble in mixed martial arts." Elgin warned.

"Duly noted," Maine filed the warning in the back of his brain and zoomed in on Chelle making her way back to his room with a light pink towel barley covering her body. "Let me check on her and make sure she alright." He silently thanked Chelle and God for an escape from Elgin.

Maine headed to his room. Cordell and his guest were still rocking and knocking in his room. In a few seconds, he planned on joining Chelle and Yonna to make some music of his own. He didn't care what Elgin did, as long as he didn't burn the apartment down and blow chunks all over the place.

As Maine turned the doorknob, he found it locked. *What the—,* Maine turned the knob again and still couldn't unlock the door. He reached above the door frame for the spare key for emergencies like this and found the key gone. He went to Cordell's room where bodies were smacking to a steady rhythm.

His key was gone too. And so was the one above the frame to the bathroom door.

"Yo, open up the door!" Maine demanded as he grew pissed. He put his ear to the door and could hear Chelle and Yonna laughing and giggling on the other side. "Shit ain't funny Chelle, open the damn door."

His banging wasn't no use. Cordell was occupied and he had no intention of breaking the door and forfeiting the security deposit. He hadn't started work yet and had no way of paying for a door to his room.

"Fuckin' aye." Maine vented as he kicked the door one last time.

He reluctantly sat on his recently worn out couch and slouched as he stared at his door.

"I think you need this more than me," Elgin handed him a red cup. He didn't care what it was, he took a sip and the scent of alcohol and the fruity mix hit his nose and lips at the same time. Having a drink wasn't the same thing as getting some ass, but one thing was for certain, Maine regretted not taking Corey back to campus. He took another sip and kicked back and waited for Chelle and Yonna to come out.

2

Willie's

"Aye man get up!" Cordell commanded as he shoved Maine's feet off the arm of the couch.

Maine's eyes popped open fast. He sat up and looked around. The guest from the party were gone. The living room smelled like lavender-scented ammonia and Febreeze. Cordell, or somebody had run the vacuum cleaner. There wasn't an empty red cup on the sofa, the coffee table or the counter.

"What time is it?" Maine lifted his arm to view the time on his silver-banded watch. "Damn, it's one o'clock."

"I know, been trying to wake your ass up for the last three hours." Cordell took a seat next to him, picked up the remote and turned on the television. "Your mama got you fucked up."

And there it was—the nightmares. The rank and horrid smell of bleach invaded his nostrils. It took a minute for Maine's vision to settle. He'd avoided the doctor at all cost but his eyelids were bothering him from time to time since she last tried to wash the gay off of him a week ago. Maine never told Cordell or anyone else that his vision was a little blurry. He'd hoped that over time that it would get better and so far, it has.

"How you say that?" Maine was in complete denial. He'd learn from Cordell to keep certain feelings about his mother bottled up.

"He ain't gonna make it!" Cordell imitated him. "Damn near scared Yonna and Chelle."

"How you get them out of my room?" Maine remembered the reason he was on the couch. The girls had promised him another round and failed to deliver.

"Felicia couldn't stop screaming my name. *Cordell! Oh god! Oh shit!* All she did was scream and yell." Cordell bragged as he switched the channel to ESPN. "Chelle banging on my door like, 'y'all too loud.' When I got out of the room, I had to set her ass right and remind her that this was my castle and I paid half the rent. Speaking of, you got an hour to get to Willie's."

Maine looked at the time again. "Oh shit."

While thanking God that the record store was only fifteen minutes, he knew he had to move fast if he was gonna get to work on time. Cordell was lucky. He got to transfer his part time job to one of the locations in Durham when he wasn't in school. Maine had the summer off, but had to show his face the weekend before classes started.

Maine quickly headed to his room and was pleased to see the door was opened. He shook his head at the well-made bed and dove into his dresser. He grabbed a pair of orange and green boxers and a matching pair of ankle socks. A beeline to the closet led him to pull out a dated orange and green FUBU shirt and some green Cross Color jeans with bright orange threads outlining the fabric. He snatched his clear shower caddy and headed to the bathroom.

In seven minutes, Maine was in and out of the shower, zestfully cleaned, dressed and doused with Ralph Lauren cologne and stepping into his Air Force Ones. Moments like this, he was glad he didn't have to wear a uniform or come home smelling like burgers and fries. He poured a dime-sized portion of Dudley's PCA over his smooth, low-cut fade and headed out of the door.

Willie's was in the Summit Shopping Center not too far from campus. A few doors down was a Foot Locker and a black-owned clothing store that had the latest in hip hop fashions. He could smell the Mrs. Winner's a block away. He'd stop there on his lunch break since he was closing the store today.

"Always punctual," Willie greeted him from the register.

"Good afternoon Old Man," Maine nodded his head and looked at his watch. He was five minutes early, which meant he could breathed for a minute before he clocked in.

"I see you're not wearing your rope," Willie pointed out.

Maine wasn't going to admit that he left it at home. He quickly scanned the store and saw the promos for Mary J. Blige and DMX's store appearance prior to their performance for NC TECH's back-to-school concert. The store was gonna be packed and he couldn't wait for the bonus that would come from helping to organize and promote the appearance. Unbeknownst to Cordell and Corey, he'd been working on his marketing plan all summer. He also done a little studying and research so he could add some current events to marketing studies.

"And if it isn't Mr. Def Jam!" Willie bellowed as he stepped down from the elevated platform and gave the shorter, stocky, five foot seven boy wonder a hug. The young man looked like Willie was gonna squeeze the life out of him.

"Good afternoon Mr. Willie." The young man edged out.

"I told you boys to call me Willie." Willie insisted. "I pay y'all to make the customers comfortable enough to buy some records and come back again."

"That's true." The man answered. "Sup Maine."

"Hey Spence," Maine played it low key and for good reason.

Academically, Spence Rowling was his biggest rival at NC TECH. They both were marketing majors and Chancellor's Scholars. Maine beat him out for president of the school's American Marketing Association chapter; Spence got the coveted internship at Def Jam. They both had their eyes on the vacant assistant store manager spot one of the graduating seniors left behind to become the financial manager for Lil Wayne.

Their competition kept it steamy in the bedroom. Maine first found out Spence's little secret after homecoming. He went to a house party one of the fraternities on campus was sponsoring. Too much green juice led to a trip to the bathroom where he found Spence smoking an upperclassmen's pipe while stroking his Johnson on the toilet. Refusing to piss in his pants, Maine relieved himself in the sink and after he shook off the rest of his drip drop, the upperclassmen leaned down and lip locked with his cock. Even with Spence having someone else's nine and a half inches of pleasure down his throat, he kept his eyes fixated on him. Later that night, he found out the short man could be his equal in a sixty-nine and threw that ass back better than a big booty Judy in a rump shaking contest.

"Before I leave," Willie brought his attention out of the gutter and back on music and money, "I'm looking at you boys to be the leaders of the crew this semester. I want to have more artists in here and I expect that you did what I told you to do when you got to New York."

"Yes sir, I hooked up with an upcoming neosoul artist they are getting ready to launch in the spring. I even got to hang with him in Philadelphia. I also got to join some studio sessions with Dru Hill. Lord willing, I'll have song on Sisqo's upcoming album." Spence revealed.

Maine did his best to hide his jealousy. The last thing he wanted to hear on his first day of work, was Spence's exploits in the music industry and him hob knobbing with the celebrities. He could picture Spence popping bottles and getting that round bubble butt bounced on a regular.

"Well, I'm proud of both of you. I'm leaving so I expect to hear good things tomorrow after church. Next week, we'll have new guys working and I need for both of you to be on point." Willie instructed as he grabbed his things and headed out. "There's two hundred and fifty dollars in the register. If a dime of my money comes up missing, I'm fucking both of y'all up."

"Yes sir," they answered in unison as he shook each of their hands and headed out. Maine watched the good-hearted pot-bellied man make his way to his pearl-colored 1989 Mercury Cougar.

"I missed you man," Spence tried to hug Maine from behind. Maine quickly stepped to the side and faced him.

"Fuck you fratboy," Maine headed to the register and typed in his passcode.

"When?" Spence licked his lips. "I been thinking about that dick all summer long. I haven't had none since you almost made me late for my flight to New York."

Maine remembered that night. He'd gotten a hotel room so he wouldn't have to go back to Atlanta right away. Him and Cordell were unsuccessful at getting Spence and Elgin to agree to room with them—which meant carrying on a higher cost for a two-bedroom apartment versus renting a spacious four-bedroom house near campus more affordably. He understood Elgin's situation because the man helped take care of his young siblings and had to share his campus housing with his cousin. Spence had the means and the ability to do so and was just selfish.

"Not here," Maine finally answered and licked his lips.

"You get on my fucking nerves, always teasing me." Spence vented as he went to the back.

By now Maine was used to this routine. Spence would hit him up for a quickie. If he was down, things were good but if Maine wasn't in the mood or had made plans to be with a female, Spence turned into a little bitch. He'd be mad for a few hours and either they'd go a few days without speaking or Maine would feel some level of guilt and given in to Spence's desire and see that ass work against his abs.

Seeing Spence storm off and move that ass made his dick hard. He looked out the window to see the lot was full and figured most of the customers were either getting shoes or clothes. They weren't buying music. He walked out of the door and didn't see any customers on the sidewalk.

Looking ahead, he saw Spence moving around in the back. Maine felt the weight of his dick getting heavy. One more glance at the door and Maine was booking it to the back of the store. He unzipped the fly on his jeans and loosened his belt.

He was going to give Spence something to cry about.

3

Back It Up

Maine grabbed Spence's arm and forced him to face him.

"I can't believe you don't have no clothes on," Spence was shocked as he watched Maine's heavy, thick dick swing from left to right.

Maine didn't respond. Instead he grabbed Spence's hand and wrapped it around his member. He looked to the front of the store and verified that it was still empty.

"This is a big ass dick." Spence marveled at the size as he unbuttoned his pants and let them fall to the floor. He stroked it slowly as he stepped out of his pants and pushed them to the side. Spence started to go down but Maine shook his head no. "You not gonna let me suck it?"

"Just watch the door." Maine commanded as he found a seat near the back of the storage room. Maine took a seat and reach out and cupped Spence's ass in the palm of his hands. In a quick motion, he surprised Spence by putting his dick in his mouth. Maine swallowed him whole; Spence's nuts relaxed on Maine's chin and his Irish Spring-scented pubic hairs tickled the underside of his noise.

"Oh shit," Spence whispered while turning around.

Maine greedily attacked Spence's dick with vigor. Slurping on it like a big straw. Almost as if he were enjoying a cup of lychee-flavored bubble tea. The head of Spence's burgeoning member punched his tonsils just right. Maine closed his eyes as he continued to feast on the meal Spence was provided.

"Damn, I've—" Spence stuttered. "I've—" Maine moved his head all the way back to the tip of the dick. Spence's head was the size of an old fashion lollipop. His shaft was a thick and as long as a king-size Snicker's bar. It wasn't as big as his but what Maine liked about it was that when Spence rode him, it jumped up and down and Spence could aim and spit with it without touching himself. "Had my dick sucked like this before."

While Maine continue spinning his head and twirling his tongue up and down the length of Spence's shaft, his finger sneakily made their way into Spence's crevice. The tip of his middle finger slowly went in a circle and deeper past the boarder of Spence's sphincter. Maine liked sucking dick, but it was all a rouse to get to the ultimate prize—tagging that ass.

"Damn, fuck!" Spence rocked. His breathing labored and he struggled to keep his eyes open. "Oh fuck," he whispered as he put his hand on Maine's head. Spence squeezed his cheeks but relaxed his muscles, allowing Maine to slip another finger in. Maine knew were Spence's spot was and in no time, he rubbed Spence's prostate with the same rhythm he sucked Spence's dick with. "You're gonna make me—"

Spence struggled to get his warning out and Maine continued handling his business. In no time, Maine got what he was working for as Spence's cum hit the back of his throat. Maine continued to suck and swallow and finger-fuck Spence into oblivion.

"Hmm—umm-umm-umm," Spence grunted low as he continued releasing himself between Maine's lips. When he opened his eyes, he remembered they were in the back of the store. "Oh shit." He panicked as he stumbled away. Spence searched for his pants until he found them near the wall. "You not gonna get dressed."

Maine spewed some of Spence's cum and his spit into his hand and reclined further in the chair while he stroked his member with his right and played with his left nipple.

Spence got himself together and the bell to the store rang. He quickly tucked his shirt in. He stole a glance at Maine, who acted like he didn't have a care in the world.

Maine slowed down his strokes. He opened his eyes and wondered how often Willie and some of his co-workers got down in the storage room. It was a nice little space and big enough to host a small party. The boxes were filled with CD's, records and cassettes and were sturdy enough for Spence to hold onto while

Maine hit it from the back. With a little effort, he could turn them into a makeshift bed for him to twist a female out on.

"Damn man you still stroking?" Spence asked as he made his way back to the storage room.

"What does it look like?" Maine got smart as he didn't miss a beat while answering Spence's question.

He watched as Spence took his pants back off and then reach into his back pocket for a Magnum. He tore the package open with his teeth and then put the condom into his mouth. Spence kneeled before Maine, stared into his eyes and paid homage. Then quickly, he used his mouth to roll the condom down Maine's thick dick. Once the Magnum was down low enough, Spence got up, turned around and reached back for Maine's dick and lined it up to where he knew he would make a perfect landing. "Hurry up and come in me. We got a customer in the store."

Spence worked himself down Maine's length and squeezed his sphincter muscle tight. He moved forward so Maine could enjoy the view of his firm, muscular ass working at a steady pace to suck Maine off. He lifted his shirt because he knew Maine liked the way his back muscles moved when Maine was hitting his spot.

"I'm ready to make my purchase!" the customer yelled out.

"I'll be out in a minute." Spence promised as he rode Maine's dick faster.

"Shit," Maine bucked faster, knowing that the inevitable was coming. His hands raced up the length of Spence's abs and chest and punched both of his nipples. "Ummphf," Maine whimpered as he bit his bottom lip. His thick dick pulsated and expanded has he picked up the speed and pumped his load steadily into Spence. When he was done, he fell back in the chair and Spence quickly got up and put his pants back on. In less than thirty seconds, Spence was back in the front ringing up the customer's order. Maine carefully unpeeled the soiled condom from his dick. He got up and walked to the bathroom and flushed the condom down the toilet, grabbed a paper towel and dampened it. He squeezed the hand soap into the paper towel and quickly scrubbed his dick and his ball and made a trip to wash his ass. He grabbed a clean paper towel to dry off and put the wet paper towel inside the clean one, balled it up and threw it into the trash can.

Maine left the bathroom and quickly put his clothes on. He was happy he'd given into Spence and let out some frustration. Only thing he hated was that he didn't have any mouthwash and he'd have to see if the gum ball machine up front was working so he could have some assistance washing the after taste of Spence's salty cum from his mouth. Last thing he needed was the taste and smell Spence's dick in his mouth for the rest of the shift.

Satisfied that he didn't look like he'd gotten into something mischievous, Maine headed out to the front and his eyes locked in on 'Keem and his girl.

"Aye Maine!" the girl called out.

Maine gave her and 'Keem a head nod.

"When you having another party?" she asked as if she were in the middle of the projects yelling to someone in a building.

"Cordell and I haven't talked about it, but as soon as we get it together, we'll put out the word." Maine saw the way 'Keem eyed him. 'Keem looked at his girl then looked at Maine. "Who you working out to?" Maine redirected the conversation to 'Keem so he wouldn't be disrespectful. Truth be told, he didn't give a fuck about 'Keem, but he was on the clock and didn't want to give Spence his spot so easily.

"I got that DMX," 'Keem's raspy voice bragged. "I don't have any new choices."

"Q-Tip's album, *Amplified* sounds like it's gonna be upbeat. I'd recommend that when it comes out." Maine suggested.

"You don't have a bootlegged copy of that joint?" 'Keem asked.

"Come on man," Maine scolded. "You know we don't sale bootlegs in this joint."

"Damn, aight."

Maine saw the way 'Keem's girl looked at him. He saw Spence leaning against the register, watching everything.

"Aight man." 'Keem looked at his girl. "We gone head out. Catch a movie and chill or something. Let us know when that party happens and we'll stop by."

"Cool."

As 'Keem headed out, he noticed his girl looking back his way. She licked her lips. Maine cracked a smiled.

"Motherfucker!" Spence gritted his teeth once 'Keem and his girl were out of the store.

"What?" Maine couldn't understand Spence's attitude.

"You fuckin' her?" Spence closed the gap between the two of them.

"When I do, I'll let you know." Maine stepped closer, ready for whatever was gonna pop off with Spence.

"Fuck you man," Spence threw up his right middle finger in Maine's face.

"We already did, but if you want to go another round—"

Spence threw up his left middle finger, abruptly cutting him off.

"Fuck you too nigga," Maine responded with his own middle finger.

And there they were—back to being enemies. A part of Maine wasn't worried because he wanted to get up with Chelle and Yonna and make them make good on their threesome promise. Then, the way 'Keem's girl was looking at him, he knew it was a matter of time when the right opportunity would come along for him to swim in-between her legs. He knew for a fact 'Keem had a big dick, so Maine was confident she could hang with his too.

And if he caught up with Corey, he was gonna apologize the only way he knew how.

"I'm going on break," Spence bumped into him like he was gonna swing.

"Do that shit again nigga!" Maine warned him.

Spence threw his hands in the air, waved them fast, inviting Maine to come down from the register, and then flicked him off with both fingers again.

"I'm getting sick of your finger." Maine picked up the pace and was ready to meet Spence at the door.

Spence stepped outside and challenged Maine to follow him. As bad as he wanted to, he knew fighting Spence would fuck up some future head and his chances of becoming assistant manager. Maine exhaled, shook it off and dug into his pocket for his phone. He tried to call Corey, but he still couldn't get ol'boy on the phone.

Damn it man, he cursed to himself.

Maine knew he needed to get Corey back in the rotation. It was gonna be a while before Spence sucked his dick again and he needed to get up with Corey ASAP.

But he had to find him first.

4

About The Summer

The rest of the shift was tense. Maine and Spence played nice in front of the customers and when Willie came back to check on some things. But when the two of them were alone...

"Why you such a prick?" Spence put it out there. They were closing the store and making sure the shelves were organized. The register was straight, being the exact amount on the tape register.

"I wasn't a prick when I was drinking your nut earlier." Maine responded without looking at him. He caught Spence rolling his eyes which only added fuel to his fire. "You couldn't keep your eyes opened or your mouth closed."

Maine didn't like to brag about his head giving skills—they were decent but the last time Corey had his dick in his mouth, his best friend's younger brother taught him some things. Judging by Spence's reaction, he aced the exam.

"Look man, I'm not with this back and forth shit with you," Spence finished his work and made his way to where Maine was. "You can't keep fucking me and then acting like a little bitch when I say something you don't like."

"I'm not the one catching feelings. Matter of fact, I'm done fucking niggas. Y'all stress me out more than the bitches do." Maine straighten the last of the CD's on the rack and headed to the register to clock out.

"If I didn't know any better, I'd bet that you told someone that before," Spence followed him and clocked out. "Who is he?"

"You gonna tell me who's dick you been riding all summer?" Maine asked.

Spence looked at the front and then all around to be sure it was just him and Maine. "Let's just say I know who's love goes deeper than the other."

Maine was shocked. It didn't take him long to figure out who he was talking about. He heard the same rumor but never entertained the gossip. Let the world tell it, all the single R&B singers were gay, all the male groups had at least one gay member and it was possible that one of the rappers were living on the down low.

"I gotta guy I call Mushroom," Maine smiled. "And he and I know why."

"So did he top you?" Spence asked.

"Nah, you know I don't get down like that." Maine defended. "We just messed around. Nothing serious."

Maine neglected to tell him about the biology teacher from high school or the couple he hit it off with from time to time. And he was certain Spence had more exploits than he was willing to share.

"And I know a producer with a fat ass." Spence led the way out of the door. He pulled out his keys and locked up once Maine was outside. "Next time I get a way to New York, I'll bring you along. There's some good ass parties and you never know who you are going to bump into."

Maine and Spence had a way of kissing and making up. The idea of going to a celebrity-filled sex party and being let in on some of the world's biggest secrets enticed Maine. He'd been to a party before and he liked to watch and participate. He wore a Robin Hood mask so no one knew it was him. Plus, he was at an undisclosed location in Florida at a house owned by a famous football player.

Aside from Spence, he never entertained too many dudes on campus. NC TECH was one of the largest HBCU's in the country and had just shy of five thousand students. It was like a big high school. Everyone knew everyone and if you didn't want someone to know something, you didn't tell anyone. NC TECH was a freaky campus and on the right day, you could catch couples and hook ups going down.

"There he go again," Spence pointed to Elgin lounging around Mrs. Winner's, "you fucking him?"

"He's straight," Maine insisted.

"Are you sure?" Spence saw how Elgin made eye contact with the two of them and headed their way.

"Of course man." Maine got annoyed. "I told you before if Cordell thought you got down, you wouldn't been offered a chance to live with us."

"Sup fellas," Elgin gave Spence and Maine dap.

"My nigga," Spence gave the taller man a hug. He smirked at Maine.

"I got y'all the two-piece meal from Mrs. Winner's." Elgin handed each of them a plastic bag with a warm food container inside. "I'm not trying to get used to the trailer food."

"I know right," Maine agreed, "they could've waited until after we graduated to renovate the cafeteria man."

"I still got my meal card and I hate that I can't transfer money from my Wachovia account to my meal plan." Spence piped in.

"Spence, you riding with us?" Maine offered.

"Naw man," Spence turned down the ride. "Remember, Vanessa's taking me back to her dorm at UNCG."

"You still fucking them white girls Spence?" Elgin inquired as they headed to Maine's car, which was parked at the end of the lot.

"Oh hell yes," Spence licked his lips, "trouble free pussy and her roommate is a freak. Plus, neither one of them makes me wear a condom."

Maine shook his head, "white pussy don't mean clean pussy."

"Yeah," Elgin jumped in, "you can catch herpes, chlamydia or some of the white STD's."

"White STD's?" Maine didn't know who was spouting more misinformation, Spence or Elgin.

"White girls don't get HIV man," Elgin touted like he was an expert. "Black girls get that shit from these down low faggots who can't decide if they like dick or pussy. White faggots don't mess around with white girls like that."

Maine and Spence shared a look. Any question on where Elgin stood with his sexuality dissipated. Subtle guilt and conviction about how their friend felt about their actions stung them each.

"Well, I'm nutting in some white pussy tonight." Spence bragged as a set of headlights flashed. "There go my snow bunny. I'll catch y'all niggas later."

Maine watched as Spence headed into the car. It wasn't too dark on an August night for him to make out Vanessa's shoulder-length hay colored hair. Vanessa was a full-figured woman who's D cups needed more support than her bra and tank top provided. Her white poodle with blue and gold Greek-letter insignia moved on her rear-view mirror as it were being taken on a walk.

"I bet that's as close to a black girl Spence's gonna get." Elgin pointed out Vanessa's affiliation with a prominent black Greek-lettered sorority. The confirmation made by the blue and gold stripped cane that rode on the back dash of the Honda Civic, and the license plate frame over her license plate.

"Yeah." Maine was still shaken up by some of Elgin's hurtful comments. He didn't see himself as a carrier of HIV and didn't appreciated it being insinuated that he'd become positive just because he had sex with men. Maine took pride in the fact he strapped up no matter who he slept with.

But he couldn't tell Elgin his true feelings. Unlike Spence, Elgin still though he was straight. Maine unlocked the door to his car and he and Elgin got in and put on their seatbelts.

"Man, Renee jockin' you?" Elgin pointed out while Maine headed out of the parking lot. "She trying to give you the goods man."

"Everyone thinks I'm trying to fuck 'Keem's girl." Maine complained. "I'm not in a rush to break her back."

"Well, you shouldn't have broke off Chelle and Yonna at y'all's party. Man, everyone's talking about how you had them screaming and hollering and calling you daddy. One of the girls told Misa that your man meat is about as long as your forearm." Elgin looked out the window.

Maine kept his eyes on the road. "Cordell was the one that had the girl screaming like a hyena."

"But ain't nobody talking about Cordell, dawg. Them girls are obsessed over you. That fight between that Zeta and the Delta was a classic."

"I did not tell them girls to fight over me," Maine's tone was cold.

"Yeah but you were fucking the Zeta all year long in and out of Club Hurston." Elgin pointed out.

Club Hurston was the library. Opened 24-7 and everything went down there.

"And you were banging the Delta while she was pledging. Had them chapters doing 'The Boy is Mine' step shows dissing each other over you. You're a legend. Only freshman to pull that shit off."

Maine couldn't deny the new found fame his latest stunt brought him. Spence's frat was pursuing him—hard and so were their arch-rivals. Spence giving up the ass wasn't supposed to be part of the bribe but it didn't stop Maine from taking it.

"I'm not chasing Renee but if she drops the panties, I'm a drop my draws and fall right in there." Maine's answer was blunt.

"And you and 'Keem will be fighting." Elgin promised.

"And I will swiftly and efficiently kick his ass." Maine boasted.

"You really think you can kick 'Keem ass, dawg?" Elgin sounded concerned. Like Maine was off his rocker or something.

"I am King David to the monkey-faced Goliath." Maine declared. "I'll send that boy crying to his mama."

"Alright," Elgin wasn't convinced.

Maine wasn't going to go out of his way to pursue Renee. That was a grown ass woman. But if it went down, it went down. And wasn't a damn thing Elgin, 'Keem or anyone else gonna do to stop it.

5

Looking for Corey

The stoop in front of the bookstore was full as young, athletic men sat and watched the fine young ladies walk by wearing tank tops and daisy dukes. Older men drove by shiny BMWs, Benz's, Lexuses and Audi's.

"Look at these old muthafuckas," Elgin pointed out while enjoying some "spirited" juice from a blue Solo cup. He was showing off his gym rat-trained abs and biceps only pushups and pull ups could buy. "And these dumb broads fall for this shit every time."

Maine glanced at Elgin. He had to admit that he liked the way his black boxer briefs hugged his boy's ass. If he looked at Elgin like that, he'd teach him a thing or two. He brought his focus in the direction Elgin was pointing at and sure enough, he saw Chelle rocking a low-cut, blue and white striped blouse and a skirt that could barely hid how thick her hips were. When she moved, her thighs and the thread of those jeans went to war.

"Ain't that Papa Green?" Maine asked, discretely trying to get a good look.

"Hell yeah," Elgin complained. "Old fucker always gets the new pussy."

Maine chuckled and shook his head as he watched Chelle put her seat belt on, pull down the visor and reapply some lipstick. "Well, he not stopping my pimping."

"Who you pimping?" Yonna walked up to him. Maine was surprised to see her seeing how she and Chelle were ducking and dodging him since they locked him out of the room. Maine took the cup from Elgin and took a sip. The lime-flavored gin hit the sides of his throat just right.

WHAT'S BEST FOR YOU   23

"Whoever I want," Maine brushed her off as he adjusted himself on the stoop. Other guys were leaning over, trying to get a good look at the cakes Yonna was flaunting in her summer dress. Even with the extra fabric, that donk couldn't conceal itself to save a life.

Yonna tried to sit in Maine's lap but he closed his legs a little and moved over to the side.

"You still mad I locked you out of your room?" Yonna asked coyly as she made another attempt to sit between Maine's legs.

"Hell naw," Maine brushed her off and looked around her. He liked the view he had facing the cafeteria. He'd been on the stoop since 10 a. m., having avoided scheduling any classes on a Tuesday. School started yesterday and the bookstore and walkway was packed. He'd halfway hoped that Corey would've reached out to him on the sly. He was looking for him and when he went by his dorm yesterday, his roommate, Melvin, told him he just missed him for class. Maine wasn't about to walk all the way from Scott Hall dormitory to Carver Hall or Merrick Hall for him not to catch Corey there.

He picked the stoop because in order to get to the mobile kitchen units, Corey would've had to walk from Scott Hall, which also was the freshman dorm for men, to the café. He would have to walk past the bookstore, unless he cut through Club Hurston, which wouldn't have made sense. If Maine sat on the stoop, sooner or later, Corey would have to cut to the café to get breakfast, lunch or dinner. Only way Maine wouldn't have missed him would've been if he got up at 5:30 in the morning and ate with the ROTC cats, and Corey wasn't the type to get up with the cadets.

Yet, Corey avoided him all lunch period.

"When you having another party?" Yonna was in his space. He put her hand on his thigh, rubbing it, trying to get his attention.

"Cordell and I haven't gotten together on that," Maine revealed. "I been in Merrick all day—speaking of which Elgin, you think Janessa gonna show up at study hall tonight at Hurston?"

"She better," Elgin nodded his head at a female that caught his eye. "Accounting 101 ain't no joke—I barely read two paragraphs of that accounting book and I already know it's gonna be a bitch."

"Yeah, some of the old heads already warned us to get a jump on that class. I can't get my marketing degree without it." Maine complained.

"I know." Elgin added. "That's my major and I already know I'm gonna need all the help I can get."

"Yeah man," Maine confirmed. "You change your major now, you could set yourself back a whole semester or a year. Or have to do a lot of summer school."

"And I don't have time for summer school." Elgin continued as he slyly took the folded paper from the young lady who passed by. "I'm trying to get right with Ernest & Young or Kimberly Clark now. I do not want to walk around with a degree in hand and only be able to teach high school or be working at some stuffy call center."

"Hell yeah, that's why I'm putting all that time in Willie's. I get my degree, get some work experience and I'm never going back to the A. I might move to New York, start a label." Maine's dreams were almost his reality. Only two things standing in his way were Spence's big head and Yonna playing with his smaller "head."

"I want to go into business with you." Yonna found her way on his lap. She indiscreetly put her hand in his navy and marigold NC TECH athletic shorts. Yonna found was she was searching for and giving it a few tugs.

"Oh yeah," Maine challenged, trying his damnest to keep mind over matter in place.

"You and I should form a partnership." Yonna squeezed his Johnson harder, determined to turn his wand into a stress ball.

"What kind of partnership are we gonna form?" Maine asked.

"One where you are gonna get your hands out of that man's pants," a booming authoritative voice yelled. "And one where you are going to keep your shirt on." Maine looked up just in time to see Mrs. Lynette Boykin throw a marigold NC TECH shirt at Elgin.

"I didn't have my hands in his pants," Yonna tried to lie.

Mrs. Lynette took off her glasses and put her hands on her hip. "You calling me a liar?"

"No ma'am." Yonna took a few steps back.

"I keep telling you, fast ass little boys that you want women who will help you build families and pass down generational wealth—not little girls who only want you because you look good, got good stroke or make a few dollars." Mrs. Lynette didn't have a filter. She managed the bookstore and to many, she was also their mama away from home. And she didn't discriminate, she got on the little girls about giving it up too easy, wearing "slut clothes" and cursing like sailors.

Elgin quickly put his new shirt on and a few of the guys were laughing at them. 'Keem walked up and stared at Maine. "Yo man, we need to talk."

Maine could see the look in Elgin's eye but he wasn't sweating it. He got up from his seat, pissed that once again, Corey eluded him. "Yo what's up." Maine was ready for whatever. He seriously doubted 'Keem would try anything in front of Mrs. Lynette but he didn't put it past him either.

"Let's go over here man," 'Keem suggested as they walked to the side of the school that ran down the local street. "I don't want these nosy jokers in my business."

'Keem had a point. To avoid confrontation, Maine followed him to the welcome gate that was next to the end of the bookstore. Under the two-story building, also held the mailroom for all the on-campus students. That's when it dawned on him how Corey could've eluded him for the past three hours. If he got a ride off campus, all he had to do was get to the mailroom and he was good.

"You think 'Nee fine?" 'Keem got straight to the point.

"She aight," Maine played it off.

"Look nigga, don't bullshit me, I know you saw me and my girl fuckin' on your couch. I'm asking because she told me she want you to hit it." 'Keem was cool as shit.

Maine was expecting a confrontation and it wasn't beneath him to throw some 'bow. "She told you that?"

"Yeah man," 'Keem wrapped his arm around Maine and huddled him closer. "We got an open relationship. When you see that I be on a different girl every so often, 'Nee know about it. When she wants to explore things with another nigga, I don't trip.

I got the biggest dick on campus bruh, but even I know a woman want to try something different."

Maine couldn't believe his ears. Open relationship? That sounded like some shit only Will and Jada Smith did.

"So here's the deal? You not the only one she got eyes on. And I'm gonna tell you like I tell the other niggas she want to fuck, I got a few rules. One, only wear a condom with her ass. Don't be raw dawging my shit cause if I catch what you got, I'm killing your ass. Two, don't fuck her in my bed—I don't want to wake up to your manfunk and shit. Number three—don't tell her you love her. I'm the only one that loves her. And four, don't hurt her. If you not feeling her no more or she becomes a pest, pull me to the side and we handle it like we handling this shit now."

Maine had to pinch himself to see if he was dreaming. And there he was. Corey was walking to the cafeteria from Hurston with his roommate Melvin and some thick chick on Melvin's arm.

Shit, shit, shit.

"Aight man, I see someone I need to catch up with. And if it goes down..." Maine tried to step away.

"I don't want to know—just take care of her is all I'm saying."

Maine still couldn't believe it. 'Keem just gave him free pass to smash his girl. Holy shit! He couldn't see himself doing the same. And he wondered what 'Keem was really into that he was gonna allow it to happen. He tried to catch up to Corey and company but just as fast as he saw him, the man eluded him.

Fuck, fuck, fuck.

It was no use. He wasn't about to sit at the stoop and wait to catch up with Corey again. In a few hours, he'd need to be ready to run things at Willie's and after he got off from Willie's, Maine was going to join the rest of the responsible students at Club Hurston. He needed to stay on top of his studies and keep that GPA up so he could get that assistant manager spot. Spence already had one up on him with the internship at Def Jam. If he didn't link up with Willie, Maine was going to be forced to find another way into a fast-paced marketing career.

"When's your next class?" Yonna met him around the corner. He looked to his old spot to see Elgin gone and a new set of students trying to run game.

"I'm off today," Maine wished he could take the words back the minute he said it. He knew Yonna was gonna try to start catching up with him on Tuesdays.

"Let's go back to your room." Yonna suggested.

Maine had nothing to lose. Corey had come and gone. 'Keem basically handed Renee to him and to top it off, standing before him was a woman that wanted nothing more but to be alone with him and was offering the panties without having to take her to McDonald's first.

"Let's do that," Maine agreed, "I parked over here."

Maine led the way to the car. He knew Cordell should've been in class and that Cordell left for the Burger King on Summit Avenue right after class. He had about three hours to kill. And Yonna was gonna help him with that.

6

Is It Worth It?

Maine's strokes were steady as he pushed his covered dick in and out of Yonna as she laid on her back. Her hands pounded the wall and her legs holding on to Maine's waist for dear life.

"Hmm," Yonna moaned, struggling to grab ahold of something.

Maine's knees supported him as he pivoted up and down, slowly increasing his stroke while twisting both of her M&M-sized nipples. The sweat and fragrance from the PCA rolled off his forehead and down his face as his king-sized bed continued to rock as he moved his hips.

He was gonna teach her about locking him out of his room—he didn't forget.

"Turn over!" Maine ordered. He was tired of looking at her face and he wanted to see his dick move in and out of her from the back.

Yonna sat up, tried to ride him a few more times. Her lips attempted to kiss his as he quickly turned his head to the side and bit his lip. Her harden nipples rubbed against his smooth chest. The scent of her being worked over got stronger as her pussy got wetter.

A little pissed that he wasn't getting what he wanted, Maine continued to rock his hips with hers for a minute. Stealing a glance at the clock, he knew he had a little under two hours to get it together so he could go to work on time.

Yonna bit the side of his neck, pissing him off and causing him to roll his eyes. "Damn," she cursed as she held.

"Let me hit from the back." Maine suggested.

"Can I lay on my stomach?"

No, Maine thought.

"Sure," Maine relented as she got up. He looked down to see a soaked condom.

Yonna laid next to him on the bed and Maine got on top of her. Disappointed that her ass wasn't as round as Spence's or Corey's but determined to make it work. He aimed his thick dick at her kitty and put it inbetween her lips. Yonna gasped and Maine pushed all the way in, his nuts kissing her thighs. His slender weight rested on top of hers as he pumped furiously, trying to rub against some tightness so he could bust and be on his way.

"Oh my gosh!" Yonna yelled.

Shut the fuck up! Maine almost told Yonna how he truly felt as he tried to race an imaginary car around the race track.

Suddenly, he saw a vision of Corey kneeling in front of him. His long, mushroom-tipped dick aiming for his lips. Maine wished he had a dick in his mouth while he was pushing his into some whiny, scandalous ho. He missed the way Corey went down on him. Maine closed his eyes and he could picture Corey getting behind him, eating his ass while threw his dick in and out of Yonna.

"Yes, yes," Yonna yelled as Maine continued his pace. Eyes closed shut, he could feel Corey's hand rubbing his ass and parting his cheeks, his tongue licking him in circles. His face felt so good as it moved in synch with his ass.

"Oh shit!" Yonna and Maine yelled at the same time. He hit Yonna's spot at the same time he could picture Corey tonguing his.

Finally, his cannon was being loaded. He could feel the eruption that was gonna fill the tip of the Magnum he wore. Yonna panted as Maine sent his strokes into overdrive. Their legs crashing against one another as Maine worked hard to get his nut. He focused his energy on pressuring his balls to shoot.

"Ah—aw-ahh-ahh," Maine screamed as he could feel his nut leaving its destination and his legs shaking.

"I'm cumming again!" Yonna yelled.

"Me too—damn—hooo!!!" Maine yelled as his dick expanded and he couldn't hold his nut in. "Oh fuck!" Maine pulled out, sat up and ripped the condom off. Thick long ropes of white milky fluid landed all over Yonna's back and a few drops made it to the back of her head. Maine continued pumping the rest out, increasing the strokes of his right hand not giving a fuck where he landed. Instinctively, his left fingers flicked and tickled his nipples. When it was over, Maine lost his balance and fell back on top of Yonna.

"Damn baby," Yonna cooed as she slowly moved her ass. The tip of his dick was lining up with her hole and he was too tired to move. Maine relaxed and gasped for air. It was a good nut and he didn't want to be forced to move. He could feel Yonna's ass moving, her pussy lips surrounding his unsheathed penis. As he breathed, Maine could feel his dick hardening again, Yonna's wetness entrapping him the way a spider's web catches and wraps around it's pray. "You feel so good."

What the fuck? Maine knew the tip of his head was already back inside Yonna, but the raw pussy was feeling good. He'd never raw dawged before and all of a sudden, he saw Yonna in a different light. *I need to pull out*, his conscious tried to warn him. His body didn't listen.

"You got a condom on?" Yonna worked her ass back, loving the way Maine's tip brushed against her clitoris.

"No," Maine pushed in deeper. "Oh, shit!"   Pussy wasn't supposed to feel *this good*. Yonna's hips were moving and soon Maine's was following her as he pushed his thick raw dick inside her. "Oh God!" The strength in his dick was returning as common sense left the back door. "This pussy good!" He whined.

"Dick good," Yonna got wetter. Her pussy squeezed tighter, latching onto his skin and without a barrier to protect the two, Maine continued to push in deeper. He wondered what he'd been missing all this time.

Maine rolled on his back and held onto Yonna tight as he continued to push insider her. Yonna sat up and rode him reverse cowgirl style. Maine got a good look at his dick going in and out of Yonna. He liked what he saw.

Yonna spun around him slowly, keeping him nestled deep inside her. "Yes," Maine mumbled as Yonna made the circle complete. Yonna leaned down closer and grinded her hips into his pelvis. Maine grabbed her ass and squeezed tighter.

Their eyes locked with one another as Maine continued increasing his strokes. Yonna getting wetter only encouraged her to go deeper. Maine sat up and Yonna rapped her arms around him. They kissed like long lost lovers and soon, Maine felt his dick getting tighter.

"I'm about to cum again!" a part of Maine wanted to push away from Yonna, but his hands betrayed him, pulling that ass closer to him. His lips found Yonna's again, each made love as they muffled the sounds of their bodies as Maine released himself inside of Yonna.

Busting the nut felt better the second time as he didn't hold back. Maine allowed himself to let go inside her and he loved the way their bodies slowed down, almost as if he were having an out of body experience. He could see himself thrusting inside her. When they were down, Yonna fell off to the side and Maine stared into the air.

"I can't believe we did that," Maine gasped for air.

"Me either," Yonna struggled to breathe.

For the first time in his life, Maine had unprotected sex and released himself inside someone. He wondered what it felt like to give Corey that attention. Or how he'd feel about Spence if he ever did that with him. He remembered 'Keem's warning—he wondered if Renee felt better than this.

Yonna got up and stumbled out of bed. "You came in me."

"I know," Maine admitted.

His body was in attendance but his thoughts were elsewhere. His dick was lip and heavy as he watched her gather her clothing and put it on. His toes still curled. "I wish I could stay with you all night." Yonna told him as she finally got the rest of her clothes on.

Maine got up and walked Yonna from his room to the front door. Oblivious to the fact that Cordell and his chick were watching television, Maine opened the door and leaned down for a kiss. And as they kissed, Maine wrapped his arms around Yonna and leaned her against the door.

"Baby, I gotta go and you got company," Yonna pointed out the fact that Cordell's eyes were bugging out.

Maine looked back, nodded his head held open the door. He watched Yonna walk out of the apartment and a few units down to her Chelle's place.

"Bruh, I know I didn't hear Yonna ask if you had a condom on and you say no?" Cordell quizzed.

"That's what I said," Maine responded as if he were on cloud nine.

"No bruh, you *always* wear a condom with these broads. Damnit man, now I'm gonna have to make sure you go to the clinic. You better not have anything." Cordell freaked out.

"I'm good," Maine closed the door and walked into the bathroom and turned on the water for a shower. He knew he needed to get ready to go to work. He almost hated it was time to go to work because he wanted to fuck Yonna again.

Tuesday, August 24, 1999, Tremaine October Winston lost his damn mind.

7

Just To Be Safe

"What the fuck's wrong with you?" Cordell scolded as he pushed Maine away from the door. "And you smell like her too. Damn it man!"

"Cordell!" A whiny feminine voice caught Maine's attention. He looked in the living room and that's when he saw her. Smooth, sand-colored skin, darker than a crème de la crème. Long, shoulder-length hair the color of burnt auburn. Smokey Topaz-colored eyes that rivaled a crayon in the Crayola box.

"Well damn," Maine stuttered. The blood flow being redirected to his little head.

"Oh hell naw!" Cordell cursed as he continued to push and guide Maine to the bathroom. "You fuck Bathsheba, we gonna be fighting."

"Do I need to come back?" Bathsheba asked.

"No," Cordell successfully got Maine to the bathroom down the hall. "Take a shower you funky ass nigga. Smelling like badussy."

"I'm good man," Maine began to pick up his feet and moved to turn the shower on. "Yo, I didn't mean to disrespect you in front of your girl man."

"You don't owe me an apology," Cordell rushed to Maine's room and grabbed his toiletry basket and brought it to the bathroom. "You owe yourself one for fuckin' Yonna without a condom. You know you ain't the only one she fuckin'."

Maine hadn't thought of all that. In the moment, all he felt was his dick going into some good pussy and not being able to pull out, even if it killed him. Cordell tossed him a wash cloth and

Maine caught it and immediately went to work to scrubbing his body with the bar of Ivory soap. As he scrubbed, he wondered if he'd caught any STD's or worse, HIV. The horrific pictures of mutilated genitals, busted lips and puss and acne filled body parts flooded his head. As he began to piss in the tub, he prayed to God that he didn't burn.

Relieved, he quickly washed up, dried and made a dash to his room. He didn't hear a trace of Bathsheba nowhere and he knew he needed to head to work. In his room, he grabbed his rope chain and threw it over his head. He grabbed a black pair of boxers and a black wife beater and some socks. He grabbed a pressed pair of black slacks and navy blue button up. He found a silver and navy bowtie and thanked God that Cordell's father taught him how to tie one. Maine stole a glance in the mirror and approved of his appearance before grabbing his lace up Stacy Adams out of the closet.

Leaving his room, he saw Cordell watching music videos alone with his feet on the coffee table.

"I hope I didn't fuck up something you had going with Bathsheba," Maine apologized.

"Naw, I'm good." Cordell kept his eyes on the television. "We'd already gotten it in at her place. Tomorrow, we'll both go to the clinic and get checked out. Don't worry. If we catch it now, we'll nip it in the bud and we can laugh and tell our kids about this shit."

Maine liked the sound of that. He grabbed the car keys from the key hook and headed out of the door. Getting in the car and heading to Willie's, all he thought about was the what if's. Maine didn't want to admit he was a little bit scared of catching a vernal disease. The more he thought about it, the more he wondered about his other sex partners. When was the last time Mr. Sanders had been tested? It was a one-time thing after lurking at the gay bar. Then there was the married couple he got with. And what about Chelle, Ariana and Crystal…

Not Cordell's ATL girl, *Ariyanna.*

First thing he noticed when he walked into Willie's was Spence's blow out Afro. Dude looked like Allen Iverson from a distance.

Spence fit in with the seventies kids, with the Afro pick and the tie die head wrap, like Jimmy Hendricks.

"My sons," Willie called them to the register. "We got something serious we need to handle."

Maine didn't like the sound of that. Other than Otis, Cordell and Corey's dad, he never heard another man refer to him as a "son" and the last thing he wanted to be to Willie was a disappointment. "I know y'all young, and them hormones are raging." Willie's voice got lower. "I'm not going to get into no squabble, but whichever one of you thought it was cute to flush a condom down the commode owe me one hundred and seventy-five dollars I had to pay to get it fixed."

Spence and Maine's eyes both got big. The condom Maine flushed down the commode would've been the one the two of them used when they got it in a few days ago.

"My bad," Spence spit it out. "I must've flushed it by mistake when I blew my nose. I'd been looking for it too—I thought I'd threw it away after I—mile high thing."

Maine couldn't believe Spence was lying and without hesitation.

"You know what I like about you," Willie pulled Spence in closer, "I like that you honest.   You manned up and took responsibility. So I tell you what—I'll let you choose to bring me my money in seven days or I can take it out of your next check."

In the back of his mind, Maine was trying to remember how much money he had in his account. He knew he was gonna have to break Spence off for the condom *he* didn't dispose of carefully.

"I think we get our refunds on Friday. I might can pay you then. Plus, Def Jam owe me one more check on Friday, so I got it. And I apologize about that."

"Aight young men, y'all are showing me that I can trust the two of you with the store again. Next weekend, y'all have three new associates to train. They'll be looking up to you and I'll be looking to see one of y'all move into the assistant manager's spot. Spence, you'll need to have a bit more discretion over your words and your actions. And Maine, you gotta make sure you getting in these artists' faces. You got independent artists trying to launch record labels—don't sleep on them boys because they not Arista or EMI."

"Yes sir," Maine took Willie's warning to heart. He knew if he was gonna grab that assistant manager's spot, he was gonna have to make sure the associates he trained were on point. And land a major promotional spot for an album release party or hook up with someone in the press.

Willie left and both Spence and Maine made sure he was outta sight before they started their routine.

"Thanks man," Maine offered.

"I'm good—technically, we both had a part in that so I'll pay half and you give me the other half by Friday. You think you can do that?" Spence checked.

"Yeah, I got it," he remembered that he didn't spend all of his refund money. Quiet as kept, Maine kept some of his money in a Sharebuilder account and he bought little penny stocks along the way. Plus, he still had the shares from the company that owned Harris Teeter when he used to bag for them and he bought a share of Nike stock for every pair of Air Jordan's he owned. Maine was far from rich, but those frugal habits Otis imparted on him, Cordell and Corey were rubbing off. "Aye man, we need to talk about something serious though."

"Yo, what's up?" Spence counted the money in the register since it was his day to oversee the transactions and run the credit card reports.

"When was the last time you got tested?" Maine looked him in the eye.

"I get tested every three months. I've already had gonorrhea and that Q-Tip in the dick shit is worse than being short." Spence admitted.

"Really," Maine was amazed. "I thought being shot was worse."

Spence leaned down and pulled up his right pants leg. Maine remembered the dark spot on both of his legs. "Bullet from the .45 went in one side and out the other. It was luck that my legs were positioned the way they were when I was running and that I didn't hit an artery. Could've got hit with both legs." Spence pulled his pants leg down. "As for the gonorrhea—I caught that shit when I got this girl pregnant in the tenth grade."

"Real shit?" This was the first time hearing that Spence was a father. He'd heard rumors about Spence having a kid hidden somewhere but he never thought to ask it. Spence was a local that graduated from Grimsley High. Everyone knew him and his notorious exploits with the women.

"Me and like three other dudes was burning. Pissing fire outta my dick wasn't cool," Spence elaborated. "I gave it to this girl I was messing with at Dudley and this dude I was creepin' with on the low at High Point Andrews. I felt guilty about that shit because the girl I was messing with didn't know she had it until it spread. I got to hold my son for a few hours before he passed on."

"I'm sorry to hear that man," Maine started to feel like shit. If he got Yonna pregnant and she had something, he'd never be able to forgive himself.

"Naw man," Spence closed the till. "I wasn't ready to be a father. Ol' girl wasn't ready to be a mother. I'm glad I lost my son the way I lost him instead of to an abortion. We found out the baby was mine *after* the fact. Real shit, made me focus on school. My mom made me promise I'd get a grip on my baby maker and until I hooked up with you, that's all I did, grip my baby maker."

Maine and Spence laughed. He knew what it looked like when Spence gripped his baby maker. Watching Spence masturbate was a big turn on for him.

"Tell you what man," Spence offered. "When you go get tested, I'll get tested with you. I been wanting to stop wearing them rubbers because that latex puts a number on my hole and shit. Plus, I like fucking and getting fucked raw."

"I don't know about all that," Maine hesitated. In his heart, he knew he wanted to get Spence's arc and feel what it would be like to walk around without a raincoat. But he knew Spence was fuckin' Vanessa and her roommate. He didn't know of anyone else he was screwing. "I'm going tomorrow or the next day— depending on when Cordell need to use the car."

"Just let me know."

Before Maine could respond, a few customers walked in. Maine went to the back to change out the shelves so he could put the new releases front and center. No major R&B or Hip Hop artist was putting anything out this week, but a few local independent joints were dropping. The locals were putting in bids to be able to open for the Homecoming concerts at the HBCUS up and down North and South Carolina. They needed the buzz and consideration to catch a major's ear.

Maine was good on the idea of Spence getting tested with him and Cordell. And he prayed to God he'd never have to feel something going inside his dick. Thought alone almost made him nauseas.

8

Me And *Our* Girlfriend

"Come hang with me tonight," Spence offered as he finished counting down his till. He and Maine verified that the money wasn't short; the compact discs and cassettes were in order, and the vinyl was arranged properly. The new releases were on the shelves, ready to be sold at the open of business tomorrow.

"Oh really?" Maine was curious. "You do remember I gotta get tested tomorrow."

"Yeah, I know we gotta get tested tomorrow, but what does that have to do with tonight?" Spence smirked. "Besides, I got plenty of condoms and don't want to be alone while I wait for Vanessa to get out of class."

Oh hell yes! Maine got excited about getting a trip inside of Spence again. He was liking the healthy and heavy rotation of ass and pussy being thrown his way. Spence gave him enough to not have to look or think about another dude sexually, except for the occasional beat off session thinking about Corey. Yonna and Chelle kept him occupied but with the women, he could always try one and let her go.

"You know where Wind Lake Apartments are at?" Spence asked as he and Maine headed out of the door.

"Yeah, that's over there by the American Flag Storage place on Church Street?" Maine smiled. He knew Spence had found a spot but didn't realize he ended up over there. "You kinda far from campus aren't you?"

"For the shit I like to do, I don't need no one in my business— that's for sure." Maine could only imagine what that meant. There were a lot of NC TECH students and young people that stayed in the northeast side of Greensboro. And Maine could only imagine the kind of shit that went down when folks weren't on or near campus. "I stay in 3811-F."

"Word."

Maine headed to his car. He took out his phone and called Cordell to make sure he didn't need the car in the morning. "Sup," Cordell answered within the first ring.

"Aye man, I was just wondering if you needed the car later tonight?" Maine asked. "I need to get with this girl for the night."

Cordell chuckled. "Whatever nigga—just be ready to pick me up so we can get tested in the morning."

"Aight man," Maine hung up the phone. Felt good to know that he wasn't impeding on Cordell's flow. Then again, he just gave Cordell the house to himself for the evening so it was possible for the two of them to stay out of each other's way.

"Aye man," Elgin yelled from Mrs. Winner's, "you give me a ride home?"

Shit! No! Maine wanted to yell but he seen Elgin walking out with three groceries bags and a carrying a gallon-size jug of sweet tea in his hand. "Yeah man."

Elgin picked up his step and made it to the passenger side of the car. Taking Elgin to their housing complex was out of the way. "I got a few chicken dinners—you and Cordell can have a few."

Cordell wouldn't get too mad at him if he dropped off some food. "What sides you get?" Maine asked as he started the car.

"One plate has green beans and the other has mashed potatoes." Elgin buckled his seatbelt. "The other has dirty rice and an extra biscuit and that's mine."

"I swear every time you leave that place, you come out with a plate. You must be fucking the manager," Maine suggested as he pulled off on the road.

"No," Elgin laughed. "Well, I do work there part time and yeah, me and one of the shorties that work there do get it in from time to time."

"My man," Maine gave him a pound. "Which one?"

"All of them off limits sir," Elgin got serious. "I'm trying to see if Shayla and I are gonna be serious or not and we trying to keep our relationship under wraps. Don't want everyone knowing we together."

"Aight man," Maine respected Elgin and agreed to keep the girls at Mrs. Winner's off limits. DMX got them crunk on "Party Up," Elgin and Maine recited the lyrics as they made their way to the apartment complex.

"Thank you for the ride man." Elgin gave Maine two bags of food and a gallon tea.

"Thanks for the food," Maine lifted the bags up and stepped out of the car. He quickly walked to his unit, looking to put the food in the refrigerator and grab a small amount of clothes to dump in his bag.

"No Corey, we are not having a party this weekend." Maine overheard Cordell talking.

Corey. His heart got excited. Maine searched for him but didn't see him. *Damn it man, he must be on the phone.* Maine thought to himself. Cordell came out of room walking around with his Nokia up to his ear. He only wore some jersey pants, crew socks and Adidas athletic sandals.

"You the one brought your ass up here for that bullshit hospitality degree you could've stayed in the A and got."

Maine didn't want to admit that he would've wanted a peak at Corey.

"Go fuck yourself."

Maine kept his mouth shut about how Cordell treated his brother. He understood, being that he hardly ever saw his older brother. Sam was almost fifteen years his senior, in his thirties, had two kids and doing time in one of the county jails south of Georgia for credit card fraud.

"Aye what you bring home?" Cordell stormed the kitchen.

"Elgin got us some chicken plates. You can pick the one you want. One got green beans and the other one got mashed potatoes." Maine hurried into his room and grabbed some athletic pants, shirt, boxers and socks. He folded everything and sandwiched it between the shirt and shirt. He also grabbed his overnight basket and grabbed a set of towels.

"You be safe man," Cordell warned. "I'm not trying to hear you whine about some shit you got that you can't get rid of."

"Aight man," Maine shrugged it off, "you do the same."

Maine wanted to ask about Corey but he knew that would raise Cordell's suspicions. He was still pissed about his younger brother being at NC Tech and he knew that like talking about their mamas, Corey was off limits.

Maine headed out on his quest for some Spence-ass. His dick got excited on the ride over and he couldn't wait to smash the boy on the bed. The twenty-minute ride seemed to go by in ten, which his dick wanting to take it's turn maneuvering the steering wheel. He found 3811 with little to no problem. Grabbing his things, he made sure the car was secure. Figuring out that Spence lived on the top floor, he tackled the stairs two at a time. Arriving at his spot he knocked on the door.

"Open!" he heard Spence yell from the other side.

Maine followed the understood command and was surprised to see Spence walking around the house with nothing on but some ankle socks. "You couldn't wait."

"This is my house, I always chill naked man." Spence insisted as he walked to the kitchenette and washed his hands. He could smell seasoned ground beef on the stove. "I'm making chili man, you welcome to have some."

Maine wasn't about to object to some chili. He watched Spence stir the ground beef and loved watching his compact body command control of the kitchen. He couldn't believe Spence got the crib so fast to cook, but the detour to his house gave him plenty of time. In a larger pot, the kidney beans, peppers and seasoning stewed. Spence picked up the pan with the beef in and slowly drained it in a small cup in the sink. Then he poured the meat into the pan with the beans.

"Let's go take a shower man," Spence put the empty pan in the sink. "Leave your clothes at the door."

Spence walked over to the sofa and removed the two seat cushions as Maine stripped of his garments. Spence then pulled out the bi-fold steel support frame that revealed a queen-sized bed, big enough for him to maneuver his lanky frame on. He was surprised that Spence slept on that, but he had to respect the fact the man had his own place. Maine followed Spence into the bathroom and gave him a hard smack on the ass.

"Keep playing." Spence warned.

Spence turned on the shower and stepped inside. Maine followed and the moment the water hit their skins, he picked Spence up and leaned him against the wall. He kissed Spence with fevor and enjoyed feeling his wet, hard body against his. Spence wrapped his arms around Maine's waist and clung for dear life. When he was ready to get down, Spence got on his knees and squeezed some soap on his hands. Without warning, Spence flicked his tongue out and licked on Maine's thickening member. Maine watched as his dick disappeared inside Spence's mouth like a Hoover.

"Damn son," Maine reached behind him to turn the knobs off on the water. He wanted to see Spence work that neck and mouth. He wiped the water away from his eyes. The strong, fragrant smell of musk-scented Dial turned him on as Spence continued lathering his body and sucking his cock. Maine grab his towel and squeezed some of the Dial soap on his body.

"Turn around," Spence commanded and as Maine complied, he felt Spence's thick tongue penetrating the crevices of his ass, tickling his hole.

"Oh shit!" Maine's knees buckled and he almost slipped in the tub. He found he bearings and leaned against the wall as Spence continue feasting and attacking his hole. Maine's toes curled and his legs wobbled and rocked, making standing in the tub difficult and dangerous. His hardened dick thumped against the tile. Spence was tossing Maine's salad every way but sideways. Spence tongue went up and Maine threw his ass back like a twerk team dancer. Maine's legs slid further apart and on the down stroke, he almost fell.

Spence backed his head away. "Let's finish on the bed. Wash me first."

Maine pumped some more soap in his hands and he gently rubbed Spence's body. He loved feeling how firm Spence's body was under his skin. Spence taken Maine's towel and started washing Maine's body with it. The two men slowly and carefully cleaned each other before turning the water back on.

A knock on the door sounded like gunshots. "That's Vanessa."

Are you serious? Maine wanted to ask. He couldn't believe that Vanessa was interrupting their time together.

"She's cool man," Spence assured as he stepped out of the shower and grabbed a body towel. "The three of us are about to have some fun now."

Three? Fun? Maine's mind couldn't function straight. He was about to fuck Vanessa and Spence. His bucket list fantasy was about to be complete.

"Hey baby!" Spence could be heard boasting.

"I see you and Maine didn't waste no time," Maine heard Vanessa say.

He told her about me? He worried. That was a no-no because Maine wasn't exactly out with his sexuality. He did his dirt in private and didn't want random niggas and chicken heads in his business.

"Naw, we didn't start, we just took a shower." Spence promised.

"Naughty boy!" Maine hurried out of the tub and dried off. With his clothes in the bag in living room, he was left with no choice but to walk out into the living room area with nothing but a towel draped around his waist. "Y'all left enough hot water for me?" Vanessa asked.

"Yeah, let me turn the water on." Maine watched as Spence followed a nearly naked Vanessa from the bed to the bathroom. After a few seconds, Spence came out and laid across the bed.

"You told her about me?" Maine was shocked.

Spence looked up and rolled his eyes. "Really motherfucker? Of course I told her you were blowing my back out. You the only one I'm gonna admit to doing that with."

Maine believed him. Spence had already admitted to fucking a few people in the music industry, but Maine believed him when he implied he was the only dude here he was messing with like that.

"Aight man, it's just," Maine sat on the bed.

"I know," Spence sat up and crawled over to Maine and straddled him. "I don't run my mouth like that. What we do is what we do. What the two of us got going is what the two of us got going." Spence looked at the bathroom as the water stopped. "And what the three of us about to do—it's going down."

Vanessa walked out of the shower and instantly, Spence's and Maine's dicks got hard. "Hmm, that's what I like, two hard dicks."

Spence got off Maine's lap and Vanessa soon replaced him. They kissed and Maine watched Spence out of the corner of his eyes. Maine ran his fingers across Vanessa's long flowing hair as she pushed him down. Maine could feel Spence getting a grip on his dick and soon, his mushroom was running across the roof of Spence's mouth. Vanessa moved her breasts in Maine's face and Maine put his head inbetween those cantaloupes and rubbed his head side to side.

"You been in a threesome like this?" Vanessa asked.

"No," Maine could barely get the answer out as Spence swallowed him whole on the down stroke.

"Enjoy," Vanessa offered as Maine nibbled on her nipples, loving the feel of harden areolas in his mouth. Vanessa mounted Maine's face and her candy-scented vagina lips were on his. As he grabbed her waist and brought his face closer to her inner thighs, Maine felt his legs going up and landing on Spence's shoulders. Maine moved his tongue in synch with Spence's, giving Vanessa the pleasure he felt. "His ass taste good baby?"

"Mmm-hmm," Spence moaned as he continued diving in.

Vanessa's waist knucked and bucked on Maine's face as he lost control, his legs doing butterflies on Spence's back. He felt his legs being held up and Vanessa turning on his face. Long hair brushed against the bottom of Maine's ass as his dick quickly went into her mouth. After a few sucks, Vanessa's tongue ran down the length of Maine's shaft, through the middle of his balls, down the base between his nutsack and his hole. Vanessa's tongue ran around the rim and soon, she was French-kissing Maine's ass the way he was French-kissing her pussy.

"Fuckin' sweat," Spence moaned as he found his way behind Vanessa. Maine looked up to see Spence's low hanging balls almost touching his chin. Maine had the best row seat as he watched Spence enter Vanessa from behind. Vanessa lowered her body on his and engulfed Maine's dick.

"Mmm—oooh—daddy!" Vanessa moaned as Spence slowly and rhythmically entered her from behind.

Watching Spence's nuts slap against Vanessa turned him on. He reached up and put tongue up, hoping to catch one of the balls on the swing. As they brushed against his tongue, he felt Vanessa sucking on and swallowing his balls.

"Oh shit!" Maine hissed as Vanessa licked from ball to inner thigh to biting on his leg back to licking the inner thigh back to licking his balls.

Spence kept the rhythm going as he turned Vanessa on her side. Maine appreciated the view as he got to lean on his elbow and watch Spence's long shaft enter and thrust inside Vanessa faster.

"Get behind me," Spence begged as he looked over Vanessa's shoulder.

Maine quickly stood up and looked for the condoms. He realized he had one in his bag and quickly grabbed one and put it on. Spence slowed down his strokes and moved him and Vanessa closer to the center of the bed so that Maine would have room. Once Maine got back on the bed, Spence came to a complete stop with Vanessa still going up and down on Spence's stroke. Maine lifted Spence's leg up and slowly guided his sheathed mushroom tip inside.

"Ahh!" Spence and Maine moaned as Spence started getting in a groove. Spence pushed his ass down on Maine's dick while driving his dick inside Vanessa. Soon, the three of them were rocking, pushing and moaning as they gathered their sensations and discovered their pleasured.

Vanessa slithered away and Spence took the cue to get on his knees, prompting Maine to hit it doggystyle. Maine straightened up and watched as Spence threw that ass in a circle and arched his back perfectly. Maine held onto Spence's shoulders as Spence gave him a ride.

"Damn y'all look sexy!" Vanessa yelled as she got under Spence and put his dick in her mouth. Spence grabbed her legs and dove his head between her legs. Spence and Vanessa yelled and moaned as Maine grunted and cursed every few strokes. As Maine thrusted inside Spence, he looked down and grabbed his two nipples and closed his eyes.

For a brief moment, he wondered if this was what it would feel like to fuck Corey from behind. He could picture his back and that nice shaped ass when he walked away. Maine opened his eyes to Spence doing pushups as he took the beating Maine's dick gave him while being nestled in the nice, wet mouth Vanessa sheltered him in.

"I'm about to cum!" Spence tapped the bed, grabbed the sheets but kept going. Vanessa could be heard swallowing and slurping. "Ahh—ahh-shi—fuck!" Spence yelled as Maine could feel Spence's sphincter pulling on his dick tighter. Spence's body moved in rapid pace of his heartbeat, shuttering as he continued to take dick while being milked by Vanessa's greedy mouth.

"Pineapples," Spence tapped the bed three times and slowly pulled himself from the middle of their love fest.

Maine laid on his back. He took the condom off his dick and threw it on the floor. The three of them moaned and cooed. Maine stroked his dick slowly, trying to bring himself to pleasure. Spence got off the bed and stumbled for a minute before he made his way to the kitchen. Maine had forgotten about the chili being on and Spence washed his hands, the stirred the pot. He reached into a drawer and pulled out another condom. "Baby, you gotta make him cum."

Without saying another word, Spence tossed the condom on the bed. Vanessa quickly grabbed it, tore it open with her mouth and showed off her throat skills, unrolling the condom carefully with her lips and tongue. She mounted Maine and slowly lowered herself on him from the back. Maine lifted on his elbows, getting a good look at her ass. He thrusted and she met him on the down stroke. Maine looked at Spence, who licked his lips then turned his attention back to the chili.

The vibrations of Vanessa's orgasm touched a nerve within Maine that made him lose control. He held her hips tight as she continued going up and down, screaming like a banshee as Maine continued pushing his tip to the spot. He focused on opening and closing of Vanessa's cheeks as he felt himself releasing inside the condom while she continued to rock around on him. As their orgasms finished, Vanessa lay at Maine's feet while he deeply inhaled and exhaled.

"Round two in thirty," Spence suggested as he poured three bowls of chili. "Let's eat."

9

Final Exam

"Hmm," Maine heard a moan as he turned over. He rubbed his eyes and noticed Vanessa eating French Toast sticks, bacon and sliced pineapples while Spence was between her legs, moving his head and tongue by the way her booty was wiggling. The sight of Spence's naked body got Maine on brick. "Look who woke up."

Spence looked up and grinned. His face was wet from the breakfast Vanessa was feeding him. He got up and walked to the kitchen, got Maine a plate together and walked back to the bed and handed it to him. "You're next," he offered.

Maine smiled and Vanessa gave him a high five. "You're handsome when you wake up," she complimented him.

"You're fine too," Maine offered. "Let me get up and brush my teeth."

Maine got up and grabbed his shower caddy and his bag. He walked to the bathroom and turned the shower on. He put toothpaste on his toothbrush and quickly hopped in while the water was still hot. Maine brushed his teeth and tossed the toothbrush in the trash. Then he quickly lathered his body with soap and gave himself a thorough cleaning.

After drying off, he headed back to the living room where Spence had Vanessa on the bed doggystyle, hitting it from behind. "Hurry up before the breakfast gets cold, I still need my leche."

Maine chuckled as he laid down and took a bite of the French toast sticks. He was impressed that Spence made them and not warmed them up in the oven. He enjoyed watching Spence put in work as he had Vanessa's legs over his shoulders, drilling her for dear life. He couldn't wait to see what Spence had in store for him.

As Vanessa and Spence orgasmed together, he continued enjoying the show while eating his food. Spence crawled between his legs, grabbed his erect member and put it into his mouth. He thanked God he was almost done eating as he almost fumbled the plate in his hand. He gently set the plate on the floor as Spence lifted his legs up and gave his balls the ultimate treatment.

"Breakfast and head!" Maine called out as Spence continued to work those tongue skills on his balls.

***

"I thought you was going to hang out with a chick?" Cordell questioned when he got in the car. Spence was in the back seat slouched. They gave each other a head nod.

"I did," Maine told a half-lie. "I just up and shaved, showered and shitted before I got here. Spence didn't live to far so I picked him up too. And Elgin is on his way out the door."

Just as he called it, Elgin and the chick he recognized from Mrs. Winner's came out of his room.

"I hope you niggas wore condoms," Cordell stressed. "We are going to get tested."

"Nigga, don't act like you didn't fuck Bathsheba last night," Maine called him out.

Cordell rolled his eyes, "I just got some head. She on her period."

"Nigga, same thing." Maine replied. He was beginning to see Cordell as a prude. He couldn't believe for all the talk and shit they experienced together, Corey was the one that seemed like the expert. Over the course of a summer, Corey lost his virginity, learned how to suck dick, been to a sex party and had a threesome. If it hadn't been for Maine giving Cordell his last condom a month ago, he, Corey and Liam could've had their own threesome going.

"Anyway, let's get to the clinic," Cordell ordered as he rolled down the window. "I don't like needles or doctor's offices."

Maine started to say something smart but then he remembered that Cordell still tripped out over the death of his mother. He watched as Cordell shouldered most of that burden while Otis worked multiple jobs to take care of the household and he helped put on the façade for Corey that everything was alright. Maine was

"My niggas," Elgin bragged. "How about our boys about to start their line soon?"

"Who?" Spence sat up. "You know we don't pledge or start no one in the Spring."

Elgin mouth dropped as he remembered Spence's Greek. "I meant at UNCG." Elgin tried to clean it up. Inward, Maine knew Elgin was cursing himself for not being discreet.

The rest of the ride went without a hitch. Erykah Badu sang about the next lifetime and Maine hoped that if there was another life, there would be no such thing as HIV tests, STDs and relationships to ruin the feeling of good sex.

The clinic they went to was in High Point, which was about twenty-five minutes from the heart of campus. The boys chose to drive that far because they didn't want any of the nosy ass students from NC Tech in their business.

"I feel like we all on that movie, *The Wood*," Elgin blurted as they stepped out of the car.

"Why you say that?" Spence asked.

"Because, here we all are, doing this test after Maine done caught slipping. It's like we making him own up to his proposal." Elgin replied.

"I was gonna get tested with or without y'all," Maine and Spence stole a glance. He remembered they almost barebacked last night. He wanted so bad but decided against it.

The boys stepped into the clinic and each of them were directed to take a number from the ticket dispenser. Maine looked at his number and the number on the display monitor. He had seven people ahead of him, including his boys. He recognized one of the girls from his Accounting class and remembered he ditched the study group he was supposed to go to last night. He also saw a young couple holding a baby. The woman had her head in the middle of *Sorority Sisters* by Tajuana "TJ" Butler.

"Number 22," one nurse called out.

"Number 23," another called out behind her.

"Number 24," another called out.

"Oh this line moving quick," Elgin let out. "We might have time to go back to the café."

"Man," Cordell grinned. "You better have one of those Mrs. Winner's plates on deck."

"I need a break from Mrs. Winner's." Elgin took out his phone and started texting. "You think Cookout open?"

"Oh hell yeah," Spence chirped. "I haven't had Cookout since I been home. I'm good for a burger, fries, corndog and a drink."

"Everybody got five dollars?" Cordell asked as he dug in his pocket to pull out a five.

"Yeah," Spence and Elgin called out.

Fuck Maine cursed to himself. He didn't have cash and none of the fast food places took credit cards. "I need to stop at the Wachovia."

"Number 25," one of the nurses called out and Elgin got up.

"Aight fellas, time to fail this test." Elgin gave everyone dap.

"Fail?" Maine questioned.

"Yeah nigga," Elgin answered. "If I fail the test, that means I come up negative. If I pass, I test positive and I pass. I wanna fail this test with a zero."

"You stupid." Maine replied as he eyed an *Ebony* magazine on the table. He picked it up to pass the time. He felt his phone buzz.

What do you want man?

It was Corey. The boy finally texts him. He couldn't believe it.

I was just checking on you. Making sure you didn't need anything.

Maine played it cool. He was happy to finally hear from his boy. He wanted to get up with him and finish what they started. Maine wanted that ass and he still was trying to figure out where and how to get it. He wasn't going to fuck Corey in the dorms because Maine didn't want to be seen nowhere near the dorms. The walls were paper thin and he hated hearing someone else's business as much as he didn't want all the niggas in his business. Corey moaned and cursed too much when he was getting sucked and about to cum. Last thing he needed was to be seen leaving Corey's room. And he still haven't figured out how he was gonna smash in the same house he was living with Maine in.

Yo', I'll be in the library tonight. I'm studying for my calculus exam.

Hell, yeah!!! People smashed at Club Hurston all the time. All he had to do was either get Corey in one of the study rooms for a few minutes or lock up in one of the stalls. He was gonna have to teach Corey how to ride a dick so they wouldn't get caught. He wanted to do more than hug and kiss and he needed more than head.

I'll be there tonight. Just let me know and we'll figure something out.

It was set. Him and Corey were going to resume their freaktivities in the library. Worst case scenario, he'd have to shell out thirty bucks for a hotel in Winston-Salem, but it would be worth the time and the travel to get some of that.

"Number 26," the nurse came back and Maine caught the way Spence was grilling him.

"The fuck you mad for?" Maine let it slip.

He knew why Spence was mad.

"I swear y'all niggas got a love/hate relationship going on," Cordell let him know he saw it too. "Y'all niggas fucking the same bitch?"

No, we fucking, Maine didn't want to spoil the surprise. "You know Spence be bugging out sometimes."

"Real shit, that's why I didn't want to live with that nigga," Cordell admitted, "he spaz out too much for me. And on top of that, he fucking that white bitch and I'm not down with that."

The revelation surprised Maine. He could count on one hand how many white bitches Cordell gave the wood to because two of them, they did together last summer when they took a road trip to Daytona Beach last Spring Break.

"Oh, aight," Maine answered. He checked his phone. No message from Corey. Maine was serious about getting it on and poppin' with that boy.

"Number 27," one of the nurses came out.

"Aight man," Cordell gave Maine a pound. "Time for me to go fail this test, too."

Maine chuckled and checked his phone. Still no text back from Corey. He didn't know what time the boy was gonna be at the library or where. The Zora Neale Hurston library had four floors and a basement.

"Number 28," Maine heard his number.

His heart dropped. He hadn't had a test for HIV or any STDs since he had his physical last year to get re-admitted into NC Tech. Everything check out negative then but in that period of time, Maine had at least twenty different sex partners. He couldn't remember a couple of their names. Maine followed the thick male nurse to one of the back room.

"Oh shit!" That sounded like Spence.

Is he in there fucking? Maine wanted to know and headed to their door.

"Your test is in here sir," the nurse called out.

"Oh," Maine backed away from the door and headed to his room. He walked in and was surprised to see only a desk and three chairs. Posters outlining the importance for prostate exams, avoiding smoking and losing weight litter the room.

"When was the last time you been tested?" the nurse started.

Maine looked at him. He was fine and that booty fit into the scrubs nice. "About last year."

"When was the last time you had sex?" the nurse asked.

Last night, Maine knew not to give that answer. "About a few weeks ago."

"Any unprotected sex, sex with someone possibly infected with HIV or STD or sex with another man?"

"Yes, I don't think so and if threesomes count."

"I'll take that as a yes," the nurse smirked.

Maine didn't like him no more. He was cute and all but now, the man seemed judgmental. "This is what we are going to do. To be on the safe side, I'm going to take this swab," the nurse reached over the counter and grabbed a packet and opened it. It looked like a Q-Tip on a wooden stick. "I'm gonna have to swab your penis for a culture sample because if you have any STD's we need to get you in for a regimen right away. Fortunately, we're in a window period so I can have the doctor prescribe a penicillin-based drug to start killing the infections should your test come out positive. Are you allergic to penicillin?"

"I don't think so," Maine wasn't sure. Hear his mom tell it, he didn't know who his real parents were or anything about their health history.

"Drop your pants," the nurse ordered. Maine complied, glad he took a shower again after he, Vanessa and Spence got it in after breakfast. "I'm going to stick the swab and move around inside your penis."

"How far in my penis?" Maine questioned.

"Just the tip," the nurse answered.

"Cool," Maine answered as he inhaled. He felt the tip of it circle around the lips of his dick, then he felt his dick being penetrated. The swab didn't feel soft at all. Maine inhaled deeply as it felt like the swab was scratching the inside of his dick. "Ahhh—damn—damn—damn—shit!!!" He looked down to see that the tip was all the way in and the nurse was pulling it out.

Maine could feel the tears forming in his eyes. "You said it wasn't going to hurt."

"I did not," the nurse quipped. "I said I was only sticking the tip in." That prompted Maine to remember every time he told that lie to some unsuspecting female he ended up smashing. He didn't like that lie no more. "You gonna be ready for the blood draw?"

"Yeah," Maine stuck out his left arm, "they got a good vein from this arm the last time."

"It's good you know that." The nurse swabbed the culture and put it to the side. He then wrapped a tourniquet around his arm and prepared the needled to draw blood. He saw three different vials that looked thicker than the average hot dog.

How does that prayer go? Maine tried to remember the Lord's prayer. It had been a while since he said it and he remembered saying it the last time they stuck the needle in him. *Our fa*—Maine barely got out two words before the needle pierced his vein. He saw the blood flow immediately. *Art in heaven. Be thy name. Kingdom come, will be done, earth & heaven—shit I forgot the rest.* Maine looked as the nurse made the switch from one vial to the next. "We're almost done," he promised.

Maine gave up on the prayer. His mind focused on how fast his blood was entering the vial. In a few short seconds, he was done.

"You have any questions for me?" the nurse asked.

"When will I get my results?" Maine asked.

"We should know your STD results in about 48 hours and your HIV results in two weeks. I would highly advise you to abstain from sex—but I remember going to NC Tech and I couldn't keep it in my pants either." The nurse went to the drawer and pulled out a small brown paper bag. "In this bag is ten different types of condoms—strawberry ones taste real good—some lubricants and small packets about oral, vaginal and anal sex. Look over the material because I'm giving you a quiz when you come back for the results."

"Quiz?" Maine asked.

"Yeah—I don't give away these goodies for free. And your penis is gonna be a little sore throughout the day but you will be fine. No medication other than the penicillin needed. So in layman's terms, no pussy, no ass, no beating off with or without lubricant and be gentle when you wash it tonight."

"Alright man," Maine chuckled. He looked at the nurse again. Broad shoulders, smooth skin, looked damn good to have a little gray in his goatee. *Daddy I want to fuck you*, Maine thought what it would be like to peel those blue scrubs off him.

"And let me burst your bubble before you get out of here," the nurse stood up and looked Maine in the eye, "you not getting *this* ass."

"What?" Maine tried to deny.

"Bro—come on." The nurse shook his head. "I seen you checking me out and if I were ten years younger and closer to your age, I'd have you climb the walls screaming my name, cause I got good dick, nice head game and an ass to die for. But I'm also HIV positive, and I try to catch little knuckle heads like you before you end up in the same predicament I'm in."

Maine felt like his eyes were going to fall out of his sockets. "You got HIV?"

"Yeah, fine nigga like me had to have it all." The nurse smiled. "I was a star basketball player, a leader in student government, one of the best steppers in my frat and I fucked every man and woman who opened their legs and if a dude had a big dick, I was swallowing them in both holes. Right before I went to Wake Forest for grad school, I found out I was infected. Tore my world up. I spent the whole year suicidal until I met a young, fine, cream-colored sister who looked like she could be a fashion model. She was on the cover of *Essence* magazine and I couldn't believe she was positive. I only thought white homosexuals and drug users caught the virus. Anyway, she spoke about her experience and how she moved forward and because of her, I went to Wake

Forest, got my masters in nursing and now, I'm a year away from being Dr. Julius O'Shea Canton."

Maine was stunned. Nurse Julius looked very healthy and his body was too tight to be sick. Nails were clean, no discoloration of the eyes, perfect white teeth.

"I take nine medications to manage my HIV and blood pressure and I take vitamins, monitor my diet, talk to my psychologist and I speak around the country representing young black medical professionals who are making it despite living with a variety of infections. I'm human just like everyone else."

"You still have sex?" Maine asked.

"Come lunch time, my partner and I will find some place new to handle that—" Julius answered. "In the meantime, go out, have fun, stay on top of your studies and no sex for two weeks. And if you're going to disobey the last order, at least wear one of the condoms I'm providing you." Julius looked at the time. "Aight, my man will be here in fifteen minutes and I still haven't figured out where we're going yet. I'll see you in two weeks."

Maine couldn't believe he was being shoved out of the office. He clutch his bag and left with a mindfuck confusion on what his life would be like if he was positive, if he still wanted to mess around with Corey and how Julius could be so happy and content despite his condition. He had more questions than answers and after hearing the door closed, he knew he wasn't getting any.

10

Club Hurston

The Zora Neale Hurston Library was lit as the bright lights beamed from the top of the five-story building. The grounds within a few hundred feet were illuminated as the darkness filled with stars and a half moon.

Corey where are you at? Maine sent a text. He missed the first study hall for the accounting class but came to this one in part to catch up with Corey. It had been a few weeks since he and Corey had any level of intimacy and he missed him.

Maine followed Spence, Cordell, Elgin, Yonna and Chelle inside as they immediately headed to the fourth floor to meet with the rest of the groups from Dr. Finley's Accounting 101 classes. Several of the students from his three sections met and arranged several study groups in which to work on the homework together and study. Dr. Finley was one of the most highly sought after professors due to launching a successful, black-owned accounting practice after a ten-year stint at Deloitte & Touche. He was a national vice-president of Beta Gamma Sigma, the prestigious academic honor society for business majors. His firm counted No Limit Records, Grant Hill, Tamia, Act-1 Group, Radio One, Inc and BET Holdings as major accounts.

Dr. Finley was known not to play games in the classroom, teaching with the passion of Bishop T. D. Jakes with the tone of James Earl Jones. Physically, Dr. Finley was a daddy Maine wanted to fuck because despite being in his early fifties, Dr. Finley had a better physique than many of his classmates. He knew by the way Dr. Finley walked in class that he was serious about putting it down and wasn't scared to try a new position.

"Y'all are just in time," Janessa could be heard announcing as the crew walked into the door. Maine locked eyes with Renee, who moved her stuff and offered Maine a seat next to her. She motioned him with her finger. Maine and Yonna shared a look before he headed in Renee's direction.

"You got your work with you?" Renee asked as she took folded papers out of her accounting book.

"I only got to chapter one," Maine told the truth as he and Spence worked on the assignment at Willie's in between dealing with customers.

"I started chapter two," Renee replied as she slid her assignment in front of him.

"Renee, you bring up a good point, where is everyone?" Janessa asked as she took her place at the head of the table. "My father works for KPMG and will be here from Amsterdam in two weeks."

"I didn't know your dad worked for one of the big four," Elgin mentioned.

"Yeah—I know I can be a jerk sometimes, but I really want that low-key. He is on my ass about making sure I stay on top of my studies, as well as get into Beta Gamma Sigma and Beta Alpha Psi." Janessa stressed. "Not to mention he and Dr. Finley were undergrads and frat."

"Oh please don't say frat," Spence looked up. "Dr. Finley is my chapter advisor and with him, I feel like got two daddies."

Three, Maine thought to himself.

"Damn, that's right. I forgot you and I are in the same boat," Janessa winked.

"Thanks for the heads up on Dr. Cooper's visit." Spence laid his work on the table. "They are trying to get me to switch from marketing to accounting, but I've made some headway at Def Jam and I really want to go back this summer."

I'm on the third floor, Corey texted back.

On my way, Maine texted as his dick jumped. He was one step closer to hooking up with Corey.

"I'll be back," Maine got up and stuffed his phone in his pocket.

"Man, we haven't gotten started," Renee pouted. He saw it for what it was. Renee had plans to get at him sooner rather than later and while 'Keem said it was cool, Maine didn't want to make his move on Renee yet.

"I'm not gonna be long, one of the guys I'm mentoring is on the third floor and I'm gonna check on him real quick." Maine lied.

He knew Cordell nor Spence bought it and he suspected Elgin saw through it too. Yonna looked at him and rolled her eyes. She was getting on his nerves with her nonverbal, passive-aggressive behavior. Maine knew he and Yonna needed to have a serious sit-down about their situation, their decision not to wear a condom and if she was getting tested. His dick itched just thinking about it.

Maine hustled out of the room and headed straight to the steps as he did not want to wait on the elevators to get to the third floor. He hadn't seen Corey since almost catching him come out of the cafeteria a few days ago and on some real shit, he wanted to see if Corey had thought about getting tested. He knew he was clean as of two months ago when he accepted the offer to attend NC Tech, but he knew that Corey smashed with Marcus andLiam and whoever else was on his dick at the sex party they never finished talking about.

In the lobby, Maine saw several students sitting at Dell computers working on papers and researching. On the side, he saw a couple of the booths were occupied. Just a scan revealed very few students moving between the aisles. His first thought was to check the three study rooms to see if Maine was in there. It would have been cool as shit to get in a little head before he headed back up to study.

In the first room, Maine could see a study group going over material. He didn't see Corey, but looked harder to see if there were an extra bag. He caught a glimpse of the engineering book and realized Corey wouldn't have been in that room. The next room was dark and Maine put his ear to the door. *Maybe my boy waiting on me in there.* Maine thought as he lightly knocked on the door.

"One minute," he could hear a gruff voice on the other side. Maine took a step back and when the door opened, 'Keem poked his head out. "Sup nigga," he gripped him up.

"Man nothing, I'm looking for my mentee," Maine looked in the room. He could see someone struggling to put their shirt on.

There were rumors about 'Keem being a freak and this incident didn't disappoint.

"Well man, I'm in the middle of my own, *private*, tutoring session if you catch my drift." 'Keem hinted as he opened the door a little wider, allowing Maine a peek inside. A young black woman was sitting at the table, appearing to be deeply engrossed in one of the textbooks.

"Aww, naw, that ain't her." Maine smirked and nodded his head. He respected 'Keem's freak game. Renee was upstairs studying accounting in their study group and it appeared 'Keem had a personal anatomy show and tell practice aide at his fingertips.

"Let me know when you and Renee link up and shit," 'Keem winked. "I'd give you some pointers, but I got to get back to class."

'Keem closed the door before Maine could respond. It occurred to him that 'Keem only had on some black boxers and maybe some socks.

As he got closer to the third study room, the open door revealed it was empty. He felt a shove push him inside and Maine turned around and almost punched Spence in the face.

"So cut the bullshit, who you really looking for?" Spence hinted that he overheard the lie Maine told 'Keem.

"Mushroom," Maine didn't bother to deny it. "Shouldn't you get back to the study session?"

"Shouldn't you?" Spence threw his question back at him.

"I will, I was just hoping to catch ole boy—that's all." Maine admitted.

"You gotta picture of him?" Spence asked. "Maybe I can help you look for him after we get this study thing together."

"Naw," Maine answered. "I don't keep pictures of dudes."

"That's cool." Spence looked up at Maine. "Maybe we can hook up with him one time once you find him. If his tip is shaped the way you say it is, I wouldn't mind sucking on it." Spence licked his lips. "Teach him a few things."

"You not gonna be teaching him shit," Maine threatened.

"I'm just saying, you captivated by this dude and I wanna have fun. You said yourself y'all weren't serious. Maybe he got caught up with something—or someone." Spence suggested.

At that moment, Maine thought about some of the shady shit he'd done to Corey. Not working with him on his head giving skills. Not hooking him up with some ass—not necessarily his ass —when he clearly wanted some. Making jokes at his expense to cover for the fact he was feeling him, especially in front of Cordell. Touching him, teasing him, always bringing him to the brink of ecstasy and no return. Pretending like he didn't know Corey wanted more than a friendship with him. Deep down, he knew he probably could've got the ass a few weeks ago and he hoped he hadn't found someone to give it up to.

Maine missed an opportunity to show him the ropes.

"Let's head back before Janessa sends a search team out to look for us." Spence opened the door. "We'll catch Mushroom another time."

Maine was disappointed. He pulled out his phone and didn't see a reply from Corey. All he knew was Corey was on the third floor, somewhere. Or at least he hoped he was. Almost ten minutes had passed and he needed to make his way back to the study group. He wasn't going to pass Accounting 101 if he didn't put in the work and just like everyone else, he needed to pass that class if he was going to get his degree. He still wanted the assistant manager position at Willies and he wanted to intern for a record company.

Defeat and a little karma slapped him once again as he gave up his pursuit. He hoped Corey wasn't in the bathroom or worse yet —he hoped Corey wasn't serving him the same bullshit Maine fed him all summer. Maine would never admit it but he was a little jealous knowing Marcus was the one that got to experience penetration with Corey. And from time to time, he beat off imagining how Corey, Marcus and Liam put in work.

"*Look Corey, just get the fuck out of here man,*" Maine's words haunted him as he made his way back to the study group. "*It's time for you to grow up. I'm not your boyfriend, never gonna be that. As a matter of fact, I'm not even with this gay shit no more!*"

Lies.

All lies. Ironic the last time they spoke to one another, Maine refused to give Corey a lift to school. Now that they were at NC Tech, he couldn't find Corey if his life depended on it.

Maine returned to the study group and sat next to Renee. He thought about her open relationship with 'Keem and his invitation to partake. She got close to him, which caused Yonna to smack her lips. She rolled her eyes at him again. Spence looked back at him and shook his head.

And all Maine could think about, was him.

11

Misunderstanding

"Open the damn door Maine, I know you're in there." Yonna yelled as she banged the door like a mad woman.

Meanwhile, Maine laid in the bed and tried to keep his eyes closed. He wasn't feeling the attention that Yonna was bringing to his spot. They weren't together—they were just using each other for sex.

Good sex.

But that's all it was to Maine and everything was fine until he took the condom off and planted his seed inside her. Now, he seemed to be reaping the consequence of those actions. Yonna was acting like she was his woman.

"Aye man, get up!" Maine could hear Cordell command as he opened the door and turned the light on in his room.

"I'm trying to sleep man," Maine turned over and brought his sheets up to conceal his nude frame.

"Bathsheba in here tripping and ready to fight her and we agreed we'd never let our women fight," Cordell reminded him.

Maine squeezed his eyes together and exhaled. He knew Cordell was taking things very slow with Bathsheba but he also knew that she was at least a contender for Cordell to barge into his room without knocking. He wanted Yonna to go to hell but he didn't want to have to get up and tell her.

Maine sat up and wrapped the sheet around his waist. He looked down and eyed his low-tops and slid into them like they were house shoes.

"If we need to call security, give me the word." Cordell suggested. "Don't put your hands on her."

Maine tried not to take offense to what Cordell was saying. He remembered Cordell being there to witness him point a gun to the woman he thought was his mother.

"Aight man." Maine promised as he stepped out of the room, walked to the living room, "if you stop banging on the door I'll open it!" Maine yelled. He waited ten seconds for silence before he made good on his promise.

"You a grimy ass motherfucker, Maine!" Yonna barged in and threw her metal baseball bat on the floor. Maine took a quick look at the door and the car he shared with Cordell before closing the door.

"You better be glad you didn't hit my shit with that bat." Maine picked it up and gripped it at his side. "The fuck's wrong with you."

"You treating me like shit, that's what!" Yonna tried to get into his face and Maine put his arm up to block her.

"Treat you like shit?!" Maine was confused. "How the fuck do I do that?!"

"Give me my damn bat!" Yonna grabbed it and tried to pull it from Maine's hand. Maine tightened his grip around it. He didn't trust that Yonna wouldn't have hit him with it.

"Sit yo' ass down before I have you escorted from my house!" Maine ordered.

"You a fucked up nigga!" Yonna pouted as she slouched on the couch.

"How is that?!" Maine asked as he stood near the door. He wanted to keep as much distance between the two of them as possible. He looked down and tightened the sheets around his waist.

"Acting like you had a problem with me earlier." Yonna rolled her eyes and shook her head. "And then you had the nerve to sit next to that skank bitch Renee. And you know she gotta man."

"DING DING DING--key-fucking words. SHE GOTTA MAN!!! Not yo' fucking ass. Let's not confuse the fact that I nutt in you for "I love you." Because let's face it, I'm twenty, I'm in school, I work and I got a big ass dick. If the world depended on my being able to spell love for human kind's survival, every motherfucker gracing this earth would be in hell because I don't know if love has three letters or four." Maine spit coldly as he looked into her eyes.

"I fucking hate you," Yonna choked and fought back tears.

"You say that like I'm supposed to give a fuck." Maine came back. "If I remember correctly—you and Chelle mess around. You've fucked 'Keem before. Spence tapped that the night he crossed. Ain't no telling how many women or men you've been with. So no, I DON'T LOVE YOU. I'm not even sure I like you."

"I don't even know why I'm tripping." Yonna got up and straightened out her clothes.

"I'm waiting on you to tell me that you're pregnant or that I have you something so I tell you that you're lying so you can get the fuck out." Maine opened the door.

"You're never getting this pussy again!" Yonna got up and stormed past him.

Maine loosened the sheets from around his waist and felt the slight breeze in the air. "My dick gotta nice hook to it, I'm sure I'll catch some new pussy before the next hour is up!" Maine leaned against the frame, not giving a fuck who could see that he was naked. He watched as Yonna walked to her apartment with her middle finger in the air.

"Fuck you Maine!" she declared as if it were going to have any effect on him.

Maine looked around and noticed a few people looking out their windows or opening the door to see the drama that ensued. Maine walked outside, dropped the bat, turned around slowly so everyone could see what he was working with, shrugged his shoulders, picked up the bat and walked back inside.

"Damn boy," Bathsheba admired Maine's physique, "you know how to put on a show."

Maine grabbed the sheet off the floor and wrapped it back around his waist out of respect for Cordell. "I gotta give the fans what they want."

"I see why that Delta and Zeta were fighting over you." Bathsheba admitted as the door knocked.

Maine looked out of the peephole and saw Elgin and let him in. "You keep breaking these girls' hearts." Elgin walked in and gave Maine some dap.

"Naw, these girls be confused," Maine defended. "One minute, they want my D. Then I give them the D. Next minute, they in love with me. It's like I got the magic stick, those cupid powers."

"Your D must stand for 'drama' because that's all it's getting you lately," Cordell called from his room.

"Who you telling?" Maine agreed. "All I do is give them what they want. I'm not responsible for how they feel afterward."

Elgin pulled a small dimebag from his pocket. "You got some rolling paper?"

"Hold on, I got some Kool's in my purse." Bathsheba got up and went into Cordell's room. A few seconds later, she and Cordell both came out. Bathsheba walked to Elgin, took the dimebag out of his hand and sat at the table. In less than thirty seconds, Bathsheba dumped the tobacco on the table, divided the weed between the two cigarette sheets and started two joints.

Maine took one joint and inhaled. "I haven't had one of these in a minute," Maine took another toke and passed it to Cordell.

"Shit nigga, who you telling?" Cordell joined in. "It thought I'd be getting blazed every day."

"Aye man, I don't run by a bag often but when I do, I share it with the homies," Elgin took a puff and passed it to Bathsheba.

"I got class in four hours," Cordell called out, "and I gotta be at Burger King today. I'm about to go back to sleep."

Bathsheba finished her tote, "I'll be back in the room in a minute babe." She passed her joint back to Maine. "On some real shit though, you need to straighten that shit out before she smash the windows out your car or worse."

"She got me fucked up," Maine replied. "Let my car get fucked up and she'll be paying for it."

"Well—fuck it." Elgin took a puff and inhaled. "I'm just glad you okay man. Terry McMillan got women out here thinking it's okay to go ballistic on a nigga."

"This ain't *Waiting to Exhale*..." Maine clapped back. "Probably should go to her place and offer her a few puffs. This is kind of good."

"Umm hmm," Bathsheba replied before she opened the door to Cordell's room, "next thing you know, she'll be puffing on your dick and y'all be repeating the whole scenario in a week."

"I'm not going to go over there," Maine promised before Bathsheba closed the door.

"Real shit, I came over here not just to check on you but to get away." Elgin leaned back in the seat. "My big brothers are getting on my nerves."

"Big brothers?" Maine gave him the side-eye.

"Yeah, that's what I said. I wasn't gonna come bother you but with Yonna making a scene, I'm knew you would be up. Just let me stay on the couch. The big brothers not gonna come mess with you in your house."

Maine caught on to what Elgin was telling him. He was shocked because he knew NC Tech didn't allow any of the organizations to have their interest meetings until the last week in January. He heard of people pre-pledging and going underground, but he never thought he'd see it up front. Maine hadn't even decided if he wanted to be Greek. He was cool with them. And he never ran out of options as far as the sorority girls were concerned. But Maine wanted that assistant manager's job at Willies and the internship with one of the record labels more than he wanted three letters across his chest.

"Aight man, you know where the pillows are at and shit." Maine pointed to the linen closet. Elgin got up and grabbed the spare while Maine took the joint into his room and chilled. He closed the door and dropped the sheets and took a seat on the bed. He opened the window and enjoyed the last of the blunt before he found a few hours of peaceful slumber.

12

Before Sex Tapes

"Oh my God, *it is* big!" One of Maine's classmates exclaimed when he walked into Dr. Finley's class. A few of the girls giggled and gave each other high five's as Maine took a seat near the front of the room. "And them gray sweatpants he wearing ain't hiding it either."

"I wonder who's the biggest between him and Donte Longstocking?" Another girl asked.

"Shit, I'd let him and Donte run a train on me and film it. I wonder how much money I could make?"

Maine arrived ten minutes early and wanted a chance to look over his notes because Dr. Finley was notorious for giving pop quizzes and Maine wanted to be prepared. He took his backpack off and put it on the desk. He reached in and picked up the accounting book and pulled out the assignments he worked on. After the fiasco with Yonna, Maine decided to get a jump on the accounting assignments and review the next couple of chapters. He had some questions and pulled out the set of the assignments he used as his notes so he could write Dr. Finley's answers and tips off the side.

"Bruh," 'Keem sat at the desk and moved it next to Maine. "Tell me your crazy ass did not walk outside and show off the goods this morning?"

"What are you talking about?" Maine tried to ignore 'Keem so he could focus on his studies.

"Dawg, let me show you this," 'Keem pulled out his laptop and opened Renee's Yahoo account. "My girl got this this morning."

"You screen her emails?" Maine quizzed.

"Nigga stay on point, I'm trying to show you something. Check out the link that says Chocolate on a Wednesday morning." 'Keem shoved his Compaq on Maine's desk.

Maine opened the email. A picture of him standing outside with his arms shrug with his thick flaccid penis standing out against his solidly cut frame.

"Bruh, I just thought I'd let you know you all over MySpace." One of the girls in the laughing group pointed out.

"Yeah, everyone's forwarding your naked pics in chain emails and message boards. Talking about NC Tech packing." Another girl pointed out.

Maine closed the link, passed 'Keem the computer and slouched in the chair. He couldn't believe his decision to bare it all came back to haunt him. Yeah, it was supposed to be a cute, innocent gesture, not one immortalized on film.

"Can you show us real quick before the rest of the class gets here?" One of the girls smirked.

Maine shook his head and smirked. He would have if 'Keem wasn't sitting in the desk next to him. He didn't want ole boy next to his wood like that. Renee walked in the room and licked her lips. She took the other seat next to him.

"We need to get up later, after class," Renee smirked, "and 'Keem, give me my laptop back."

'Keem handing the laptop across Maine's desk and Renee grabbed it. Maine moved back to make sure he didn't get hit. Spence walked in, glared at Maine and went right to his seat. Spence tripping didn't faze Maine not one bit, he dove into his studies. He really needed to ace the pop quiz he felt Dr. Finley was getting ready to hand out.

"Aye bruh," hearing Cordell's voice caused him to look up, "you know they talking about you all over the school. They almost mobbed me and Bathsheba as we tried to get out the door. They almost tore my pants off and shit."

Maine felt bad. He didn't want Cordell to bear the consequences of his antic. He could see a crowd of girls gathering around his apartment trying to gain entry.

"Class will start in a few minutes," Dr. Finley stormed inside. His navy and yellow cardigan with NC TECH down the left side with the school's shield on the right brought out the blue and yellow bow. His average-sized frame failed to conceal his workout regimen and his smooth skin defied his age. Dr. Finley looked more like one of Maine's running buddies than his peer.

Black don't crack.

"Maine, grab your things and see me outside." Dr. Finley eyed Maine and waited for him to move.

"I had some questions about the assignment." Maine raised his paper.

"We'll talk about it outside."

"You're kicking me out?" Maine huffed, still not barging from his seat.

"Not exactly," Dr. Finley admitted. "Just come outside."

"Motherfucker," Maine mumbled under his breathe. Now showing what he thought was a small audience his dick was about to cost him his education. He needed to stay in school for Willie to consider making him assistant manager. And he couldn't go back to the A—Eric wasn't going to let him stay with him with both Cordell and Corey at NC Tech and he didn't have nowhere to go.

Maine grabbed his stuff and stepped outside. He looked Dr. Finley in the eye as his professor leaned against the door. "You sir, are very impulsive."

"That I am." No use in asking if his professor saw the picture —he wouldn't be outside the classroom if he didn't.

"Look—I'm not gonna beat around the bush. I'm putting you out for the day. I want this to die down for a minute. It took me ten minutes to get to class to calm down after everyone had been forwarded your infamous nude pics. I don't know what it is with you and the other men who feel like you've got to show off what you got." Dr. Finley scolded.

"It's not like that." Maine defend. "Me and the girl I'm seeing got into it and—"

"Excuses are tools of the incompetent—and I know you are far from that." Dr. Finley cut him off. "The dean wants to put you out—but a few of your professors and I are coming up with an alternative, since technically, the incident happened off campus and the university doesn't have jurisdiction. And by the way, thank you for not acting on impulse and honoring Aaliyah's request to pull your thang out."

"So what about my assignment? And aren't you giving a pop quiz?" Maine asked.

"I tell you what. I'm not giving the class their pop quiz today—but you better make A's on all your assignments from here on out. Since I'm your advisor, I will be meeting with you between tomorrow and Friday to discuss this situation in a more private and professional setting that doesn't take away from my instruction time. Check your emails."

Maine lowered his head and pulled his homework out. "Thank you for letting me turn in my work." He gritted his teeth. He wanted to kick Dr. Finley's ass but his accountability checked him on that. It was his fault for being put out.

"I'll see you Friday in class. And if I were you, I'd head to Dr. Dudley's office. She has the rest of your assignments. She may even let you use the spare office to get some of your work done without any distractions." Dr. Finley suggested.

Maine could tell the suggestion was not a request. Dr. Dudley's office was on the top floor and he knew there were very few classrooms up there as the building hosted a mini library, a few conference rooms and offices. Taking the stairs was the best route and Maine knew he needed to face the music.

13

Put It Out There

The walk to Dr. Dudley's office was longer than Maine anticipated. He wasn't out of shape but he didn't expect to stop and switch his bag from one shoulder to the next. Dr. Dudley was his Introduction to Business professor and she stayed on Maine about getting his work done and maintaining a good G. P. A.

"Come in," Dr. Dudley invited him once she saw him through her cracked door. When Maine walked in, he admired the diplomas hanging on her wall; the pictures of her children and grandchildren. NC Tech and her sorority's blue and gold paraphernalia all over the room.

"Thank you," Maine acknowledged as he walked in and stood next to the chair, waiting to be invited to have a seat.

"Don't thank me yet," Dr. Dudley looked up. Her mane flowed with silver and violet hair reminiscent of Storm from the X-Men and fell on her shoulders. She was a tall woman, about three or four inches shorter than Maine. Despite her age, she was firm and fit. "I would ask you what possessed you to walk out of your house butt ass naked, but I'm afraid I'm not gonna like the answer."

Dr. Dudley had no filter and reminded him of the strong women of the Black Panther Party for Self Defense, which she also was a member of in the seventies.

"I don't have a good answer," Maine admitted.

"Well, for my marketing class, I need you to focus on product and placement and to begin thinking about the changes you would make to the recording industry." Dr. Dudley handed him a stack of papers. "Those are a copy of my notes for the day and, Dr. Gerber wants you to review chapter three in your microeconomics book—sounds like you might have a quiz or test next period. I'm going to get ready for my class that will arrive in thirty minutes. I'm going to unlock the door to my spare office. Various professors will be checking in so no funny stuff. And you are limited to one guest that you can review material with and study. Staying in the office will count as being present for class. I'll see you before you leave for Willie's."

Maine followed Dr. Dudley out of her office and into the spare one, which was bland with crème walls. Only a cherrywood, executive-style desk with three chairs furnished the room. Maine put his bag on the table and took a seat opposite from where the professor would've sat.

"And Maine, don't have none of these hoes in this office and you better be fully dressed when I come back." Dr. Dudley pulled no punches.

"Yes, ma'am." Maine answered as he looked over the assignments.

"'Keem, I see you made to the study session." Dr. Dudley's voice caused Maine to turn around. "This is not the locker room. I better not come back and see a party and loose girls up here fighting for either one of you."

"Yes ma'am." Maine and 'Keem repeated.

"I got a belt and some heels. Don't make me take them off."

'Keem stared at the door making sure Dr. Dudley was gone while Maine went back to reading his notes. "That old lady is wild."

"That old lady is about as crazy as my mama." Maine paused. It had been the first time in a while that he acknowledged his mom, out loud, in some time.

"Man listen, Dr. Finley went over debit and credit accounts and showed us how to use the T-account. This shit is harder than I thought it would be." 'Keem lounged as Maine made notes while looking over the papers.

"Where's your book at?" Maine asked as he dug into his bag for a highlighter.

"Renee got them notes for me," 'Keem bragged as he pulled out his Razr and started texting.

"You aren't helping me texting and shit. I gotta get some work done so I don't get no further behind than what I will be." Maine went back to his studies.

"Don't trip." 'Keem looked out the door and then moved his seat closer to Maine. Maine could smell his Curve cologne and Right Guard deodorant. "When you gonna make a move on Renee?"

'Keem was getting close—too close.

"Ain't that your girl?" Maine was annoyed. He really wanted to stay on top of his accounting studies and at least look at the marketing notes before Dr. Dudley got back. He knew she would quiz him on the work he'd done. Maine realized if he was going to get an internship at any record company or move up at Willie's, he'd have to keep his nose clean and minimize his distractions.

"Look man, I told you the shit was cool." 'Keem held his composure while putting his hand on Maine's knee. "Renee and I are into some freaky shit and we wanna let you in on the fun."

'Keem's hand traveled up Maine's thigh and got to the midway point. Maine looked up but didn't stop him. 'Keem gave him a quick thigh massage and put his hand away.

'Keem wanted an answer and Maine gave it to him. Maine found out one of 'Keem's deepest secrets.

"So you really want me to meet up and do your girl?" Maine leaned closer to 'Keem. He brought the book and the notes closer to the middle of the table so he could pretend like he and 'Keem were doing some studying.

"I wanna watch, and maybe join ya'." 'Keem put his hand on Maine's thigh again. Maine tried to fight the urge to reveal his erect but 'Keem was rubbing his thigh the right way. Like a genie in a bottle, Maine's dick was making its presence known. "The girls were right—you do got a big dick." 'Keem's voice got deep as he started to lower his head. "I can't wait to suck it."

'Keem reached the top of Maine's sweat pants and pulled Maine's dick out. It pulsated, recognizing the familiar touch of another man. Maine looked back at the door and made sure the coast was clear. 'Keem got his head under the table and kissed Maine's mushroom head. 'Keem put Maine's tip in his mouth and gave it a few quick sucks. 'Keem's tongue caressed the under sided of Maine's tip then licked the precum from the slit.

"Yeah," 'Keem brought Maine's pants back over his erection. "I can't wait to suck and get fucked by that."

"You're bi?" Maine asked, readjusting his pants and looking back at the door. He couldn't believe 'Keem boldly teased him like that.

"I'm whatever makes my dick hard and Renee happy." 'Keem grabbed the notes from the table and brought them to his face.

"She know about you?" Maine wasn't convinced that Renee was cool with 'Keem being on the DL. He'd heard of cuckolding, but only thought white people were into that shit.

"She watches me like I watch her."

Maine tried but couldn't focus on his assignments. He couldn't believe that part of his dick was in 'Keem's mouth and that he had an invitation to tap that ass, too. He tried not to get too excited but the thought of fucking 'Keem and Renee intrigued him just as much as trying things out with Spence and Vanessa. In the back of his mind, he was trying to figure out a way to get a threesome with Spence and 'Keem off and running. It's been a minute since he'd been with two men and Maine wanted to try that again. This time it would be different because Spence and 'Keem had their own girls. Maine wouldn't be a third member of a couple's sexual escapade, he'd be a willing participant.

"Yo, explain to me what this T-account shit is." 'Keem requested. "I'm still lost."

'Keem passed the notes back to Maine. Maine looked them over and then pulled out a fresh sheet of paper. Maine spent the next fifteen minutes going over the accounting concept when the door opened.

Dr. Dudley took a few steps in and inhaled, "ahh, I'm glad it doesn't smell like teen spirit up in here."

'Keem and Maine looked at each other and shook their heads. "Give me more credit than that Dr. Dudley, I know how to keep it in my pants." 'Keem defended himself.

"Umm hmm, you think cause I'm old enough to be your grandma you can tell me anything." Dr. Dudley eyed him as she took another set of papers out of her bag and laid them on the table. "I managed to get your communications teacher to make you a copy of her notes too. You need to see her tomorrow during her office hours."

"Yes ma'am, and thank you." Maine glanced at the notes.

"Oh, don't thank me yet. I still have some work to do. In the meantime, stay on top of these notes and 'Keem, walk in late to my class and you'll find yourself in the lounge. I'm sending Niger up here to work with Maine." Dr. Dudley instructed as she walked out.

Niger was the teacher's assistant getting his master's in supply chain management. He graduated with a transportation and logistics degree last year and spent part of his time working with DHL and their expansion into Greensboro.

"Looks like my time is up." 'Keem got up and put his drawstring bag on both shoulders. "If you free tomorrow, stop by after you get off at Willie's."

"Cool," Maine gave him a pound that turned into a handshake. He watched as 'Keem opened the door and walked out. He never paid too much attention to 'Keem's basketballs that were struggling to stay within the confines of his navy sweatpants. He licked his lips then turned away.

He couldn't wait to get it in with one of the star players of the school's football team. And his girl was a freak too. A small, gentle voice warned him the opportunity was too good to be true, but Maine was all too ready to take a dance on the wild side.

14

Been There, Done That

"I would ask some questions, but I don't know if I want to know the answers." Willie started when Maine walked in the door.

By this point, Maine was tired of everyone pointing at him, elders asking what possessed him to walk his naked ass outside. Spence ignoring him then grilling him like he wanted to say something. The girls boldly walking up to him asking him if they can see his dick or trying to cop a feel. The dudes acting like they didn't get the emails or see his pics all over Myspace.

"Can I say I'll never do it again?" Maine asked as he punched in. He was glad that tonight was Spence's night off. Generally, they both stayed away from the store when they had off so they could study and get into some stuff.

"No—I was your age once. There's always a way to do stupid shit again and to top what was done the last time." Willie closed the register and handed the store key over to Maine. "Don't have no girls walking around here naked and if that Yonna chick who was screaming at you the other day comes in here—call the police. I don't want her in my store acting a fool."

Willie gave Maine a hug. He was glad that somehow, Willie heard something closer to the truth about what really happened when he decided to walk outside and bare all. Willie was the first person to mention that he'd been provoked all day.

As soon as Willie left the store, Maine got to work straightening the shelves and plotting how the visit with Mary J. Blige and DMX was going to go. Fortunately for him, he was going to be able to use some of his ideas for his marketing class project and the application of the experience would help him long term.

A young man walked in with a low-cut fade. He was a nice pecan color and an even swimmer's build to support his slim, six foot frame. Maine got a look at his face and he smiled.

"Donte." Maine came from behind the register and gave his classmate a grip.

"Damn nigga, if I didn't know better, I'd think you were trying to come for my spot." Donte and Maine clapped hands and he immediately made a bee-line to the old school hip hop section.

"Naw player, that was a one-time thing." Maine was sure of himself. He knew that Donte Speaks, known to the rest of the world as Donte Longstocking, was the school's resident porn star. Part of the reason Maine didn't fear getting put out was because Donte had been making videos while still attending classes at both NC Tech and neighboring Gilbert State University. Donte was one of the first amateur adult video stars to go pro and make films in Vegas and all over the world.

"I came to get some music for my next video, but I don't know what I want to do." Donte picked up a few CDs then put them back how he found them. "I'm supposed to be doing these chicks from the West Coast but I've already made videos to Snoop, Tha Dogg Pound, Too Short and Luke Campbell."

Maine was clueless as to how to help him. Admittedly, he caught a few of the flicks when they got bootlegged to Napster or Limewire. It was almost the best way to catch porn and not get caught. He knew Donte's dick was a good inch bigger than his and thick. He also liked how muscular Donte's back looked and how he always knew some twisted, freaky, sexual position to bend a female in. And Donte pulled some women. From black girls to Asian chicks—tall, short, fat, skinny, fine and ugly. Donte got that dick hard on command.

"Have you tried some of the underground rappers or the southern rappers?" Maine suggested.

"Man, I did a parody of The Ghetto Boy's 'Mind Playing Tricks on Me.' They are still pissed at me over that shit." Donte pointed out as he looked at a few more CDs.

"I remember that *Booty Playing Tricks On Me*." Maine admitted.

"It's one of my top selling videos and streams," Donte smiled. "I paid for the use the song and they still being salty. I hope we don't end up in court. I'm sick of looking at the inside of the courtroom."

Maine's thoughts of fame and glamour disappeared as he pictured Donte paying an assload of money in lawyer's fees and court cost. Almost made his little brush with the pics being all over the place look like child's play.

"How did you deal with everyone seeing you naked?" Maine got serious. If anyone in his life understood what he was going through right now with the mixed and conflicting emotions, it was Donte. Donte been through the fights with Gilbert State University, barely escaping expulsion himself.

"Man, I had to learn the business side of the adult film industry quick." Donte schooled him as he finally found a few UGK and Three Six Mafia CD's. "That's why I worked three jobs so I could buy and trademark my Donte Longstocking name. I bought my website, brokered a deal with MySpace for my own page and took classes with some of the best adult film makers so I could learn to make my own music. Believe it or not, when I was in LA, I caught Master P and Michael Jackson having a private conservation after the Soul Train Music Awards. They invited me to the conversation. By this point, I'd incorporated and owned a few businesses that managed my career and my images. Master P offered me an internship in New Orleans to work with No Limit Records film division. Michael Jackson offered me the best business advice ever—always remain in control. I operate by them four words."

"You ran into Michael Jackson?" Maine couldn't believe it.

"Everyone is not as judgmental and besides, it was a quick pow-wow that may never happen again. He hooked me up with a company that does music sample clearances, so I can avoid future mishaps. It's the same one a lot of rappers use." Donte and Maine made their way to the register. "So I'm gonna repeat to you what the King told me, always remain in control."

In the back of his mind, he knew he didn't want to make it as an adult video star. He didn't like all the people he saw in front of the camera and didn't want to have to smash people he didn't want to.

"It sounds like I need to find out who took my pictures." Maine inquired as he rang up the CDs.

"Yeah, that's your best bet." Donte pulled out a black American Express card made out to Donte Longstocking Enterprises, Inc. Maine took the card and swiped his order. "Legally, whoever took the pictures owns the copyright to the image. But money talks and maybe, I can help you with that. You gonna be in our microeconomics class on Friday right?"

"Yeah."

"Cool, if you can get an answer by then, I'll have my people draw up a contract so that we acquire ownership of your pictures. In exchange, I want you to come with me when I make my next film. You don't have to be in front of the camera, but I want you to see what a day in my life is like before you decide to do any additional footage." Donte offered.

He knew Donte was about his business. Silently, he admitted that he admired how Donte balanced running a profitable entertainment company while going to school full time. Donte was doing what he wanted to do in terms of learning from college and putting it to work for him.

"I see I got some work to do. Whoever took the pictures most likely lived in the same apartment complex because that's where it went down. I think I'll offer a reward." Maine completed the transaction and handed Donte the bag with the CDs.

"Yeah—be sure to say that the person getting the reward has to provide or be willing to lead you to the person who can show proof that they have the negatives. Pictures can easily be duplicated but not necessarily the negatives." Donte advised.

"You've given me a lot of help." Maine and Donte gave each other pounds.

"We have to help each other out here. I've been there already. Now it's up to you to decide where you wanna go with it. I'll catch you later."

Maine watched Donte walk out of the store. It felt good to finally talk to someone who didn't judge him perse. Now more than ever, Maine needed to find out which of his neighbors took the pictures and get the negatives. Even though he hadn't taken business law yet, he knew he would need to reach out to one of the professors who may be willing to help him out. With Dr. Finley and Dr. Dudley willing to help him stay in school, he figured between the two of them, they'd help him with that.

Elgin rushed into the store with a paper in his hand. "Have you had a chance to check the mail?"

"Naw man," Maine replied, wondering why he was waving the paper.

"How about, I gotta go back and get tested again?" Elgin slammed the paper down. Upon closer look, Elgin appeared to be crying.

"Are you for real?" Maine came from behind the registered.

"My life is fucked up!" Elgin's voice got deeper and slightly slurred.

"Don't say that," Maine wanted to be optimistic while fearing his own answers. Even with the HIV scare, he slept with Spence and Vanessa and let 'Keem suck on his dick a little.

"I got herpes man—that shit is incurable." Elgin dropped a bomb that Maine wasn't ready to hear.

Maine had hoped that if he had something, it could be cured by penicillin or some other drugs. He knew HIV was incurable and would lead to AIDS. He never considered herpes or some other STD's that he might have to take pills for for the rest of his life.

Maybe he shouldn't have let 'Keem suck on his tip.

Maine looked at Elgin's results. His chlamydia, gonorrhea and syphilis tests came back negative. His HIV test came back inconclusive.

"So they gotta redo your HIV test?" Maine asked.

"Yeah, they gotta redo both the HIV test and the herpes test. They said that having herpes can trigger a false positive HIV test —that's why it's inconclusive. I just came back from the nurse where she said they have to verify HIV using Western Blot testing."

"So when you going?" Maine asked.

"I gotta go tomorrow." Elgin answered.

"Aight cool. I'll go with you. When I get home, I'll look at my results. Have you told anyone else?"

"Naw," Elgin folded his paper up and put it in his pocket. "Cordell at Burger King and you know he'll start tripping and fuckin' up people's food. And Spence's with the big brothers doing something. Man, I may never become frat with this shit."

"You being positive for HIV or herpes or anything else don't have nothing to do with you being a brother. Remember, one of the AKA's got that shit from her boyfriend and them girls defend her like a hawk. She don't ever go nowhere alone and they whole chapter ready to throw them blows for talking slick." Maine pointed out. He knew the girl and almost messed with her and he knew she was positive before the rest of the school had found out. "And you remember when one of them had their baby shower/party last year, they only asked people to bring baby items and clothing and they gave that way to a local charity that helps mothers living with HIV."

"Yeah man," Elgin smiled and wiped his eyes. "I had fun picking out that baby Allen Iverson get up with the matching shoes."

"I told you to buy some pampers—but Cordell and I pooled together to buy six cases of baby formula because the girl he was talking to at the time said that's what they needed." Maine reminisced.

"Cordell was trying to be extra. Plus, his girl trying to be an AKA this year so I know she had something to do with that. My back still hurts from carrying all them cases." Elgin chuckled.

"Boy bye." Maine shook his head. "You were the main one trying flex."

"Damn right," Elgin bragged. "I love the girls who wear pink and green. Plus my sister one, even though mom's a Delta."

Maine forgot Elgin had an older sister. He hardly saw her and Elgin hardly brought him up. Elgin having herpes put a new wave of fear into his heart for his own status. He didn't know what he would do if he had HIV, herpes or some other disease he couldn't get rid of. He liked to fuck too much and couldn't see living life without some ass or pussy to pass the time.

"Can I stay here till the shop close?" Elgin asked. "I don't want my cousins in my business and I really don't want to be alone right now."

"Yeah man, just look busy." Maine suggested.

Maine knew the risks of his lifestyle. Being that he slept with men on a semi-regular basis, he always stayed on top of the new diseases and the risks associated. Most hookups, the guys asked and bragged about their latest test results as many of the men he messed around with, Spence included, tested every three months. Up until now, Maine always gauged his results by the information shared by his last three partners—and Cordell since they were known to fuck the same females from time to time.

Elgin threw a monkey wrench into that whole plan and now more than ever, finding out who took them pictures was important. The King of Pop was right—always remain in control.

15

Guilt For Blessings

Negative…non-reactive…not detective.

Words that should've made Maine happy instead brought a level of guilt. Later that night Cordell and Maine opened their results together at the dining room table. Spence would confirm that his results were similar, too.

Who did Elgin fuck? Maine wondered.

Elgin was far from ugly and truthfully, if it weren't for their friendship and if he gotten down, Maine would easily fold Elgin up the way he does Spence. Hide him from Cordell the way he does Corey. Nothing about their hookups would be normal.

Elgin has big dreams. Working for a big six accounting firm. Graduating with degrees in political science and accounting on time. Obtaining an MBA. Joining Spence's frat. Starting his own firm that would provide services for Maine and Cordell's chain of restaurants.

Cordell had to work so Maine and Spence were waiting out in a room of a private clinic that Elgin's older sister arranged for him to retake his HIV and STD tests.

"This shit could've easily been us," Spence passed Maine's results back to him.

"You think," Maine pouted back.

It shouldn't have been either of them. They were young black men barely turning twenty and still getting into their prime.

"We not invincible man." Spence looked at the door. "As much as I like to fuck that could've easily been me. You know how many men and women I've had since I was thirteen? I lost count after one hundred."

"Who you telling?" Maine added. "I get it in myself. Women find me irresistible and niggas like you…"

"Think you're nothing but trouble." Spence cut him off then smirked. "But you're good trouble though. You get in touch with Mushroom yet?"

"No—I need him to get tested though." Maine revealed. He pulled out his phone and texted him again.

"I think Mushroom giving you a taste of your own medicine." Spence looked at Maine and shook his head.

"How so?" Maine wondered as he stared at the phone, waiting on Corey to text him back.

"You told me over the summer that you thought Corey wanted more and that you were fucking around to avoid him." Spence refreshed Maine's memory.

He did tell him that. The night after Corey asked for some ass after eating Maine out on the bathroom sink with his legs over his shoulder. Corey's dick was so brick, Maine knew he wanted more than his cakes.

"But let me be clear with you," Spence leaned closer, bridging the gap. "You will never be able to play me and do half the shit I think you did to him."

Maine rolled his eyes and leaned back in the chair.

"You can get mad if you want to. We in an open relationship so I don't have no say in what the fuck you do. But I know one thing, you better wear a condom if you fucking these other niggas and bitches. Yonna better be the last one you slide up in raw." Spence grilled him—he knew Maine was avoiding him but he held on knowing Maine wasn't going to be able to avoid him for long.

"We in an open relationship nigga?" Maine questioned.

"Who else you fucking?" Spence got straight to the point.

Other than Yonna, Chelle and the possibility with 'Keem and Renee—no one. Spence was the only dude Maine was fucking and truthfully, he fucked Spence more than he got it in with any other person combined.

"But you dating Vanessa," Maine pointed out.

"And, I'm letting you fuck her." Spence clapped back. Vanessa was privy to Maine's little secret. She was all the way at UNCG and couldn't do any real harm—but still. "And when Sierra come around, we can really have some fun—but Sierra don't like that bi-shit. We can tear them bitches up."

A pang of guilt hit Maine in his core. Spence was proposing a half-hearted, non-committal relationship based on sex and some level of loyalty. He knew Spence would never love him the way Corey did. Corey wanted total commitment and was willing to give all of himself to Maine. He knew Corey wouldn't cheat on him but he didn't want the stress of having to hide his relationship form Cordell. True, Cordell was gonna flip if he ever found out that Spence and him were more than frenemies and co-workers. Cordell did a poor job at hiding his anti-gay stance and that's why Cordell never knew Maine had the feelings he had and Corey stayed in the closet.

"So we officially calling ourselves a couple now?" Maine clarified as he wondered who was sucking Corey's dick and if he'd get another chance to again.

"Open, relationship," Spence stressed. "I'm basically saying Vanessa my main chick. I fuck Sierra only when Vanessa around— she and I don't get down without her. I know you not committing to me but check it. When you and I fuck, we can take the rubbers off. But the minute you fuck another nigga or bitch raw, we done."

Maine thought about it. He wanted to slide up in Corey raw so bad, but he knew he could meet Spence's stipulations. Truthfully, he didn't want everyone in his business and he fought to keep his private life as private as could be. He wanted to fuck 'Keem and Renee but had no intentions of getting with them on a regular. He just wanted to try them once or twice if he liked it.

"You trying to take my spot at the store though." Maine brought up the one sore spot. He liked Spence because he was not only ambitious but making moves to create a better future for himself. Despite his feelings being a little hurt that he didn't spend the summer in New York's Def Jam offices, he was slightly happy that he lost to Spence and not someone else. He and Spence were stronger together and their group projects showed that.

"I can take what's mine," Spence smiled.

Before Maine could counter, Elgin came into the private room where Spence and Maine were hanging out.

"I'll find out in a few days if the herpes results are confirmed," Elgin's solemn voice matched the dark clothes he wore for the occasion. "With this Western Blot test, I'll get my results in a week. If I'm positive, they want me on meds as soon as possible."

"We gonna claim you not positive." Spence boldly declared as he stood up and gave Elgin a hug.

Maine didn't want to see him positive either.

"I'm trying to figure out how I'm gonna tell this shit to my mom." Elgin wept as tears flowed freely from his eyes. "I'm not supposed to be HIV positive man. I'm not the only one out here fucking."

More guilt. Maine knew he had enough pussy and ass for a few niggas. And the line to jump on his dick stretched from the Aggie Stadium to Carowinds. "This shit ain't your fault man." Maine promised.

"They asked me to write down a list of my sexual partners." Elgin wiped his eyes as they left the clinic. "I don't remember all the people I slept with this summer."

"Seriously?" Spence tried not to judge as he counted his own number with his hand.

"Well, what happen was I want to this private swingers party in Miami in June and for a weekend, I got it in. Single women were giving it up. I was fucking other dude's wives while they were watching. Me and one of my homeboys from high school ran through so many chicks—we thought we were back in high school." Elgin admitted as they got in Maine's car.

"Has he been tested?" Maine asked as he put the key in the ignition.

"I haven't been able to reach him."

Spence and Maine shared a look. Something about that story didn't add up. Maine didn't suspect Elgin of getting down but he didn't put it past the homeboy.

"Do we know this nigga?" Spence asked the question before Maine could.

"Damn, that's right, you did go to Grimsley." Elgin put his seatbelt on. "How well you know the people from Mt. Tabor?"

"Shit, I forgot you was from the 336 too. Everyone went back and forth between the Tre and G-Boro to fuck. I probably do know him or at least heard of him."

Elgin exhaled. "Jermaine Reynolds."

"Wait a minute!" Spence got excited. "Star basketball player that plays for Clemson?"

"Yeah." Elgin whispered.

"That nigga is legendary." Spence revealed. "Clemson a big fuckin' deal so you probably not gonna catch him on the phone no time soon. But on some real shit, that nigga getting a lot of pussy and not just them girls from Clemson either. That dude go on the road and March Madness is crazy."

"How you know?" Maine wondered as he made his way back to their apartments.

"When I was on line, we had to visit some of the bruhs in Kentucky. It was one of the few times things didn't get too crazy. Big bruhs let us loose during one of the Greek events on campus. Damn it man. I'd never been with a non-black woman before that weekend. After that, I learned to appreciate all shades of the rainbow."

"I bet you did."

Spence caught Maine's hidden remark. "But man fuck it. You still our boy, no matter what. You still have great character, you're forward thinking, a Godly man who just let his dick catch him in some shit. But on the real, I got faith you gonna pull through this and almost all your dreams are coming true." Spence patted Elgin on the shoulders and gave him a massage.

"Aye man, if you wanna stay with me and Cordell tonight, our house is your house." Maine offered. "I don't think you should be alone right now."

"Yeah man, as soon as Maine drop y'all off. I'm going to go borrow his car and get some of my shit too."

Maine shook his head. He loved the idea of the four them watching each other's back. When they arrived at his apartment, he handed Spence the keys to his car. He walked with Elgin to his place to help him get his stuff. Once they headed outside, he noticed a familiar face standing outside his door.

"Corey?"

Corey looked at him and barely cracked a smile.

16

Look What The Cat Drug In

"Corey, it's nice to see you!" Maine exclaimed as Corey extended his arm for a handshake and Maine reached out for a hug. "Oh, it's like that now?"

"I'm learning not to confuse myself." Corey answered and he gave Maine a hug.

Corey didn't wrap his arms around him like he expected. It was more like a "side/we just boys/or I'm only doing this to be fake" —kind of hug. Maine looked around. Elgin was still in his house, and Cordell was nowhere to be found. Spence had his car and it would be about thirty minutes to get to and from his spot. For the first time in a long time, Maine and Corey were alone.

"Yo, come in real quick," Maine invited as he took his key to unlock the door.

"Cordell was on my case about getting tested. I told that fool NC Tech had that done when I got my physical." Corey started walking away from the door.

Maine had opened, but then pulled the door closed. "You not gonna come inside?"

"Why?" Corey looked at Maine funny.

Maine remembered how fucked up he treated him. Slamming the door in his face when he asked for a ride home. A ride Cordell and he had promised in an effort to derail taking Corey to NC Tech so they could get to their welcome back celebration.

"Cordell ain't home. And it's been a while." Maine observed his surroundings.

"Yeah I noticed." Corey looked away. Maine noticed that Corey appeared to be distracted and he didn't remember seeing anyone else with a car that could've dropped him off. Maine knew the next bus wasn't coming for another thirty minutes. "I had hoped to catch Cordell before he went to work."

Maine took a step toward the door. He motioned for Corey to come inside. Corey followed him and he felt like he made a step in the right direction. Maine celebrated on the inside while he plotted on how to get Corey off before Elgin or Spence came over. Corey had on an extra-long shirt, some baggy jeans and some fresh Air Force Ones. He smelled nice with the Jordan cologne he wore lingering in the air. His low cut was fresh and his hair formed a nice crown on his head. His body got a little thick...mostly in that ass Maine wanted to tap.

"Surprised it's not a club up in here." Corey noted as he took a seat on the couch.

"Man we don't party all the time." Maine countered as he took a seat next to him. It felt good sitting next to him. "We take breaks on Thursdays and Sundays."

Corey shook his head. "Yeah, right."

"How's school?" Maine felt the need to catch up with his boy. He missed his summer fling and having Corey in the flesh was working on him. He was glad that he and Spence were in an "open" relationship because Maine was "open" to getting it popping with Corey.

"School is school. My roommate and his girlfriend are cool." Corey mention.

"Girlfriend?" Maine was confused. "Ain't we too early in the school year to be claiming girlfriends?"

"If he like her, I love her." Corey answered. Maine put his hand on Corey's knee. "Patrice's cool. She bought food for the room last week."

"But y'all freshmen." Maine couldn't believe it. "Ain't been here a week and already professing love and shit."

"Melvin's cool. He told me his older brother's gay. I feel safe enough to tell him I am too." Corey confided.

Maine let his hand move to Corey's thigh. "Oh yeah. I bet your boy gets down."

"Nah," Corey shook his head. "You should've seen the way he had Patrice's legs over his shoulders while he was pounding her and kissing her. And that's a big girl he was pushing on like that too. I walked in on them by mistake, but I'll admit it, I stayed and watched for the view. Have to admit, I loved watching the sweat

"Yeah. I think they met at Summer Orientation and just kept up with each other. Melvin looks like a small power forward but he got a lot of muscle." Corey bragged.

"He look like he stacking that Freshman 15 kinda heavy." Maine threw some salt so he could see where Corey's head was at. He didn't want to admit it but he hated the idea of Corey smashing Melvin or anyone else.

"Melvin just wears them supersized clothes and shit. Only thing fat on him is his dick." Corey defended. "I didn't think anyone could have a bigger dick than Troy but I was wrong."

"Troy?" Maine jealousy reeked.

Corey smirked. "Troy took me, Liam and Walt to the sex party the night you was entertaining that Build-A-Bear looking chick."

"Shaniyah is not a Build-A-Bear," Maine shoved Corey in an effort to instigate a play fight. He hoped they'd get close so he could make his move.

"If you say so." Corey didn't take the bait.

"Look man, I'm sorry I fucked you over." Maine laid down his last card. He knew he was wrong for being shady toward Corey but he didn't want to have to say I'm sorry.

"I'm good." Corey answered. "I learned how to make it. That walk back to NC Tech with a bloody nose wasn't no joke. But I had to grow up some time."

Maine felt guilty. He knew he'd slammed the door in Corey's face but he didn't know he'd caused him to have a nose bleed. "When Spence gets back, I'll take you home."

"Spence?" Corey questioned.

"He's just borrowing my car." Maine offered. "Let me make it up to you real quick." Maine went for the kill. He had Corey on the couch and his hand was on his waist, moving forward to undo his jeans.

"Make what up to me?" Corey questioned.

Maine could see Corey's chest rising and going down a little. He worked fast to undo the pants so he could dive in and put that mushroom tip in his mouth. Corey wasn't stopping him. This was a good thing. He felt Corey's neatly trimmed pubic hair and reached in and pulled it out. The man musk turned him on. Maine was determined to fix everything with some apology head. He looked Corey in his eyes—he looked just as good and sexy as he did the first time he blew him off. Corey's hand crept down Maine's back, pulling his shirt up.

Maine gripped Corey's growing dick and stroked it a little. Maine could hear his heart beat a little faster as he put Corey's thick mushroom tip in his mouth. Maine went for the down stroke and came back up.

BOOM! BOOM! BOOM!

"FUCK!" Maine lifted his head up quick and pulled his shirt down. Corey worked to put his dick back in his pants and adjust himself. "That's Elgin—he's rooming with us tonight. Family emergency."

Maine got up and went to the door. He looked back to make sure Corey was presentable. Corey pulled his vibrating phone out and answered it. "Hello."

Maine opened the door and seen that Elgin carried his backpack over his shoulders. "Aye man, I'd a been here earlier if Janessa hadn't called. She wants to do a study group tonight. I called Cordell and he said as long as everyone brought something to eat, we could have a study party here."

Fuck! Fuck! Fuck! Maine vented. He couldn't go off on Elgin because the whole reason he was home was so he could support Elgin in his time of need. Maine dug in his pocket and pulled out his phone. For the last ten minutes while he was trying to get a nut with Corey, he missed Cordell's call.

"Aye, this is Corey, Cordell's younger brother." Maine made introductions.

Elgin and Corey exchanged head nods as Corey was still on the phone. "So y'all in the area?" Corey got up and straightened up. Elgin headed to the bathroom. "Okay, I'll be outside." Corey made his way to the door. "Thanks for letting me in. I'll catch up with Cordell later."

"Cool—we'll catch up later too." Maine promised.

"Oh yeah." Corey walked up to him. "I don't like unfinished head."

Maine smacked Corey on the butt. "Smart ass."

"You not getting none," Corey vowed as he made his way out the door. He saw the blue Honda Accord and noticed Melvin sitting in the passenger side.

"We'll see." Maine's dick got hard. Corey got closer and lifted Maine's shirt.

"Aye, y'all, give me a minute." Corey closed the door and dropped to his knees. Maine looked in the direction of the bathroom and he helped Corey push his pants down. Corey gripped Maine's pulsating tool and put it in his mouth. Corey's other hand cupped his cheek with his middle finger creeping to Maine's whole. As Corey licked around the tip and went all the way down to base, the tip of his finger went deeper inside Maine. Maine felt his tip go past Corey's throat and as he clinched, he felt more of Corey inside of him. He weakened as Corey demonstrated the perfect mastery of his gag reflex while fingering his rim. Corey slowly moved his mouth to the edge and pulled his finger out of Maine's ass, then quickly got up. "We even now."

"Motherfucker," Maine shoved his dick quickly in his pants as he heard the bathroom door open.

Corey threw Maine the peace sign and rushed to his car. Maine shook his head.

"Corey not staying with us?" Elgin asked.

Maine closed the door. "Naw man—he gonna meet up with Cordell later." Maine told his story as he made his way to the kitchen. "You want anything?"

"You got the menu for some Chinese food?" Elgin asked. "Yonna and Chelle said they'd put in for some wings and Renee want pizza—so 'Keem gonna bring some Dominoes when they make their round to Scott Hall tonight. His homeboy said the delivery man already tipped them off that they were coming to the dorms tonight. And 'Keem already got like three boxes each of pepperoni, sausage and cheese pizzas put aside. Janessa said she picked up the Chinese food tonight on her way."

"So who else is coming?" Maine gave his place an overview. He was glad it was clean.

"Ion know." Elgin replied. "You know once these negroes get here, ain't nobody gonna want to leave. Bathsheba probably coming over so you know her and Cordell gonna be in his room all night. Chelle and Yonna gonna try to take over your room again. I'm gonna give Janessa the keys to my place and let her sleep in my bed just in case she don't want to be on the floor. And you know Renee and 'Keem gonna want the couch."

"They asses can stay on the floor." Maine pouted. "You get the couch—no, scratch that. You can have my bed for the night. Just turn the mattress over."

"Maine, you don't have to—"

"We good." Maine cut him off. "This was supposed to be your get away and I want you to be comfortable. I just wish someone was bringing a drink."

"Hpnotiq and Hennessy, right?" Elgin pulled out his silver Razr. "Aye DayQuan, can you get us some Hpnotiq, Hennessy and some Courvoisier?" Maine listened in on his conversation. "Aye, Spence will be here in about ten, fifteen minutes but none of the others. Park at my place and walk up. It'll be a lot of people from our accounting class at our study party tonight."

It felt good for Maine to see Elgin in good spirits. And to see that Corey had forgiven him for being a jerk. He was gonna get with Corey about that unfinished head. He wanted that nut in his mouth again. Spence walked in without knocking and had some grocery bags filled with four different types of Doritos chips, orange and cranberry juice and Sprite and Coke. "I hope Cordell bring some double cheeseburgers or some shit because I'm hungry."

Elgin quickly pulled out his phone and started texting. Maine shook his head. Settling the score with Corey was gonna have to wait. He had a study party to get ready for which meant he was cleaning the bathroom and pulling out the linens from his bed.

It was time to party.

17

Study Party

Ain't no party better than a Cordell and Maine party—unless it's a Cordell and Maine *"study party."*

Across Cordell and Maine's compact poker table that doubled as a dining table laid a spread of potato chips, Dorito chips, salsa, rum cake, wings, Sprite, Coke, Grey Goose, and double cheeseburgers and Whoppers from Burger King. Dominoes pizzas and Chinese food lined the kitchen counter.

"Man, if I see one more word problem," 'Keem complained from the living room. "Babe, fix me an Incredible Hulk."

Maine caught that Renee rolled her eyes in the kitchen. She had sought solitude as the half of all three sections of Dr. Finley's Accounting 101 class came in and out of the study party. There were so many students seeking solitude and sanity that another group of students were set up in Elgin's apartment and another group of students were in Yonna and Chelle's apartment. And the students traveled back and forth between the three apartment units that thankfully were in close walking proximity to one another.

"Here, let me help you," Bathsheba offered as she got out of Cordell's lap and put her books to the side. She and Maine knew that once 'Keem started drinking, Cordell wouldn't be too far behind, trying to keep up. The second chapter was kicking their ass and they needed to stay on top of the classes if they were going to succeed.

Bathsheba took the cups and took a count of all the men in the room. She fixed five drinks and made sure they got equal parts of Hypnotiq and Hennessy. "We're going to be spending a lot of time together. We need to create a study party fund." Bathsheba suggested as she gave each of the men a cup.

"You think?" Spence took off his glasses and put his book down. "Thank you," he took his cup from Bathsheba.

"And you know we gotta take Accounting 102 next semester and we better stay with Dr. Finley for that." Elgin suggested as he took his drink and a sip. "My sister said it wasn't good to go from one accounting professor to the other with the first two classes because everyone has a different style."

"I'm not even trying to hear about Accounting 102," Maine took his cup, "thanks Bathsheba. I just want to get passed chapter three."

Bathsheba took two sips from Cordell's cup before she passed him his. "What you do that for?" Cordell complained as he took his cup.

"Renee drank out of 'Keem's cup already." Bathsheba passed 'Keem his cup. "She's wearing darker lipstick so that helps me keep up with which cup was his. And I wanted a sip so I could decide if I like it or not."

"Do you?" Cordell asked as he took another sip.

"A little. I'm old school. I like Grey Goose and orange juice." Bathsheba answered as she took her seat back in his lap and put her books in her lap.

"I haven't heard gin and juice since Snoop." Elgin bragged as he took another sip.

"Man, who you telling?" 'Keem replied. "Isn't Janessa's boyfriend like Snoop's cousin or something?"

"Yeah, he related to Brandy and Ray J too." Spence pointed out.

"Mr. Def Jam, are we going to use this material in the real world?" 'Keem asked as he took another sip of his drink.

"Yes." Spence answered as he leaned his head back on the couch. "We use all of this shit from marketing to sales to logistics. Every major in the School of Business and Economics is used in this internship. The communication majors have it hard because they don't have the business background—that's why many of them get MBAs after their undergraduate degrees."

"With accounting, we gotta make sure the money's right at all times." Maine cut in. "Peachtree and Quickbooks can only do so much."

WHAT'S BEST FOR YOU 97

Maine stole a glance at Spence. He could see his boy was tired. He'd co-lead the study session with Janessa and traveled between the three houses as frequently as she did. He also knew that Spence was about to nod off in a few minutes.

Bathsheba and Cordell started giggling as they passed their cup back and forth and Maine knew it was a matter of time before the two of them ended up in his room.

"Next time, someone needs to bring a joint." Renee got up and stretched.

Maine studied her. She was nice and firm and shaped like the big booty girls in the Sir Mix-A-Lot video. Renee caught Maine looking at her and smiled. 'Keem caught him looking at her and too and grinned. In the back of Maine's mind, he couldn't wait to get the party started with both of them. But he also knew this wasn't the time or the place. Despite the fact that Elgin was hosting a crew of other classmates who heard about the study party at his place, Maine was going to honor his word and let Elgin sleep in his bed. He still needed to be around friends as he dealt with whatever the news of his HIV and herpes status was. Elgin seemed calm and focus.

"We about to call it a night," Cordell slurred as he tried to stand up with Bathsheba still in his lap.

Bathsheba took his cup, "yeah, we are going to call it a night and this drink is about to be done for too." She took the rest of his cup and downed the contents as if she were drinking water.

"Let me go check on the people at my place real quick and make sure they are okay." Elgin got up and headed out of the door.

"And I'm gonna check on Yonna and Chelle's spot. I haven't heard from them all night." Spence looked at Maine—knowing the reason why Yonna especially was keeping her distance.

Maine watched as the living room emptied. Renee got up and started closing the bags of food and putting different things away.

"Why don't you come back to Renee's with us?" 'Keem invited. He'd moved closer to Maine on the couch. "I want some dick." He spoke in a low voice.

"Not now man." Maine answered as he watched Renee while 'Keem's hand rubbed his inner thigh. Maine moved his hand away.

"I promised I'd look after Elgin and make sure he got to the hospital if need be."

"That nigga look fine," 'Keem disregarded the plight for Elgin's well-being. "He walking back and forth between his place and yours." 'Keem leaned in closer and put his arm around Maine's shoulder. "If you not going to give me the dick, why don't you just say that?"

Maine rolled his eyes. He kept looking at Renee. A part of him felt like this was a set up and that she knew that 'Keem was making his move on him. Maine reached his hands to 'Keem's lap until he could feel his hardening junk in his hand. Maine gasped. He stole another look at Renee, then looked around the room and then looked down at what he'd grabbed from 'Keem in his hand.

He was slightly disappointed. Maine wasn't a size queen but 'Keem wasn't packing what Corey and Spence brought to the table. Maine pulled it out for confirmation. Most of the weight in 'Keem's package came at its girth. He was about a thick as a beer can, easily. But the length…Maine knew he had six inches between the tip of his middle finger to the end of his wrist and 'Keem was more than an inch short of that.

How could this be? Maine was baffled as he jacked 'Keem off while making sure the coast was clear. He tried to ear-hustle his way into Cordell's room to find out if Cordell was hitting it yet. Renee was texting someone in the kitchen, seemingly paying attention to her phone. 'Keem steadily rubbed Maine's thigh, trying to make his monster come out and play.

What Maine liked about Spence was that when he rode dick, more than half the time, Spence's dick was super hard. Maine could feel every time Spence bounced up and down on his dick because Spence's dick would thump on his abs in a steady beat. If he pre-cummed, it would be like playing connect the dots because Spence's tip almost never landed in the same spot twice. And Maine liked looking at dick, just as much as he liked grabbing it and sucking it.

'Keem wouldn't be able to hit the back of his throat. His dick was designed for fucking pussy. It was the perfect girth to rub a clit and fill up a mouth. Maine knew too many bottoms who'd hurt 'Keem's feelings he bought that overheated hot dog to the table.

Maine let him go and he got up and checked on Renee. He watched as 'Keem took another sip of his drink and pretended to read his accounting book. As Maine got closer, he saw her texting someone furiously. He knew her fingers were tired because it was annoying having to move a key three times to get to a single letter and don't let it be a capital letter.

"Come here," Renee whispered and reached out for Maine's hand while motioning for him to get closer to her. "Please fuck me before you fuck him."

"I can't tonight," Maine decided to be blunt, treating her with the same level of rejection he'd just given 'Keem. "My room isn't free and I promised I'd watch after Elgin to make sure he don't have to go back to the hospital."

"Is he okay?" Renee's concern seemed genuine. Opposite of what 'Keem offered.

"We don't know." Maine answered. "He's fine now but if someone gotta take him to the hospital at three in the morning, I'm that dude."

"That's why he's sleeping in your room tonight?" Renee inquired. "I saw him bring his stuff over and put in your room as we got in. I thought you might be fucking him."

Maine's eyes grew wider. "What makes you think that?"

"You see who I'm fucking." Renee answered.

She had a point.

"We love each other—even when we get on each other's nerves and be wanting to kill each other—we deeply love each other. 'Keem got his flaws but aside from all the macho exterior is a good man—that can ride some dick. And God knows I love to watch. And he can fuck too."

Hell naw, Maine thought to himself. "We'll have our day." He promised Renee. He had plans on how he was gonna get at her before he'd have to break 'Keem off because both of those events were happening sooner rather than later.

"I guard his secrets like a hawk." Renee warned Maine as they heard the door opened. "As he does mine. Whoever I allow to get near 'Keem has to be someone I trust with my life because the way we are set up—if his secret gets out, we both go down. I'm putting in too much work to be a top shelf NFL wife to let our open relationship destroy what we've built."

Renee gained Maine's respect that day. At first, he thought she was nothing more than a gold digger trying to ride 'Keem to the top. He could see now she was much more than that. Everyone knew that 'Keem was destined to go to the top. And Renee was forward thinking. Manipulative and calculating in how she acted and reacted to 'Keem's antics. Maine could see she thought things through, then acted accordingly.

Spence walked in and he eyed Maine as he took his place back on the couch. Elgin followed inside and headed straight to Maine's room. They could see 'Keem and Spence making small talk.

"Now I know who the boyfriend is." Renee winked at Maine.

"I don't have a boyfriend." Maine denied.

"That's not what Spence's eyes are saying." Renee stated the obvious. "He's cute. And he's 'Keem's type. If your boy is down, y'all can definitely make it a threesome. It's been a while since 'Keem's had one of those."

Maine studied the two of them talking again. "Oh yeah?"

"'Keem is verse bottom, leaning more on the bottom side when he's with a man. When he's with a woman, he's a dick-laying machine. But with men, he doesn't mind being submissive. It's almost like a weight has been lifted off his shoulders and he can switch roles."

The thoughts of Maine, Spence and 'Keem getting it in filled his mind. Maine loved that idea and he knew Spence would go along with it. And he still wanted some of Renee too. "Can I see you tomorrow? Maybe after you get off from Willie's." Renee suggested.

"Yeah?" Maine agreed, paying more attention to 'Keem and Spence than Renee. "Where's 'Keem gonna be?"

"Watching." Renee answered plainly. "He loves to watch other men fuck me and the loves watching videos of other men fucking him. Something about the way an man's ass moves when he's laying pipe turns us both on."

"I can see how you're made for each other." Maine suggested.

"You get us," Renee leaned up and gave Maine a slow, seductive kiss, "and soon, you'll get to have us both."

Maine was surprised as he and Renee locked lips again. Out of the corner of his eyes, he saw Spence fuming. Renee ended the kiss and Spence got up and stormed into the kitchen.

"Nigga really?" Spence vented as he followed Maine outside.

"Don't be so loud." Maine warned Spence. "Cordell and Bathsheba can still hear us, even if they are fucking each other's brains out."

Spence walked away and rubbed his hair across his freshly platted cornrows. "You be careful motherfucker. You know her man was just a few feet from y'all."

"I know." Maine smiled. "I'll explain everything when it's me and you."

Spence looked away. "Aight. Don't get into no shit you can't get yourself out of."

Maine heeded Spence's warning as he watched Spence grab his sleeping bag and lay it on the couch. He stripped down to a wife beater and some boxers that highlighted the shape of his bubble butt. Spence stepped into the bag and used his folded clothes as a pillow. Maine went back into the kitchen trying to put all the food away—and figuring out how he was going to make everyone happy.

18

Another One

Maine woke up with 'Keem wrapped in his arms as he spooned him. His muscular body felt nice as Maine's hand rubbed 'Keem from his shoulders to his ass.

Maine enjoyed switching off between Renee and 'Keem for the past three days and he felt like the couple were in competition with one another. Renee boldly sucked him off in the parking lot of Willie's despite it being broad daylight the day after the study party. 'Keem surprised Maine by sucking on his big toe while Renee was riding him. Renee made pineapple pie filling and licked it all over his body. She even put some on icing on his cakes and then grubbed on them like they were the last meal. 'Keem had Maine nutt into a blender, added some chocolate protein mix, milk and ice and then drank the last of the shake during their accounting class.

Maine didn't think he, Spence or anyone in the world were ready for what they came up with next.

When Renee and 'Keem weren't trying to out-do each other with all the freak shit they were into—they tried to out-do each other when they were into it. In Maine's eyes, 'Keem definitely put the pipe on Renee when he was digging her out missionary style. And watching his back, ass and leg muscles move turned Maine on. And as it turned out, 'Keem had almost an inch on a beer can when fully aroused, which made sucking his girthy Polish sausage a challenge. Renee was the MVP as she took 'Keem's dick down to the base and managed to lick the balls too.

But that nutt was just as sweet as Corey's.

A firm grip on Maine's morning wood brought him back to reality and he could see 'Keem reaching behind while tooting his ass in Maine's direction. 'Keem lifted his right leg up and lined Maine's tip with his warm, hungry hole without looking back. As the tip of Maine's dick started to brush against 'Keem's lightly-haired hole, Maine began to retreat.

"What you doing partner?" Maine turned on his back and began to sit up.

"I needed to get fucked!" 'Keem gruffed as he got on his knees and began to straddle Maine. 'Keem's tightly muscled body was distracting as it moved to perfection.

Maine put his hand on 'Keem's hand, trying to guide his dick away from him and looked him in the eye. "We used the last condom last night."

'Keem rolled his eyes and continued to move his ass on Maine's tip. "So—I liked to get fucked bareback. A nigga nutting in me makes me cum faster."

Maine backed away. "I'm not into raw dawg." At least he wasn't into it with 'Keem. He and Renee were freaks that made the sex Maine experienced seem like child's play. And with the way Renee and 'Keem made love to each other and battled for Maine's affections, he knew it wasn't much between the two of them they didn't do.

"Maaannnn!" 'Keem whined as he retreated. "We fucked like six times last night—I was trying to waked up to number seven. See how much we can do this in twenty-four hours before we got to play Florida A&M."

"Whatever man," Maine got up as he walked around 'Keem's suite comfortably. Unlike most of the football players, 'Keem had a private efficiency at the top of a convenience store that only Renee knew and 'Keem's closest friends knew about. The view saw the stadium 'Keem played his home games and the construction they were doing for the new building for the School of Business in clear view. "Knowing your ass, Renee probably helped arranged some freaky shit in Tallahassee."

"You need a way down there?" 'Keem stood behind Maine and looked over his shoulder at the view. Maine could feel his dick rubbing against his ass crack. A total violation of the top code, but with the way 'Keem ate that ass last night, making him call for his daddy and bitching him out, it was a code Maine would only allow 'Keem to break. "Say the word and I'll have one of the alumni book you a flight. You may have to fly from Raleigh-Durham though."

"I'm good on the flight." Maine leaned his head back. He could feel 'Keem kissing his neck and closing the distance between them. 'Keem's body felt so good against him. It been a while since Maine had someone close to his height or thick in stature. "I gotta run the store tomorrow and you know I gotta face Spence."

"Nigga you don't got to explain yourself to me." 'Keem started massaging Maine's body and he started loosening up. Maine didn't know it but his body was tense. "You grown, I'm grown. I know being from the Peach State you probably got them Miami palm tree niggas on lock."

"No." Maine admitted. "I don't get around like that." Maine closed the blinds. "I thought you were more discreet."

"I am," 'Keem defended himself. "I'm not out there like that. But I'm into a lot of shit most people can't get into. Renee and I are very selective in who we meet up with in our intimate sessions. The guy I'm gonna fuck while I'm down there is one of the drum majors. Six foot two, smooth brown skin and got a little beef on him—and he a freak. We fucked before and keep in touch via AOL IM and shit."

"Word?" Maine was surprised. "I didn't think you keep up with dudes like that."

"Man, when I'm all alone, all I do is trade pics on these message boards—from the neck down though. I watch Tagazz and DawgPoundUSA—and PapiThugz when I want that Latin shit. When I got a little extra time, I get on the chat line or read the stories on Da Site."

"I don't watch porn," Maine told 'Keem.

"Lies," 'Keem sat on his bed and played with his dick.

"Okay—I watch some porn like if someone else have it on. I have sex regularly and I pretty much go with the flow." Maine sat next to him.

"So you bottom and shit?" 'Keem started to nibble on Maine's nipple.

'Keem loved to bite and Maine discovered he loved to be bitten while being fingered. "Hell naw, never that."

"You know how many fingers I got in your ass right now?" 'Keem grabbed Maine's dick and swallowed him whole without slurping. Maine could feel him pushing his digits as his head moved up and down. Maine tried to come up with the strength to answer 'Keem's question but the sensations being applied to his dick and his ass were causing palpations. He grasped at the bedsheets and couldn't hold on. "I almost got three fingers in that ass…if I get another, you'd be able to take my dick if I were offering.

Shit! Maine cursed himself as the unthinkable happened. 'Keem was hitting a spot he didn't know he had and Maine felt a tingle in his toes. Maine hissed and moaned as he lost control of his dick and his ass. 'Keem continued to push the fingers in fast and steady as Maine could feel his loins gather together for a nut. 'Keem was good—one of the best head givers around and he always brought Maine to submission. "Da-da."

"Mmm-mmm," 'Keem moaned as Maine's nut started to drown his tongue. 'Keem moved his tongue slowly as he slurped up his breakfast and swallowed every drop. 'Keem sucked Maine's dick deeper inside his mouth, the tip of Maine's head reached 'Keem's tonsils and massaged it. When 'Keem was done drinking, he slowly released Maine's dick and make a "pop" noise with his mouth. "Thank, you," 'Keem slurred like a drunk.

"Damn boy," Maine grabbed 'Keem's head and rubbed his nearly bald head. "I didn't think you'd get that out."

"I was thirsty and I haven't had nothing to eat but your dick and ass for a minute."

It was true. For the last twenty-four hours, Maine ditched classes and called out of work to stay locked into 'Keem's suite. He felt guilty because Spence wasn't there and a part of him wished Corey was around to enjoy the ass too. And the ass was plentiful. Worthy of a feature in Sir Mix-A-Lot's video. Calls from Spence were met with half-lies as he didn't want to admit that 'Keem was putting it down.

And he still wanted that threesome. When 'Keem found out Spence got down, he begged Maine and Renee to hook it up.

Maine invited him to the suite and Spence said no—in part because he had to be the responsible one and cover Maine's shift.

"If I was into dudes exclusively, it would be just me and you." 'Keep declared as he got up and washed his hands in the sink. It dawned on Maine that 'Keem hadn't had any clothes on for most of the time he was there.

Neither did he.

"What makes you say that?" Maine continued to lay in the bed. He was still trembling from the orgasms 'Keem gave him.

"We alike in a lot of ways," 'Keem opened the refrigerator and pulled out a carton of eggs. "We know how to go out and get what we want. We're both ambitious as fuck. We smart. We like Spence."

Maine shook his head. "You beg."

"Ain't too proud for that. TLC taught me well. Cause I need it in the morning and the middle of the night."

Maine could hear the song in his head. Left Eye must've met 'Keem almost ten years in the future cause Maine knew he was who she was talking about.

Soon, the suite smelled like scrambled eggs, fried potatoes, cheese grits and beef bacon. *'Keem can cook,* Maine admitted as he got up and made his way to the bathroom. After relieving himself and washing his hands, he walked out and picked up his dirty draws and put them on.

"Nigga, if you don't take them dirty ass clothes off. I'm not putting nothing on." 'Keem fixed their plates and set them on the table. "We can eat on the bed if you want."

"Cool," that made Maine comfortable as he grabbed his plate and sat on the edge of the bed. As he tasted some food, he was impressed with 'Keem's skills.

"I noticed you did that yesterday. Wash your ass and put on them same dirty ass draws. I told you we could wash our shit together. I don't have no diseases you need to be worried about." 'Keem walked around and picked up their clothes and Renee's panties and put them in the small washing machine he didn't notice next to the bathroom.

"Old habits die hard," Maine ate and laid in the bed. He was feeling 'Keem's company. He almost didn't want to leave, but he knew he couldn't call out of Willie's today.

After the clothes got done, Maine and 'Keem bathed and played in the small ass shower they barely could fit in. He was happy to be fresh and clean and after he got dressed and stepped out of the suite, happy not to be cooped away from campus.

As he and 'Keem walked to campus, they laughed and joked some more. It was cool seeing a different side of 'Keem. Made him respect him even more. The honk disturbed their groove and as they looked back, Maine recognized Vanessa's car.

"Dr. Finely told us to meet him at the library," Spence pushed the door open. "Y'all heading in the wrong direction." Maine and 'Keem took the open invitation to get a ride to the other side of campus. As they got adjusted, Spence turned down the Ruff Endz blasting from the car. "I guess y'all enjoyed y'alls little honeymoon or whatever."

Maine couldn't believe Spence was getting in his shit.

"Yup," 'Keem didn't deny it. "Only thing missing was you. The three of us need to get it popping soon."

Spence looked at 'Keem from the rear-view mirror. Maine shook his head and focused on the students walking and bullshitting on the way to class.

"This weekend," Spence's answer caused Maine to perk up. "We both got Sunday off and after I go to service, I'm free. We can chill at my place and study. The three of us."

"Ask and ye shall receive," 'Keem smirked.

"That's not the way the Book works." Maine smarted off.

"Shittin' me," 'Keem replied as Spence parked the car. "I just asked for two dicks and I'm getting them on Sunday. God works fast if you ask me."

Maine and Spence shook their heads as they got out and walked to Hurston. Spence was blessed to find a space close to campus. They saw Dr. Finley standing outside with a group of students.

"I hope we are not having class outside." Spence secured his bag over his shoulder and picked up the class.

"He ain't that crazy." 'Keem was convinced.

"Keep telling yourself that." Spence mumbled. Maine caught the subtle hint and knew Spence may know what's up.

"Good to see the rest of the class join us." Dr. Finley motioned them over with his hands. "I brought you to Hurston today because the City of Greensboro is undertaking a major plan to redevelop the businesses that are in north eastern parts of the city and that border our schools. Your project for both Accounting 101 and 102 will start here. I want you to spend the next hour traveling the area, meeting different business owners and discovering their needs. Some of them need business plans, others need help assessing their financial affairs. Your assignment will be to help a business assess those needs and put the tools I will give you to use. Maine, we've decided that you and Yonna will work with the business we've chosen inside. Everyone else can pick their partners."

"Are you serious?" Yonna yelled. "This is not fair."

"Keep your business out of the street and I'll be fair. If you refuse, both of you fail this class." Dr. Finley stated plainly and the way he glared at her let everyone know he wasn't joking.

Maine cursed to himself but he didn't dare challenge Dr. Finley. He hated the idea of having to work with Yonna. But he knew this was a test. Maine would have to show that he could overcome the obstacle and get the job done.

"Fine," Yonna stormed into the library.

"Dean Hardy is waiting on the two of you inside. You'll receive further instructions from him." Dr. Finley advised as he nodded for Maine to follow.

Maine looked back at his class and then marched inside. He knew Dean Hardy had something sneaky up his sleeve and he didn't think he was going to like it.

19

Why Can't She Just Go Away?

Maine followed Yonna in the library and Dean Hardy waved them over to his table. Dean Hardy stood five foot nine and was imposing on most students. Maine knew to stay off his shit list because he taught the International Marketing Strategy class he needed to graduate.

"My two lovebirds," Dean Hardy's voice reeked of sarcasm. He stood next to a younger lady who looked like she was barely out of high school. "I want you to meet Malika Saudi. She's a sixteen-year-old senior at Dudley High School. In addition to be a future NC Tech student, she the owner of Saudi's Sweetness."

Maine and Yonna looked at each other. Saudi's Sweetness was a quaint bakery and smoothie shop in the Friendly Shopping Center. It was one of the few black owned businesses in the shopping mall and Maine used to buy his mom the confections every now and then. "Your mom doesn't own the store?" Yonna was impressed.

"No, it's hers." An elder woman who wore a burgundy khimar that covered her head, neck and shoulders. It contrasted with the full body black thobe that did little to conceal the body underneath. "I'm her older sister, Salma."

Maine and Yonna shook their hands.

"I'm trusting that the two of you will work with Salma on helping Malika expand Saudi's Sweetness. I expect greatness from the two of you." Dean Hardy left them alone and attended to others in the library.

"Are y'all dating?" Malika's voice lacked the innocence once assumed a teenage Muslima to have but instead was bold and brash like she was from the Bronx.

"Hell no," Yonna looked disgusted as she stared down Maine and then caught the look in Salma's face. "I'm sorry. We're not dating."

"Okay, I saw the looks the two of you exchanged with one another and I just wanted to make sure we can get right down to business." Malika wasted no time stating her concern. She picked up a white three ring binder in front of her. "I have ideas about expanding into a second location and doing more with the store I have now. I want to use every inch of space in my store as possible. I make okay money, just a little shy of one hundred grand a year, but I'd like to make ten times that amount by time I graduate high school."

"Girl," Yonna put her hands on her head, "you make me feel very unprepared for life." Yonna took a seat and accepted the binder Malika handed her. Malika waved the binder more forcefully at Maine, who took it after looking away from Salma. "You're sixteen years old, own a business and speak as if six figures was nothing."

"My husband and I teach my sister that money is only a tool that can be used to gain wise men the ability to provide charity and fools the means to destroy their homes." Salma nonverbally commanded Maine to have a seat. "We do not want Malika lavishing in the material things many Americans seem to be interested in. We want her to do great good with the blessings Allah has given her."

Maine looked at the packet, avoiding direct eye contact with Yonna and Salma. Saudi's Sweetness has only been operational for two years, and in that time, they've managed to double their sales while decreasing their operational cost. Maine wished he'd brought his laptop so he could look at the store's website.

"As you can see, Malika is very aggressive and has strong ambitions for her future." Salma spoke. "I want her to be cautious and realistic about her growth plans. And I need her to have balance. Education and opportunity go hand and hand I do not want her to sacrifice her academics in pursuit of wealth."

"How do you manage everything?" Maine was intrigued. He couldn't believe Malika was dancing her under a table with her business acumen.

"My brother-in-law runs the store in the day time. My sister helps too sometimes. I use my lunch breaks and study hall to prepare for tests and exams.   When I get off school, I go to Saudi's and then I study there two in the down time. I hired two of my classmates and so we study together sometimes." Malika stated.

"Where the two of you come in is that Malika needs help in defining and pitching her ideas to others. I could help my sister, but I also have a two-year-old and a one year old that I tend to. My husband have them now so I have a break from them but this is life. I like that my sister can pursue her dreams and has created something that has been able to sustain us all."

"I think we can learn as much from you as you can from us." Yonna complimented.

"Well, let's exchange numbers. I guess we can meet a week from now, after Fall Break and solidify the details and begin to craft a plan." Salma took out her phone and she programmed Maine and Yonna's number as they gave them to her.

Maine watched as Salma and Malika grabbed their stuff and leave. "I didn't think you liked Muslims." Yonna vexed as she grabbed her stuff.

"The correct term is Muslima and I'm attracted to what I'm attracted to." Maine retorted as he put the binder in his bag. "I just want to be successful and if helping the young lady make her store better is what I got to do. I already like what she sales, now I like her too."

"Malika is too young for you." Yonna raised her voice.

"Naw, Salma said she married and I'm gonna respect that. I do have boundaries." Maine defended as he and Yonna left the library.

"Shit, you could've fooled me. Messing with me and Michelle, and I heard you did it with Renee last week." Yonna walked out of the door without leaving it open for him. Maine shook his head and followed her out.

"I'm grown and I can do what I want." Maine started to say something else but he noticed Elgin sitting on the bench outside of the library. Yonna kept running that mouth and Maine tuned her out as he took a seat next to Elgin. He could see that his boy had been crying and he knew that whatever was going on was not good.

"I'm positive," Elgin blurted out. "Mother-fucking-positive and I got herpes."

Maine felt his heart drop. "Are you serious?"

"You act like I would tell you that shit just for kicks." Elgin covered his head with his NC Tech hat. The tears still fell heavy and Maine could tell Elgin was heaving.

"Look man, let's go to my house." Maine suggested as he looked around. He didn't want nosy ass students catching his boy crying and offering fake concern.

"Man fuck that." Elgin muffled through his hat. "I know you didn't drive and that you spent the past three days fucking 'Keem."

"What you mean?" Maine was in denial. He'd never shared with anyone about his sexuality. He started re-evaluating his presentation because he thought he was staying on the DL.

"I know you and Spence fucking—that boy got a thing for you. I can see that shit in his eyes. Cordell may not notice that shit but I do. I see a lot of shit. Just like I know you and Cordell used to pass Yonna and Chelle around like they toys you exchange for Christmas. I know Janessa been wanting a nigga to fuck, but I can't give to her what someone or some people gave to me. I know y'alls dirt but I couldn't tell you who gave me HIV or herpes or if I got it from one chick or two." They sat in silence. Elgin was spilling out his feelings without a care to the world and all Maine could do was just listen. "You know the minute it gets out that I got this shit I'm gonna have to transfer schools."

"Don't let these motherfuckers run you out of here. You can have a long and productive life…"

"I'm trying to figure out how I'm going to pay for twenty three pills a day." Elgin cut him off. "The doctor told me my pills are gonna cost fifty-two hundred dollars a month. I don't have that kind of money or have any idea on how to get it."

"You got insurance?"

"NC Tech's insurance plan only covers part of the cost...and that's just for the meds. I have doctors to see. Health regimen to maintain. And still focus on getting a degree and finding a six-figure income."

Maine felt guilty. On one hand, he only was getting tested to make sure Yonna didn't give him nothing because he was too lazy to put a condom on. His boys went with him for moral support. No one guessed that one of them would come back infected.

"And now Dean Hardy wants me to help a medical doctor who provides low-cost family care expand his practice when he can't get his customers to pay." Elgin vented. "It's like Dean Hardy found out all our little dirty secrets and just using the teachers to exploit us."

"I'm sure Dean Hardy didn't know," Maine defended.

"Just walk with me home man," Elgin got up and Maine followed him. He hated he didn't drive. But he let Cordell keep the car so that he could get away and have fun with Renee and 'Keem.

"Come to Willie's with me." Maine suggested. "I got to be at work anyway and Spence will be there too. Willie not gonna say shit, just say we working on our accounting homework. He supports education."

"I just want to be alone," Elgin cut Maine off again.

"Hell no!" Maine stood in front of him. "I don't trust you to be alone right now and even if I did, I don't want you to be. You're coming to the store with me and the three of us are gonna work and chill until Cordell gets off. And we'll figure some shit out."

"You and Spence better not ditch me to fuck," Elgin warned.

"Let's keep that between the three of us." Maine looked around. "Everyone don't need to know how big a freak I really am."

Elgin didn't respond. He cried as he and Maine made the long walk to Willie's. All Maine could think about was how to make sure Elgin stayed sane.

20

Before I Self Destruct

Elgin slept peacefully on the couch with Maine's comforter over his body. His long legs hung off the arm as he struggled to use the other side as a pillow. Cordell, Spence and Maine took turns watching over their friend. Bathsheba, Vanessa and Sierra, Vanessa's roommate took turns cooking and cleaning house and relieving the men so they could go to class and take breaks.

"I hope you weren't up all night," Cordell broke Maine from his daze. He'd been watching Elgin like a hawk, especially after the last suicide attempt. Elgin had intentionally walked in front of another student who was driving a little too fast through campus. If Maine hadn't of thought to grab him, Elgin would've been hit. Instead of being thankful for being saved, Elgin seemed frustrated and upset.

"I'm scared to close my eyes." Maine admitted.

Cordell pulled up a chair and sat next to Maine. "You're smothering him."

"You watched over me when I had a gun to my head in the tub." Maine defended, whispering in a low tone. Memories of his own suicide attempt fresh in his mind. Sitting in a tub full of bleach after his mother insisted on washing "the gay" off of him.

"I gave you some distance man," Cordell replied. "After you turned the gun on your mom, I realized then that all I could do is help you from a distance. You have yet to tell me what everything was about in the first place."

Checkmate. Maine had no intentions on telling Cordell that he still dreams about sucking Corey's dick, or letting the boy eat his ass. How he wants to be the first to deflower Corey and give him some of that big dick on the couch Elgin is sleeping on. Truthfully, Corey might be the only nigga that Maine might consider giving the cakes to—that tongue game is nice and he had a hunch that the dick wasn't wack. Plus he's watched Cordell fuck plenty of chicks so Corey had to pick up something somewhere.

I'm bi, Maine thought about telling Cordell his deep, dark secret. Elgin already knew and Maine still hadn't figured out how he got caught slipping. Maine and Spence were careful to only have sex at Spence's spot or at different hotels in Winston, High Point or Burlington. Maine only fucked chick at their spot.

Cordell had warned him when he straddled Corey on the couch and pretended to be a stripper over the summer. That's when he felt how hard Corey's dick got. That's when he first discovered that his suspicions about Corey's sexuality were true. Maine would never admit it but he wanted Corey, even then. He loved the fact that Corey wanted him too and did everything out of Cordell and their father's eyesight to show him.

Everything Maine needed to know about how Cordell felt about his sexuality could be summoned up in that one statement. Confirmation that only a select few people could be invited inside the closet that Maine kept the keys for. His mother found out and if her reaction was typical of how everyone responded to being gay or bisexual, he didn't want anyone else to know his secret.

"So you not gonna tell me why you had a gun to your head?" Cordell brought him back in focus.

"I'm just tripping man." Maine stood up and realized his legs had falling asleep. He couldn't sit back down for fear of cramping and trying to walk was a task in and of itself.

"If it weren't for them girls and Spence keeping you occupied, I'd be worried about you." Cordell went in the kitchen and reached for the Frosted Flakes.

"Spence?" Maine choked. *Did Cordell know?* Maine still was trying to figure out how Elgin found out his secret. He thought he and Spence covered their bases. Were they that obvious that they were fucking?

"Between working at the store and y'all competing for them marketing scholarships and that position at Willie's, Spence keeps you on your toes." Cordell answered.

Cordell didn't know. His secret was safe—kinda. He still needed to find out how Elgin knew.

"But tonight, take a break," Cordell continued. "Check this shit out though. Corey and Melvin got placed on suspension at their residence hall because Melvin and his girlfriend don't know how to keep it quiet when they fucking."

Maine chuckled. "Are you for real man?"

"Dad called us on three-way and Corey told him how Melvin and his girl fuck like rabbits. I know he's not lying cause I walked to Scott Hall to check on him one night and all I could hear was 'oh God, oh God, Melvin, Melvin' through the damn door. She must've been a virgin, screaming like she never had dick before. And she a big girl too so I know Melvin gotta put in extra work to get them strokes in.

"Anyway, this motherfucker asked Dad if he could borrow some money to put Liam in a hotel because he promised his friend they could hang out during fall break. Dad's ole cheapskate ass told Corey that Liam could stay with us."

"Oh hell no!" Maine shouted. "You cannot be serious?!"

"Dad on some little guilt trip because he didn't buy Corey nothing for his room and shit and to get out of it, he promised him our space. I told pops, he better give us that hotel money cause another mouth to feed means we need some food. And Liam ain't staying here for free. Pops was like he'd give thirty dollars cause he wasn't putting Liam in no room so he could fuck some bitches. I told Corey, he better cough up some money too cause thirty dollars ain't gonna cut it. And I don't care if you can get a Motel 6 for that price or not. I'm supposed to be on break, not babysitting one of Corey's punk ass friends."

"Aww hell no." Maine cursed. "I don't like Liam."

"Look man, it's just for two days. I just came from meeting Corey, Melvin and Patrice at the library and shit. Patrice fine for a big girl and she carry her weight well. Melvin better watch out before I pull this dick out and wipe her down. Anyway, she felt guilty about them being in trouble and shit so she gave me one hundred dollars to drive Liam around and wash his clothes and shit." Cordell dug in his pockets and pulled out three twenties, two tens and four five to try to convince him.

"I'm a fuck that little nigga up." Maine shook his head.

"Y'all handle that shit in your room." Cordell offered. "I'm gonna haze his little ass, though. He gonna watch Elgin for both nights while he here and that nigga gonna detail our car. I ain't forgot how he fucked some little freshman freak in the backseat of my uncle's Jeep two years ago. Uncle Roy let me borrow his spare vehicle cause Dad couldn't get me and Corey a car because he was paying Mom's hospital bills. I had to pay Dad back the money he gave Uncle Roy to get the car from the tow people and the money to have it detailed. And on top of that, Uncle Roy is making me buy the Jeep from him. I got six more months to make payments and that green bitch is mine."

"How much are your payments?" Maine wondered. He remembered Cordell getting in trouble behind Liam but he didn't know it was like that.

"I been giving Uncle Roy a hundred dollars a month. But here's the thing. Uncle Roy will only take a hundred dollars a month. He said he wanted me to remember this shit so that when I got the Jeep, I won't be careless with it this time."

Maine shook his head. "I tell you what Liam owe me some money so I'll make sure he pay me that before he leave. I'll give you twelve hundred for your half of the car. That way you can just pay Uncle Roy off that. Use the hundred a month for maintenance and get that title just in case you end up having to trade it in."

"Uncle Roy let me drive the Jeep occasionally so I know it hasn't been sitting. Plus one of his girlfriends' been keeping the oil change and brakes on it and shit." Cordell assured him.

"Someone at the door." Elgin walked in and rubbed his eyes together.

"Let's get these little niggas." Cordell and Maine raced out of the kitchen. "Get y'all's asses in here!" Cordell opened the door and dragged Liam, Melvin and Corey inside. Maine made eye contact with Corey and Liam. Melvin looked away. He had to admit, Melvin was a little cutie with that Afro pic sticking up from the back of his head. Liam was aight. His candy stripped Yankees hat was titled to the back with his extra-long white and Columbia blue shirt tucked into his baggy stone blue pants. The left pants leg was rolled up to the knee. "We gonna lay down some ground rules so no one gets fucked up these next two days."

"I should've went to my mamas for this shit." Liam rolled his eyes.

Cordell grabbed Liam by the shirt and lifted him up. "I'ma put your ass in a body bag you get smart with me again."

"Put him down," Corey tried to help free Liam from Cordell's grip.

"Ain't been here ten seconds and already almost got fucked up," Cordell straightened out his fit. "Like I said, I got rules. You ain't fucking no bitches in my house." Cordell counted them out to make a point. "Only niggas getting pussy in here is me and Maine, cause we pay the damn bill. And you giving me my money back for fucking that bitch in my uncle's Jeep."

"How I know you was gonna bring this shit up?" Corey vented.

Cordell got in Corey's face and looked up at him. "You got something you want to say motherfucker! I can throw this little nigglett out in the street."

Maine could see that Corey wanted to pop off, but he backed off. "Man chill. We need a place for Liam to stay and we really don't have no one else to call on."

"That's what I thought," Cordell shoved his finger in Corey's forehead. Corey balled his fists, looked up in the air, shook his head and pouted but he fell back cause he didn't want it with Cordell. "Like I said, no fucking in our house. No partying in our house. And I don't give a fuck where you go, your little ass better be in this house before ten o'clock."

"Ten o'clock?" Liam pouted. "Where the fuck is my mama?"

"Cuss at me again little boy." Cordell was in Liam's face. "The only reason you here is because me and Elgin out-voted Maine's ass and let you stay."

"Dad gave you thirty dollars," Corey threw that fact in his face.

"And my girl just gave you one hundred." Melvin stepped back and put his arm up. "And you not gonna jump in my face like that. Corey's brother or not, I will fight you and make you give my girl her money back and we can get someone else to house Liam."

"Aight, aight, aight," Maine jumped in-between Cordell and Melvin. He really didn't want to see no one fighting, especially

WHAT'S BEST FOR YOU 119

when they still had to watch Elgin's suicidal ass. "Liam gonna stay, but me and this little negro about to have a talk first. Follow me."

Maine looked back to see Liam following him to his room. "Y'all go get his shit." Maine commanded as he opened the door to his room and once Liam followed him inside, he closed it. "Have a seat." Maine offered Liam a chance to sit on his bed.

"I think I'll stand." Liam walked around Maine's room and walked around. "Cordell don't know do he?"

"No, and I plan on keeping it that way." Maine moved in front of Liam. "On some real shit, I never addressed you about that shit you did to Cordell 'cause that was real foul."

"I didn't mean to get caught." Liam admitted. "I thought that pussy would've been tight and I couldn't gotten a quick nut. I didn't expect her to be as wide as Niagara Falls. And I apologized to Cordell about that shit. I don't know why he bugging about it now."

"Aight so look—since you the reason the Jeep got impounded, you owe him $150 that he had to pay to get it back and you owe him $125 he paid to get it detailed." Maine laid down the law.

"Done," Liam moved into Maine's personal space. "Don't think you gonna get away with fucking Corey over. I know about how you slammed the door in his face and made his nose bleed."

"That ain't none of your concern." Maine answered.

"Naw nigga, don't run now." Liam warmed up. "I listened to you defend your best friend, and I'm gonna stand my ground for mine. Got this nigga falling in love with you and shit and you doing him all kinds of wrong, bitch."

"Who you calling a bitch?" Maine looked down at Liam, waiting on him to make the first move.

"You Khadijah." Liam bucked and looked Maine up and down. "That's my best friend, and soon he gonna be my nigga, so you can forget about chasing him. I'm putting my lock on that tonight."

"Didn't y'all do that threesome with Marcus?" Maine brought up. "He might try to claim Corey."

"Marcus too busy going from Emory to Morehouse to Clark Atlanta doing freaky shit. He ain't even thinking about Corey. But

Corey stay on my mind. That's the only reason I ain't fuck Cordell up because I don't want Corey to think I'm some man beater."

"Whatever man," Maine backed down and sat on his bed. "I bet you don't get the draws, my nigga."

"I bet I do." Liam smirked. "Corey and I got some unfinished business to attend to and *you* not invited."

"You just mad my dick bigger than yours." Maine tugged on his shit. "You should be on your knees sucking it right now."

Liam walked up to Maine, sat on the bed and put his hand in Maine's pants. He whipped it out and massaged it a little. "Your dickhead ain't no bigger than a Blow Pop. I can't suck on that."

Before Maine could make his next move, Elgin walked into the room without knocking. Liam quickly moved his hand without knocking. "Y'all good in here? Corey said they got everything out of Patrice's car."

"Yeah we good. I'm just politicking with this motherfucker though." Liam got up and headed out the room. "Ain't no beef in here."

Maine rolled his eyes. He couldn't believe Liam tried to play him like a sucker. There had to be a way for him to get that little nigga back.

***

"Shh," Maine whispered in Liam's ear.

Bathsheba decided to host Cordell at her place for the night and Cordell offered up his room for the night. Elgin had taken Cordell up on the offer and washed Cordell's sheets and put some clean ones on the bed. The washing machine was still going by the time Liam got back in before ten o'clock. He and Maine played NBA 2k on the SEGA Genesis and continued to talk shit to one another throughout the game.

Spence was invited to hang out but chose to hang out with Vanessa and Sierra. Spence did offer for Maine to make a threesome a foursome, but Maine opted out because he didn't trust Liam not to sneak in no dudes or females on campus. Liam was a hit and drew a crowd wherever he went. Liam quickly drew attention from the New York/New Jersey crew who paraded him around like he was an "authentic New York nigga." If only they knew he was really from the A. Some of Corey and Liam's high school classmates hung out at Putt Putt and Steak N Shake.

Maine hated the idea of not being around Corey and Liam. He could picture Liam doing everything with and to Corey that he wanted to do. Maine's dislike for Liam was rooted in the underlying feeling he had that Liam wanted Corey all to himself.

And he was right.

Corey ended up shooting Liam down. Liam was eating two cups of blueberry yogurt. Maine watched as Liam piddle and moved his spoon from one cup to the next.

"Shh," Maine whispered in Liam's ear as he snuck up behind him. "Wrong with you?" Maine asked as he walked to the fridge in search of a beer. In getting all the extra food for Liam, Corey, Patrice and Melvin to be walking in and out of the house on, no one thought to get any beer.

"Don't want to go to New York in the morning." Liam looked at Maine then looked back down. "Tired of hooking up with these down low niggas on the subway or in the park. Half these motherfuckers homeless, technically."

"So why go back?" Maine asked.

"I go to an Ivy League School, I've already met some good connections in the industry. I've done a few print ads, nothing major." Liam put his spoon down.

Maine thought he'd recognized Liam from one of the ads in the hip hop magazine. He decided not to bring it up though. "You should just go back to the A. You get the same opportunities there that you do in New York now. A lot of record companies are in the A."

"And them same niggas have to fly to New York when it's time to make a decision. I need to be around a nigga that cut a check."

"True dat." Maine replied. "So you gonna sulk for the last few hours while you here?"

"Naw, I'm about to go beat off and then take a nap before we head to the airport." Liam admitted as he got up and threw the yogurt in the trash.

"Beat off," Maine laughed at him. "Why you gotta beat off?"

"I ain't bust in a few days and I don't have no one to get off with." Liam was about to walk past him until Maine grabbed him by the rim of his jersey shorts. "Maine let me go."

"Maybe we should finish what we started." Maine pulled Liam closer to him. "You was gonna give me some ass until we realized I didn't have a condom."

"Man, I can't," Liam started to say until Maine put his finger on Liam's lips. He reached in Liam's pants and pulled his dick out. It was nice and meaty and looked semi-erect. Maine quickly got a nice grip on it and put it in his mouth.

"Shh," Maine instructed as he went down on Liam all the way to the base. He stuck his tongue out and licked his balls.

"Damn," Liam whimpered as he looked around and put his hands on Maine's head. Liam peeled out of his shirt and let his pants fall to the ground. Maine picked Liam up and put him on the table and continued his oral pleasure as he let his pants fall to the ground. He lifted his head up to make sure he could hear Elgin's light snoring. Satisfied he wouldn't be disturbed, he backed away from Liam and took his shirt off. He kissed Liam on the lips, pleased with how juicy his lips looked. "I got a condom in my pants pocket." Liam told Maine.

Maine grabbed Liam's pants and dug around until he felt the condom packed. He was happy to see the condom was lubricated and feel it's slickness as he unrolled the condom on his thick dick. He discreetly spit in his hand and rubbed it along his length. He scooted Liam down until half his ass was off the table. Liam opened his legs wide and when Maine entered him, he wrapped his legs around Maine's waist.

Liam pulled Maine's head down to kiss him. Maine could feel Liam stifling his moans. When they broke free, he could see Liam's eyes rolling to the back of his head. Maine got a good grip on Liam and swiftly scooped him up off the table. Liam's eyes and mouth opened in shock.

"You never had that before?" Maine asked.

"No hmm," Liam whispered and bit his lip as he worked on riding Maine's length. Liam underestimated Maine's strength and Maine underestimated Liam's flexibility. On the downswing, Liam let both of his hands touch the floor and he started guiding Maine's thrusting with his hips. "Keep going."

Maine loved the view of Liam's dick and balls jumping up and down as he fucked him while Liam did a handstand. Maine continued thrusting inside of Liam until his dick slipped out. Liam landed on his feet and walked to the sink. Liam leaned over and Maine wasn't too far behind him, lowering his back with his hand, forcing his head in the sink. Maine picked up his legs and dove right back into his ass. Liam grabbed a hold of the sink and kept moving his ass on Maine as he continued to go further back. Maine had Liam to where he had to hold on to the edge of the sink for dear life because the rest of his body, including his head was now about three feet above ground. Liam looked like he was Superman flying low stretched out across the kitchen floor. His body was now a plank being pounded smoothly as Maine moved his legs up and down.

"I'm coming," Liam took his right hand off the sink to touch his dick but then he put it back on the sink quickly. Maine continued to hit that spot until he could feel Liam quench his as muscles tight and contract. Maine started releasing himself inside the condom.

He put Liam down and backed away and peeled the condom off. Liam left spots of nut all on the floor and the cabinet doors. "Damn, I never been fucked like that before."

"You're one of the most flexible." Maine complimented. He'd never had nobody bend on him like that when they were riding him.

Liam's body shuddered and Maine enjoyed the view from behind. "You gonna have me walking funning at PTI."

"You'll get to rest." Maine laughed.

A knock on the door disturbed their groove. "Oh shit!" They both exclaimed as they quickly rushed to put their clothes on.

"You can't tell Corey," Liam quickly pulled his pants up and tucked his shirt inside.

"You can't tell Cordell," Maine tried to tuck his still erect penis in his pants so he could conceal it.

"They'll kill us." They mimicked in unison as they straightened each other's clothes out. Liam hopped on the couch and Maine answered the door.

"You ready to go?" Corey asked as he walked in without acknowledging Maine's presence.

"Damn best friend," Liam checked Corey. "You gonna be rude to Maine like that?"

Corey looked back and forth between the two of them. "Is your bags packed?"

"Yeah man, I'm ready." Liam grabbed his bags that were already in front of the couch. "Thank for letting me crash at your place man. I really appreciate it."

"No worries." Maine smiled.

"I'm glad we put our differences aside." Liam gave Maine a hug before he left. "I can stop calling you stuck up."

"I'm gonna start calling you Flex."

Liam chuckled and shook his head. "Tell Cordell I said we even. I better not have to clean that nasty ass car again."

"Aight man." Maine watched Liam walk off. The boy was still trying to walk that dick out. He hoped Corey didn't notice. He watched until Liam's bags were in the trunk of Patrice's car and they pulled away from his apartment. He looked back in the kitchen and he could hear Elgin still lightly snoring in Cordell's room.

Maine went into the kitchen, dampened the paper towel with a little dish soap and got on the floor like Cinderella and began to scrub the ground and the cabinet door. He could smell the funk the two of them created just minutes ago and his dick got hard again. Maine focused on the task at hand and by the time he was done, there was no evidence that Liam had left his mark.

21

Man, Man, Man

Corey yawned as he stretched on the sofa chair. His eyes were heavy from staying up watching over Elgin last night. Maine watched him from the hallway. Corey was extended out the slit of his boxers and his precum glistened. The morning wood was no joke as Corey fought a losing battle trying to control it.

"So you spying on me now?" Corey called out as he stood up and looked around.

"Ain't no one spying on you." Maine came from the hallway, fighting his own battle. "Your pants are under your foot."

"Thanks," Corey replied as he put his shirt on. "I don't see how you do it man. My brother and his girl fuck like rabbits. I swear, if I hear *'Cordell, oh Cordell, oh God, oh God, yes Daddy'* one more time."

Maine chuckled. "I get it in too so I can't say shit. We're not always under the same roof so that makes it bearable."

"I just slept right through it." Elgin sat up and rubbed his eyes.

"I'm just glad I didn't room with y'all." Corey pulled his pants up and straightened himself out.

"You say that like you don't be getting..." Elgin jumped in.

"I gets it in." Corey revealed. The fact caught Maine's attention. Corey getting his had Maine feeling some kind of way. Forget that he had Spence and 'Keem and a plethora of females.

"Oh word?" Maine tried to be inconspicuous. "You breaking them freshmen girls' hearts already?"

"Naw, I messed with a senior during Fresh Faces. Then Melvin talked me into banging this one girl who swore up and down she thought I was cute."

"Word?" Maine couldn't believe his ears. Corey got him some pussy. He can finally spell vagina. Unfucking believable. Maine would've paid good money to see that. "So who was better?"

Maine read between the lines. He knew that Corey most likely pulled one of the DL senior boys that was always thirsty for new meat. Everyone banged a freshman during Fresh Faces—that was part of the initiation.

"The senior was more of my speed. The girl was aight. I busted twice with her, but I won't be doing that again." Corey confirmed Maine's suspicions.

Well, at least he tried it and can say he don't like it. Maine thought to himself.

"On the real, thank you for letting Liam crash here these past two days. I'm glad you and Cordell didn't kill him." Corey extended his gratitude.

"We came to an understanding." Maine smiled.

He knew Liam wasn't going to tell Corey their secret. That would've caused all kinds of commotion and drama.

"I'm glad y'all got along because I know how headstrong Liam can be." Corey continued. "He'll get his mind set on something and be ready to action."

"We settled our beef." Maine thought about how Liam flipped on him and took the dick while doing a headstand. He wondered if Corey was that flexible. Thinking about Liam made him wonder how the threesome with Liam, Corey and Marcus went down.

"I'm gonna head out," Corey grabbed his small backpack and threw it over his shoulder. "I gotta brush my teeth and get in my own bed and sleep."

"Don't you got class?" Elgin asked.

"I can miss today." Corey was confident.

"Aw hell, that's how it starts." Elgin warned. "Next thing you know a whole week will have gone by and you'll be like 'what happened?'"

"I'm good, I promise," Corey gave Elgin a pound. He waved Maine the peace sign and headed out the door.

***

"We should've picked 'Keem up." Maine barely looked up from his Accounting 101 book. The lessons kept getting harder and

Maine knew he was going to need every second of studying he could get.

"Nah," Spence insisted. "He said he had to do some stuff with the team. He's trying to get out here without drawing a lot of attention."

It made sense. 'Keem was one of the most popular guys in the school and when he wasn't on the football field handling his business, he was partying and bullshitting and causing a ruckas.

"So we really gonna be up for this?" Maine asked as he looked up from the page he was studying. "Last time I tried to get in a threesome, one of the guys bailed on me."

"You ready to take this dick?" Spence walked up to Maine and took the book out of his lap. Spence unzipped his pants and his hardened penis fell at attention. Maine studied its length. Spence wasn't as big as Maine but he was a far cry from small. Maine liked his ass to be teased, not touched.

"I'll never be ready for that," Maine conceded as he leaned forward in the chair. "But I can't wait to watch you stuff 'Keem with it." Maine extended his hand and gave Spence's dick a firm grasp. Maine pulled Spence closer to him and extended his tongue, licking the slit of Spence's dick. Slowly, Spence's throbbing mushroom head pushed passed Maine's barrier and he sucked on it like a lollipop. Hearing Spence moan encouraged him to go for the kill. In one swift move, Maine sucked Spence in like a Hoover and once Spence's dick hit the back of Maine's throat, he held him until neither of them could move any further. The scent of Spence's musk turned Maine on as he continued to maneuver his mouth up and down Spence's shaft. He could feel Spence's cold finger caressing and twirling his hardening nipples.

The knock on the door interrupted their moment. Maine let Spence go and laughed as he watched Spence struggled to put his dick in his pants. Maine sat up straight and grabbed the book so he could look like he was reading before 'Keem walked in and stole the show.

"My niggas," 'Keem greeted them at the door. In his hands were bottles of Hypnotiq and Hennessey. "My boy is hooking us up with some cheeseburger and vegetable lovers pizzas and from Dominoes and he agreed to get us some of those extra large wings from China 1 Buffett. He gonna run by here before he stop at Cooper Hall, I hope you don't mind."

"Hell naw I don't mind," Spence grinned as he took the bottles. "Free food is always good."

Maine almost felt guilty for not bring anything, but he gotta supply dick to feed Spence and 'Keem. That oughta be enough.

"What up V?" 'Keem gave Maine a pound.

Maine returned the gesture. He looked 'Keem over. He smelled good in Irish Spring and Curve. He could tell by the way his meat stuck out in the front of his gray NC Tech sweatpants that 'Keem wasn't wearing any draws.

"You got any downstairs neighbors?" 'Keem asked.

"Yeah but we straight," Spence returned with three shot glasses. "They'll be partying after a while so it's all good."

"Spence, you did a good job with this spot. A lot of college students from all over stay out here." 'Keem complimented. "Renee and I are thinking about moving out here next year or whatever."

"Yeah man," Maine agreed. "It's not too far from campus, real discreet. Close enough to catch a short bus ride if you had to and far enough for motherfuckers to stay out of your business."

"I heard that," 'Keem added. "What business y'all end up getting with Dr. Finley's class?" 'Keem downed his drink in one shot. "Renee and I are working with an elderly couple looking to sell their tax preparation business."

"Me and Chelle are gonna help this lady who is trying to create a black owned bookstore down the street. Seems pretty cool. But I think she don't have the best people around her watching her back." Spence answered.

"Yonna and I are helping a high school student expand her business." Maine replied.

"Saudi's Sweetness." 'Keem inquired. Maine confirmed with a head nod. "Ole girl is dope as shit. I wish I had the heart to do what she did when I was young. I'm not gonna front, when I grow up, I wanna be just like her. My dad stressing me about getting back into the mosque and saying my prayers and shit. I like Allah, he and I are cool. But I like dick too and I gotta find a way to have them both."

"You're a Muslim?" Maine was shocked.

"Yeah, I hope that's not a problem." 'Keem jumped on the offensive.

"Naw man, I had no idea, that's all."

"My real name is Dawid Aakil Hakeem Allah—prince of the wise and intelligent rulers under Allah. I Americanized my name because I wanted my talent to speak for itself. I don't want to be the athlete that is Muslim. I just want to be a good football player. Truth be told, y'all and Renee are only a few who are in on some of my secrets and in in a few minutes, y'all about to get to get into a few more."

'Keem got on his knees and got inbetween Spence's legs. Maine glanced at the clock and realized they had about fifty minutes or so to get it in before the pizza boy showed up. Maine got on his knees and got a good view of 'Keem handling Spence's business. Spence's body quivered as it surrendered to 'Keem's thick, juicy lips and expert tongue working it's magic. Maine stood up and pulled off Spence's shirt. He could feel his boy under him enjoying the pleasures that attacked his body.

Maine pulled off his shirt and he could feel 'Keem tugging at his pants. 'Keem sucked him off too and he struggled to capture his balance as he got hooked up with the same treatment Spence got. Spence got on his knees before Maine and he and 'Keem took turns licking the length of Maine's manhood and teasing his balls. The view from up top was magnificent and Maine couldn't wait for this threesome to be off the charts.

Spence laid on his back and he pulled 'Keem's pants down. He used both of his hands to part 'Keem's ass and he dug his tongue right into 'Keem's sweet spot. 'Keem shuttered and moaned as he rode Spence's face. He grabbed Spence's legs and curled him up in a ball and put his face on Spence's hole. Maine watched as the circle moaned and rocked without him. He laid on the floor and put his head where Spence's dick was and quickly put it in his mouth. As he pleasured himself, he went from Spence's dick and 'Keem's dick. Moans of pleasure could be heard as Spence and 'Keem continued to devour one another like Thanksgiving plates.

"You top?" Spence broke free and asked.

"I prefer not to, but I can." 'Keem answered. "Can both of y'all fuck me at the same time?"

"Word?" Maine had always wanted to try it.

"Yeah. Maine, since you are bigger, you will need to lay at the bottom and Spence will have to have his legs over yours when y'all line y'alls dicks up." 'Keem suggested as he grabbed some Astroglide from his bag.

Maine got up and took and seat across from Spence. Spence put his legs over Maine's as 'Keem suggested. As they scooted across the floor and met dick to balls, their asses kissed. 'Keem tossed each of them a Magnum and gave them time to cover and lube their jimmies.

"Should one of us loosen you up first?" Spence suggested as he went to work on his piece.

"You gotta thick tongue my nigga. I'm loose, trust me." 'Keem stood over the two and put both of their lubed dicks together. Maine and Spence were amazed at how easily 'Keem opened up to accommodate the both of them as he lowered his ass upon them.

"Oh shit!" Maine and Spence yelled as they slowly rubbed their dicks against each other, trying to fuck 'Keem. Maine got off on the way his balls rubbed against Spence's and kept pace with one another. 'Keem was in full control of the boat and Maine and Spence had no choice but to enjoy the ride and respect the power 'Keem put into his bottom. 'Keem closed his eyes and hummed as he rocked his hips on the dick, chanting and singing, hypnotizing everyone under the sound of his voice.

When he was done, 'Keem got off and the laid on his left side. "Fill me up."

Maine was courteous enough to let Spence get the ass while he stuffed 'Keem's face. He loved watching Spence lay next to 'Keem and put his covered penis deep inside 'Keem.

"Yeah boy!" Spence yelled. "Been wanting this."

Maine watched as Spence danced to a new rhythm inside 'Keem. Soon, Spence scooped 'Keem into his arms and started to piston fuck him. 'Keem continued to show the two of them he could take whatever they dished as he continued swinging and moving his hips as if he switched gears. Maine loved watching

Spence attack the ass and it was good to see him give the dick as good as he took it.

Spence eased off and 'Keem got on his knees, putting his face down, ass up. The proverbial tag, Maine switched places and grabbed a new condom and put it on. He slammed into 'Keem's ass and watched his backside as 'Keem soon took over the thrusting and was massaging Maine's dick for him.

'Keem sat back and stood up as Spence began to use his face like 'Keem used his waist. Maine looked up and loved the peace and serenity in Spence's eyes as he was getting his satisfaction.

Spence reached for the last condom and put it on. Maine wanted to watch the two of them fuck again and was happy to switch places. Spence got behind 'Keem and dug into him. Maine stroked his dick as he watched Spence's ass part on the upstroke and clinch on the down. Spence swiftly threw his arms back and formed a table while allowing 'Keem to spin on him like a mechanical bull. 'Keem leaned back and Spence laid flat. Then, like a WWE wrestler, Spence wrapped his legs around 'Keem's and started choking the shit out of him. 'Keem's eyes rolled to the back of his head while humming, never breaking the smile that plastered across his face.

"Fuck that nigga Spence," Maine encouraged. "Beat the shit out of him."

The dance was causing Maine to grip his dick harder and stroke faster. 'Keem and Spence turned on their side. "Come fuck me," Spence offered as he continued to stroke 'Keem.

Maine quickly scanned the room and realized his first hunch was right. They were out of condoms. "Ain't no more rubbers man."

"We good, I trust you." Spence kept stroking into 'Keem's backside.

Maine smiled as he laid beside Spence. Spence lifted his leg up, making it easy for Maine to get to his hole. Maine was nervous. He always teased Spence, pretended like he was gonna put the dick in, but he never dropped it in raw before. Spence slowed his strokes and Maine lined the tip of his penis in. When Spence pushed that ass out, Maine pushed in. With one stroke, Maine was in and he held his spot. Feeling inside of Spence without restriction was like heaven. Felt better than Yonna. Spence reached back and pulled Maine in deeper, using his own waist to synch the strokes.

Maine tried to hang, but he couldn't. Like a virgin who'd never had any ass before, Maine's dick expanded and he could feel his nut ready to rip loose. "Yo, I'm about to cum."

"Cum in me." Spence continued moving his hips, taking the dick and delivering the strokes at the same time.

Maine tried to hold on, stay in the ass a little longer but it was no use. As Spence cried and cursed into his own orgasm, Maine felt his dick expand wider and his soul leaving his to be with Spence's. Maine grunted and cursed violently as he thrusted his hips deeper into Spence. Spence turned his head back to kiss Maine and as their lips met, their tongues made love, never wanted to let go. Maine never felt no ass or pussy like this. As he looked into Spence's eyes and kissed him, letting the last of his orgasm tremble through, he felt like he could give it to Spence like this all the time.

'Keem rolled onto his stomach, Maine and Spence rolled onto their backs. The living room smelled of sex and sweat and the three were too weak to do anything about it. They struggled to catch their breathe as that had been one of the most thrilling encounters either of them had ever had.

"Y'all two the kangs." 'Keem rolled his sweaty body across Spence's and Maine's stomach. He picked off the condom from Spence's dick. 'Keem devoured the nut inside and the last drippings as if he were scraping the plate of a well-cooked meal. He grabbed Maine's dick and greedily claimed the last he had to offer. "Can we go again in fifteen minutes?"

"After we get some pizza," Spence laughed.

"Yeah man, I need some food in my belly," Maine added. "And we gotta get some more condoms."

"Aight man," 'Keem got up and pulled out a twenty from his pocket. "One of y'all need to get the rubbers cause I need to be here to make sure we get our food."

"I'll go," Spence volunteered as he got up and walked to his bed and put on some pajama pants laying at the edge with a worn T-shirt. "Y'all behave."

WHAT'S BEST FOR YOU 133

Spence opened the door and walked out. Maine laid out on the floor, in awe over the fact that he not only got inside Spence raw, but he let himself go.

"That's the first time y'all hit it raw?" 'Keem cuddled against Maine.

"Yeah man," Maine admitted. "I see how that causes problems."

"Yeah. Niggas be out here equating raw sex with love. Do you love him?" 'Keem asked.

"I like him more than I like a lot of people right now," Maine answered. "I guess I can love him, and that will come at some point."

"You be careful and don't tell him that." 'Keem answered as a knock on the door interrupted their moment.

Maine swiftly got off the floor and searched for his clothes. 'Keem put his sweatpants back on. Maine headed to the bathroom and turned the shower on. He washed up, enjoyed the way the water felt as it ran down his body. The door opened and Maine slid the shower curtain open. He was happy to see Spence stripping off his clothes, rushing to join him.

"That was quick." Maine moved toward the back of the shower.

"I hope you didn't use all the hot water," Spence jumped in. "And the store wasn't but a few minutes away and there was no line. In and out."

Maine looked down at Spence. He couldn't believe moments ago, he was inside Spence the way he always thought he'd be inside his wife or long term girlfriend. He knew at that moment that whatever he and Spence had was special. He pushed Spence closer to the front and got on his knees. He put his face between Spence's ass and dived in.

22

Bound 4 Life

The sheets Maine and Spence were supposed to be under struggled to stay on top of the bed as Maine moved his feet, and turned away from the man he was cuddling with. He wanted to go back to sleep but seeing the clock reading seven fifty three am, Maine knew it was a matter of time before Spence's alarm rang.

It had been a week since Maine and Spence made the decision to stop wearing rubbers and the consequences have been drastic and severe. After going to a group therapy session with Elgin, the group of friends decided their boy was stable enough not to have to watch over them. The fact they came up with a plan to deal with Elgin's HIV status and mental health was commended. Elgin began to resume the life he had—working at and flirting with the girls at Mrs. Winner's; getting on top of his academics and diving in head first into his business classes. Elgin and Janessa began to hang our more socially. For a moment, that concerned Maine but the doctor told all of them that as long as Elgin stayed on top of his medications and wore condoms every time he had sex, he would be least likely to infect new sex partners. Elgin also began dressing up and hanging out with the brothers of Spence's frat more often.

Bathsheba became the unofficial third member of the house, chipping in on rent and food. Most of the time when she wasn't at work at Borders or studying with her laptop and four textbooks all over the table, she was huddled in the room she now shared with Cordell. And they got it in.

Other than entertaining Bathsheba, Maine hardly ever saw Cordell. On Monday, Maine broke Yonna off with some "we can't fuck no more/apology" dick after things didn't go well with

Saudi's Sweetness. On Tuesday, Maine and Spence traded off between Vanessa and Sierra after they worked a huge release day sales event. Wednesday brought a night of hanging with Renee and 'Keem. Renee was trying to get a game of Phase 10 going and a party but her friend's dorm but a couple of the invitees bailed.

Thursday was Maine and Spence day. The two were inseparable. They hung out in the cafeteria trailer and then studied at the library. Maine was even allowed to be on the fraternity plot and have a few drinks with some of the older brothers. Later that night, they met up with some of their classmates at the McDonalds on Bessemer Avenue and that joint turned into a club inside the fast food joint. Ludacris was getting the crowd hype as his old-school mixtapes were passed around like they were new again. Juvenile had everyone backing their asses up and the way the classmates and some of the locals were grinding, one would've thought they were at Freaknik from the early nineties. Later that night, Maine and Spence couldn't keep their hands to themselves. If Spence wasn't riding Maine's dick on the sofa, Maine was crying "uncle" over the dinner table as Spence at that ass like it was the last supper. Maine would have on all four hunched over him like a dog in heat. Spence would retaliate by controlling Maine's dick with his ass as he got fucked over the porch rail while smoking a blunt.

When they woke up on Friday, they went to classes, did their job at Willie's and had a repeat of their night cap. Saturday morning, Spence left Maine a key to his apartment while he went to spend the day dealing with frat-related stuff while Maine pulled at double at Willies. At first, he wasn't going to work so hard but then he thought about the assistant manager position and how bad he wanted it. Sony Entertainment and Capital Records opened their internship application period and Maine was on top of getting those assignments down. He still kept his eye out for an opportunity at Def Jam, in part so he could spend the spring and summer with Spence.

Maine turned on the television and could hear the news reporters talking about Y2K and what was going to happen to the banks and computers once the clocks turned 1/1/2000. Maine focused his attention to the bottom of the screen. He read the market information and followed the stock. For the most part, his portfolio was doing well and Maine was pleased that he'd be able to replace the money he was giving Cordell for the car in no time. Nike was doing well and so were WorldCom, Enron, Chase and AOL TimeWarner.

"You believe the hype?" Spence asked as he turned over.

"What hype?" Maine continued his focus, waiting to hear news about the company that owned Harris Teeter, Diego and Yum Brands.

"This Y2K bullshit," Spence leaned over and faced Maine. "I feel like they doing this shit to cause a panic and to get us ready for some new world older bullshit."

"I'm not stuntin' it." Maine replied, keeping his eyes glued to the television.

"I was reading *Behold a Pale Horse*, they talk about shit like this." Spence got up and stretched.

Maine caught the view.

"That dude said HIV and AIDS were created to rid the world of blacks, Hispanics and homosexuals. Let him tell it, the government is hiding the cure." Spence paused spitting knowledge to go through his ritual fifty pushups and crunchies.

"You stay up on them conspiracy theories." Maine commented as he got up and did his own set of pushups.

"I don't trust the government," Spence admitted as he struck a Yoga pose. "Never had, never will. I think Ronald Regan put them microchips in the dollar bills and that's how Monica Lewinsky got caught sucking Bill's dick."

"Seriously bruh," Maine smirked. The Spence he loved and loved to hate was emerging. Maine made it a point to avoid debates with this nigga because Spence never knew when to let a point go.

"Hell yeah. And these fuckin' Republicans got everyone thinking they are the morality police. Have you read the impeachment files on President Clinton? Those documents are steamier than a Harlequin romance novel—I almost beat off."

Maine shook his head. "Heel boy."

"I'm serious. And speaking of beating off—when was the last you got it in with Mushroom? That is Cordell's younger brother, right?"

Shit! Shit! Shit Maine cursed to himself. He hoped he wasn't talking in his sleep and talking about the boy. If Elgin hadn't of been in the living room a week ago, Maine would've taken that chance and tried to see if Corey would've given him the ass. Maine felt like he was so close, yet so far away from the promised land.

"I haven't fooled with him since the summer," Maine kept it honest. He and Spence worked hard to get their relationship to where they trusted one another. "I would've messed with him last week if the opportunity presented itself but it didn't."

"You should bring him here." Spence offered.

Maine looked at him. "You serious?"

"Hell yeah. I need some fresh meat and if he's what you say he is, I won't have to worry about Cordell trying to whoop my ass." Spence shadow boxed. His flaccid penis bounced from one thigh to the next as he kept in pace with his movements. "Tomorrow, we got these new team members coming into Willie's and we gotta get these knuckle heads in shape."

"You right about that." Maine admitted. "If I can get in touch with Mushroom, I'll see what I can do about getting him to come over."

Spence stopped and grabbed a set of towels out of his linen closet. "That's what's up. I'm gonna get ready so I can take Vanessa to church—you want to come with us."

"Naw, I'm good." Maine passed. He didn't feel like running back to his apartment to change and if he was going to be in the house of the Lord, he at least wanted to look presentable.

Maine heard the water running. He could feel the weight in his dick getting heavy. He laid back on the bed and turned to BET. *The Bobby Jones Gospel Show* did what it was supposed to do, bring that morning wood into line. He reached on the edge of the bed and brought the sheet up to his neck. He listened as a choir and an ensemble sang different renditions of church hymns he'd grown up to when his mom used to take him to church. He turned the channel and watched the country music television show. He didn't really care for the music, since he associated with confederate flags, racism against blacks and hypocrisy for talking about the same subject matter rappers dealt with. Maine changed the channel and reluctantly kept it on the show that was a true rip off of *Living Single*. The show had no originality and was only popular because it's white cast members behaved in a way that flaunted their entitlement.

Where are The Golden Girls? Maine wondered as he skipped channel after channel. He didn't even want to watch the show, but watching four elder women keep it real about life, love and the lack thereof secretly kept him entertained.

"I'm surprised you didn't come in here and join me," Spence walked out of the shower drying off his body. The water looked so animated rolling down his skin.

"I was looking for something on the television," Maine got up and walked to Spence. "Maybe you and I can have shower time after we get off work."

"Naw, baby," Spence moved around Maine. "I promised Vanessa I'd spend the night with her. She ain't seen me in a few days and I don't want her getting too suspicious."

"Oh yeah, that's cool." Maine felt rejected. "I take it Sierra is with her man?"

"Nah, Sierra's mom is in the hospital so that's why you haven't seen her." Spence slipped into so low-cut red briefs and some red, white and gray diamond black socks. "You gonna stay at my place or are you gonna head back home?"

"Man, I'm gonna go back. I may check on Elgin, see how he doing." Maine offered.

"That's cool." Spence had buttoned up a white and grey pin-stripped shirt and he was jumping into some pressed gray slacks that was hanging in the closet. A few sprays of the Nautica cologne and a quick bowtie later, Spence looked his Sunday's best. "I'll call you after I get out of service."

Spence walked up to him and kissed Maine on the lips. Spence's tongue broke past Maine's barrier and danced with him. Maine was tempted to pick Spence up, throw him on the bed and get it on, but Spence pushed him away. "We'll finish this up on Monday —promise babe."

"Promise," Maine watched Spence walk out of the door.

As the door closed, Maine felt like a part of him was walking out of the door too. He wasn't in love, never been in love before. He wondered if Corey would've left him in an empty apartment to tend to a boyfriend or his brother. Maine got back in bed. Spence's scent invaded his nose and soon, he was touching himself, wishing Spence was between his legs, and not attending to his girl.

23

Fresh Meat

"Aight fellas," Willie called Maine and Spence to attention. One of the young high school girls had her fingers all through Spence's blow out Afro. Willie shook his head. "You getting too old for that."

"Aww man, you know I'm not gonna…" Spence started to explain but Willie cut him off.

"Set the example," Willie scolded as Spence took a step up to the register. "I do appreciate the both of you coming in early and on a Monday when I know y'all got a day full of classes. However, I've chosen three new employees I want to work with. They should be on their way in at any minute."

On cue, a young man wearing a white shirt with black slacks walks in the door. The black braided belt wrapped around his waist tightly, but still gave him enough room to sag his pants a little. His high top slanted to the left to the little, like Kid from Kid N Play and skin tone was a shade darker than a white corn chip. Not too far behind him was a short, thick girl with long cornrows braided down to her bra strap. The lack of makeup emphasized her rough features. Maine was convinced she studied the movie *Set It Off* because she has Queen Latifah's movements in that movie down to a T. The last young man to walk into the store was short but muscular. His bald fade was tight and his waves were perfect. His skin was filled with light acne at the top, but his eyes gave away his soft features. He barely showed Maine, Spence or Willie any eye contact.

"I'm glad y'all are on time, I like you already," Willie was just as friendly to them as he was to Maine and Spence on their first day. "The guy with the Afro is Spence and he'll be teaching you how to do stocking and inventory. The guy with the fade is Maine and he'll be teaching you how we do customer service, phone etiquette and how to prepare for the start and close of your shift. These two gentlemen will assist me in teaching you everything you need to know to be successful at working at Willie's.

"I'm going to step out and I'll be back in about an hour or so to check on you and see how you do. You'll go on a small break and then you'll get to clock out at nine thirty."

Each of the new employees shook their heads.

"I'm Alize," the hardcore looking chick introduced herself and gave Maine and Spence firm handshakes. "I'm a senior at Grimsley High School and I'm looking to major in marketing at NC Tech next year."

"I like you already," Maine chuckled. "Looks like we'll get to help you settle into your major and get you started at Tech the right way."

"I'm Broadus," the taller, lanky fake Kid from Kid N Play introduce himself. "I'm a senior at Smith High School and Snoop, Brandy and Ray J may or may not be my distant cousins. Still trying to find that out."

"You going to college?" Spence asked.

"I'm going to The Winston-Salem State University—gotta get out of G'Boro, been here all my life." Broadus answered. Maine saw Spence tsk.

"Going to the wrong high school and to the wrong college," Spence vented.

"You must've went to Grimsley," Broadus smirked.

"Damn right."

"No sirs, we not doing that in here." Willie spoke up. "Keep that rivalry BS outside my walls—Spence!" Maine could see the disappointment in Willie's face. "Travis introduce yourself."

"I'm Travis," the short quiet man quickly waved his hand and put it back down. "I'm home schooled and I don't know if I want to go to a black school or a PWI. I just know my mama put in this program so I could develop some people skills."

"Your mama put you in the right place." Willie shook his hand again and put his hand on his shoulder. "I'm step out—all y'all behave and if you break anything, just know it's coming out of your first check and the time and labor it cost me in administering your ass whooping."

"Yes sir," the three new employees replied in unison.

Everyone watched as Willie left. The sounds of gum smacking grew louder before Alize blew the biggest bubble and let it pop. "Okay y'all—before we get started, I got some of my rules I need to go over with y'all. One, I hate my name so don't be calling it on a regular. Two, I may look and act like a dyke, but I like dick. But I don't want your dick," Alize pointed to Spence, "your dick, your dick or your dick." She pointed to everyone else. "And lastly, I got a ten month old son and my baby daddy be tripping, so my sister may have to bring him up here from time to time so I can handle my business."

"Aight—we won't call your name on a regular. I have a girlfriend, kinda…" Maine replied to Alize's list of demands.

"I actually have a girlfriend." Spence butted in.

"And what's your son's name?" Maine inquired. Secretly, he liked that Alize was a little hood and thought she'd bring a different flavor to the store.

"Amaru Goines." Alize stated fact. "I named him after my favorite rapper and my favorite author and not his punk ass daddy."

"You got one more time to talk about my cousin like that." Broadus warned.

"Boy bye—you need to worry about why your girlfriend cheating on you with the whole basketball team and half the lacrosse team at High Point Andrews. And if you see your punk ass cousin, please tell him he already owe me fifteen hundred in child support and don't think cause he don't want to pay that I won't get my money." Alize got in his space and put her hand in his face.

"Why don't we take you?" Spence stepped down from the register and grabbed Broadus' arm and led him to the back. "We'll get you started back here learning the inventory. Let's leave her and Travis up here to learn how to clock in and clock out."

Good thinking, Maine thought as Alize eyed Spence and Broadus as they went into the stock room.

"Travis, I hope you aren't nothing like Broke Ass because he like to run his mouth too much and I'm not trying to have a whole bunch of problems where I'm trying to make this paper." Alize put her hands on her chest.

Travis shook his head no.

"You better start learning to speak up before people start thinking you're gay around here. You don't want to be one of them feminine acting, Avon Skin-So-Soft type of dude. You better get you some DMX in your voice."

Note to self—do not get caught with no dude in front of Alize, Maine thought to himself as he eyed Alize. He was convinced that Willie had to know that Alize was a ball of fire and ready to strike without warning. Knowing her, her bite was probably as loud and vicious as the dog she sounded like.

Travis didn't respond to Alize. He just shook his head and looked off into space. Travis reminded Maine so much of Corey that he wondered about him. He had a hunch that Travis might've been gay—but any chance of him acting on it diminished greatly with Alize's discouragement.

Maine showed Alize about logging in and out, demonstrated professional courtesy when answering the phones and displayed detailed product knowledge in reference to the artists whose music they sold during the time period. In an hour, they switched places with Broadus and Maine got the work with the young man one on one. Broadus seemed to emulate Maine's mannerisms and even took the lead in persuading a customer to buy a Missy Elliot album.

Willie was pleased with the progress the new employees were making and told them they had great first day. After they left at nine thirty, Willie, Maine and Spence stayed to help Willie close.

"So what y'all think?" Willie asked as they left the store.

"Alize may be the leader of the group, depending on how she work things out with her baby daddy." Spence answered as he mimicked her voice.

"She's a sweetheart. Don't let the hard exterior fool you. She's guarding herself and navigating the world as a mother without the support of most of her family." Willie defended her. "She got big dreams and as long as she keeps those legs closed, I believe she's worth helping with that."

"Broadus learns very fast and loves to stay busy." Maine took his turned. He really liked Broadus and saw bits and pieces of himself in him.

"Broadus likes to fight but I believe if we can keep him occupied, we can keep him from falling into the same trap his older brother got into." Willie revealed.

"Where's his brother now?" Spence asked.

"He gets out of prison later this year and I want to have that boy on the straight and narrow so I can focus on helping his brother get back into civilization the right way. And I know Travis needs work, but the boy is gifted. He knows Sarah Vaughn, Ella Fitzgerald, Duke Ellington, Miles Davis, John Coltrane and he can slowly decipher the lyrics to a Bone Thugs N Harmony song to where I can understand it." Willie told them.

"How long have you known him?" Maine asked.

"I've known his daddy since we were boys. He's not going to say it but his parents are my age." Willie got in his car. "He's their miracle child because they'd been trying to have him for twenty years. When they got him, they shielded him from everything and now, we're taking the first steps to showing him the rest of the world. I'm pleased with y'all so far. Each of you are showing me that you have what it takes to be my assistant. I do want them to see y'all working with them together, not just individually."

"Yes sir," they replied as Willie closed his door.

Maine and Spence each headed to their cars. Maine knew that Spence was going to Vanessa's to spend the night. A part of him had wished that he and Yonna weren't on bad terms but he knew he needed some time to himself. He needed to figure out how he could be a good leader to Alize, Broadus and Travis and how the four of them were going to help him achieve his goals.

24

Another Sad Study Party

"I hate this damn class!" Janessa vented as she tossed her book on the dinner table. Elgin looked at her and smiled. "You think this shit funny."

"Baby girl, you got to chill for two minutes and give me a chance to explain the concept to you." Elgin picked Janessa's Accounting 101 book off the table and handed it to her.

"I'm with Janessa, I feel like throwing books and shit." Renee joined in as she put her book on the side. "Spence, how long is it gonna be before the chicken chili is ready? A bitch is stressed and hungry."

Maine looked at Spence who smiled at him. Instead of ordering out, the classes pulled their money together and brought enough ingredients for Cordell, Spence and Chelle to cook for everyone. The study party grew from the faith few to all of Dr. Finley's sections and all of Dr. Cooper's sections, plus some students from Bennett College, Gilbert State and UNCG. Accounting 101 was kicking the whole city of Greensboro's ass and about seventy accounting students found their way to Cordell and Elgin's for the block party.

"And I thought I told you cover up your hair!" Renee yelled as she got up from her chair. "If I find Afro in my food, you gonna find my fist in your face."

"Ma calm down," 'Keem held Renee back.

"Let me go man, I'm getting up to get us some drinks." Renee walked to the table with 'Keem staying close behind her. On one side was bottled water, cans of Food Lion branded soft drinks on the other side, Jack Daniels, Jim Bean, Chardonnay and Seagrams made their presence known. Spence's frat brothers made a punch that was disappearing fast in the center of the table. No telling what was in it except the noticeable pineapple chunks and Jell-O shots that lined up on opposite sides of the bowl.

The smoke from the grill Cordell was manning wafted in the apartment and the turkey burgers and chicken hot dogs made Maine's stomach sizzle. He wanted some of the barbeque baked beans Cordell made from scratch without the bacon to accommodate the Muslims who were studying with them. He got up and stretch and headed to his room so he could get some fresh air.

Maine laid on the bed as he thought about accounting and marketing and wondering how all this was going to help him be an assistant manager at Willie's or get him an internship at Sony. Interscope Records wasn't opening their internship session this year and Maine was a little bummed about that.

"Mind if I come in?" Yonna asked from the door.

Maine nodded his head. Yonna came in and took a seat at his desk.

"I'm glad Malika and Salma are pleased with the work we are doing for Saudi's Sweetness." Yonna made small talk. The project was going well and forcing the two of them to gain a better understanding of the earlier accounting concepts and work together. "Malika said they might be on their way and that Farooq may come too. One of Malika and Salma's cousins want to prove they can run the store unsupervised and they may stop of here to test that theory. Plus, Salma said she could probably help us apply this in a practical sense."

"I didn't know Salma was an accounting major," Maine straightened up.

"Yeah. She worked for Ernest & Young when she's not helping her sister run her empire." Yonna reminded him.

"I think that's where Elgin is looking to go." Maine mentioned.

"Elgin is really on top of his shit, and he breaks it down easy for me to understand." Yonna admitted.

"That's his major." Maine pointed out. He opened the window, letting some of the cool late September air come in the room.

"What y'all doing for Homecoming?" Yonna sat on the bed.

"We're taking a pass." Maine smile as she sat on the edge next to her. "We don't have no older family members to impress, and friends dropping by to see us and I know I'm going on the plots to eat."

"I thought the Sigmas and Zetas banned you from the plot at the fiasco with them and the Deltas last year." Yonna brought up.

Maine chuckled. "Me and the Sigmas cool. I actually like the chapter they got up here. Dudes are cool and real social. They're diverse and I feel like I can be me around them. It's like them and the Iotas—they're like real niggas, not some stuck up, arrogant, assholes who think they're God's gift to women and think they are better than someone because they got money."

"Oh shit, let me find out you trying to pledge Sigma!" Yonna exclaimed.

"If I pledge anything, you'll see when it happens. But on the real, I don't know if I want to be Greek or not. I need to get some things out of the way first so I can start my business when I graduate." Maine admitted.

"I'm surprised you not trying to pledge Spence's frat." Yonna moved in closer.

"Nah—like I said, I'm don't know if I'm gonna pledge anything or not. Don't think Cordell is that interested though but he hang with some of the Alphas and Sigmas. We haven't really talked about it."

"The AKA's are having a line next Spring and I've been focusing on accounting and getting my information together." Yonna stood up and stretched. "Between me, you and Chelle, the treasurer of the chapter is my half-sister and their chapter advisor is my aunt. I don't tell nobody we're related cause I'm not trying to come in on legacy. I want them to like me for me, not because of who my family is."

"I respect that." Maine answered.

"My mom's a Zeta, and I haven't figured out how I'm gonna tell her blue and white is not for me."

Maine laughed.

"That's not funny."

"That's the funny thing about wanting to be Greek. Everyone stresses and puts all their energy chasing three letters and a brotherhood and sisterhood. For a few weeks, we forget we're college students and go through hell." Maine stood up. Yonna grabbed his hand. Maine looked at her and he helped her off his bed. He was tempted to close the door and give her the business but he didn't want that relationship with Yonna anymore. The fact they had the conversation showed how far they'd come since the incident that forced them to have to work together. "I'll be out in a minute."

Maine watched as Yonna went out. He put his hands in his pants and pressed the tip of his penis, praying to make the erection go away. Once it had subsided he headed to the bathroom and washed his hands. He came out and bumped into 'Keem.

"What's good man?" 'Keem asked as he looked around.

"You tell me." Maine whispered.

'Keem pushed Maine back in the bathroom. "I need some dick."

"You gotta condom?" Maine asked as 'Keem's touch undid the hard work Maine made to make his erection go down. 'Keem shook his head no as he continued to massage Maine's tool.

"In my room." Maine offered. "I got some in a big fish bowl next to the lamp with some small packets of lube."

"Cool," 'Keem gave Maine a kiss. The punch was on 'Keem's lips and as 'Keem headed down the hallway to get the items needed, Maine made a quick exit. He looked to see where Spence was and how close the food was to being ready because he was more hungry than he was horny. Most of the classmates took a break from the studies and enjoyed the food. He looked outside and seen Spence and Elgin heading to Elgin's apartment.

Damn, Maine thought to himself. *I really wanted to get it in with him. It's been a week.*

After have all the bareback sex he wanted with Spence, the last thing he wanted to do was go through the hassle of stretching out and unrolling the latex barrier on thick dick. And he didn't want to deal with unrolling the condom and accidentally pulling on one of his pubes either. Shit wasn't fun.

'Keem waited by the bedroom door and Maine nodded for him to go inside. Maine looked around and didn't see anyone looking in his direction. He headed to his room and closed the door and locked it. He pulled a comforter from the top shelf of his closet and rolled it up in front of the door.

"We gonna have to be quiet because if I put on some music, they gonna know something." Maine warned 'Keem as he kissed the back of his neck and rimmed his sweat pants. As he pulled them down, he admired the red and black jockstrap he wore. The ass stood out like a ripe peach, ready to be bitten into.

'Keem kissed Maine again but Maine wasn't feeling it. "Your bed make a lot of noise?"

"Naw, we good, just lay on top of it. Don't take nothing else off." Maine instructed. He watched as 'Keem laid across the bed. Once the condom was snug on his dick, Maine crawled on top of 'Keem and looked down as he guided himself inside of 'Keem. Once he was inside, he stretched on top of 'Keem and kissed him on the lips. Their hands met and interlocked at the top of the bed. Their legs struggled to interlock due to them both having pants on. Maine and 'Keem continued to kiss as Maine gave 'Keem the dick he desperately needed.

Maine and 'Keem stopped kissing and stared at each other for a minute. They looked up out of the window and looked back down and kissed again. Maine couldn't believe 'Keem's ass was so tight and he knew whatever exercises 'Keem was doing to keep that sphincter muscle strong was on point. 'Keem had a firm grip and applied enough pressure to bring Maine to his point of ecstacy soon.

"I'm gonna cum." Maine warned him as he went back to kissing 'Keem.

'Keem rocked his ass faster and squeezed tighter. Maine wanted to scream and yell because the nut was feeling so good, but he focused on kissing 'Keem. For the first time, Maine was fucking a dude in his house and he was disappointed it wasn't Spence. But 'Keem was a great substitute. Maine gasped for air and then bit his lip as he let himself go inside the condom as he plowed harder into 'Keem's ass. 'Keem kept throwing it back and squeezing tighter, making sure Maine was fully relieved. Maine surrendered by rolling off of 'Keem and quickly pulling the nut filled condom off his dick. 'Keem got in his favorite position and licked the nut from the Maine's dick. He then turned up the used condom and drank the nut from it.

"Now I can eat." 'Keem stood up and pulled up his pants. He picked up the used condom wrapper from the floor and put the drenched condom inside of it.

"You're so fuckin' nasty." Maine shoved 'Keem as 'Keem crawled back on his bed and opened the window. The two of them looked out and 'Keem crawled out and landed on his feet.

'Keem leaned on the window frame. "Everybody gotta fetish nigga. I like nut and I like that I like nut. I suck dick because that's the best way to get it. I like when it shoots fast and hits the back of my throat just right. I like all the flavors and I like the way it feels when it sits in my gut." 'Keem gave Maine a quick peck on the lips. "You better find yours and embrace that shit."

Immediately Maine's came to mind. He liked his ass licked and played with without penetration. At first, he thought that made him verse until Corey asked for some ass. He'd never been in a position where he'd been closed to being penetrated. A lot of dudes and chicks wanted him to fuck because he had a huge dick and he knew how to use it. And Corey worked Maine into a frenzy that night in the bathroom when he stayed over his house.

You know I'm a top. Maine declared.

He wasn't teasing. As far fetch as it may sound, he realized that he had a limit when it came to anal sex. Maine loved ass all day long and he loved sucking dick. But a man would never get behind him and penetrate him.

Getting ate like a Georgia Peach was Maine's fetish, and he embraced it.

25

Better Future

Maine and Yonna walked inside Saudi's Sweetness and were amazed at how Malika brought the Candyland game to life. The smell of candy and cake almost hit them with a sugar rush. Each of the places on the board game were in similar locations in the store. The jeweled candy sparkled like rhinestones and shined brighter than the gems one would buy from KAY Jewelers.

"Didn't this place have an Operation theme a few months ago?" Yonna asked as she looked around. She opened the cake stand labeled for samples that housed the game pieces they made. Yonna gave Maine a yellow game piece and when he put it in his mouth, the pineapple flavor hit his tongue and made him smile.

"Yes," Malika answered. "We switch the themes every few months to enhance the customer experience and to motivate them to come back if I had the manpower and the resources, I'd change the theme every week."

Yonna bit into her orange game piece. "This is peach!" Yonna jumped up and down like a little girl. "You got skills girl."

"It's chewy and don't contain gelatin, which is a byproduct of pork." Malika highlighted as she bit into her own red piece. "Believe it or not, mine is passion fruit. I try to switch it up every now and then."

"Also, Malika does a good job of incorporating the themes into her sales pitches and some of her candy and bakery designs." Farooq pointed out as he removed a Candyland-theme display featuring one of the game pieces.

Maine noticed Farooq. His sand-colored skin hid any clue that he had African ancestry. His full nose and lips were as ancient as the original sculptures on the pyramids. Under his white linen pants, Maine could tell he was hiding the shape of a basketball player. The face they could look each other in the eye was appealing too.

Despite Farooq's sex appeal, Maine respected that he was Salma's husband. Married men wasn't a territory Maine knowingly ventured into. Maine prided himself on that moral and for that reason, he turned away from Farooq so that he wouldn't have to face him for a length of time.

"I'm impressed that she's doing all this." Maine brought his mind back to the conversation. "I really can't believe she's running things."

"Of course I would be," Malika stood next to Maine as she handed him a portfolio. "I learned at an early age that I couldn't just file incorporation papers, hand out business cards, tell everyone I own a business and sit around and look cute." Malika led them to a table she had set up near the register. "I cook, I clean, I count the money, I handle human resources issues. I give up a lot to be the boss."

Maine could imagine. He knew that if he had to choose to put down a few thousand to start a business or start creeping with Yonna again, Yonna would be screaming and hollering soon.

"Do you ever have fun?" Maine asked as he took a seat.

"I go to pre-planned, scheduled parties at school and the community, provided they don't interfere with my observations of special religious celebrations or prayers. I don't do surprise parties often but I'm always surprised when I get to go." Malika answered.

"We make sure she enjoys some form of teenage life." Farooq interjected as he took a seat right across from Maine. "We were young once and in my case, I wasn't always a Muslim. My mother was Muslima but my father was Buddhist and they let me choose. I did my dirt until Allah got me in order."

That's what it was. Farooq was a hustler. Under the Islamic garb was an old fashion New York hustler he'd seen on the rap videos and in some of the street lit books he'd discovered. Maine always liked the guys hardcore and he had more fun topping "bad boys."

"Malika has her quarterly statements and the bank statements, which is good. Does she have a petty cash or incidentals?" Yonna asked as she scanned through the portfolio.

"Yes, very small amount." Malika answered.

"I ask because what I'd like to see is maybe a more definitive statement that shows where some of the breakdown is. We have a lot of expenses that are rolled into marketing. Maybe we could look at either streamlining some of the services and/or eliminating the ones not producing results." Yonna suggested.

When Maine looked at the balance sheet again, he did notice that the marketing expenses were high. It didn't seem like she was getting the best bang for her buck.

"Well, I pay for radio advertisement..." Malika started to say.

"Where?" Maine wondered. "I listen to both 102Jamz and 97.1 WQMG and don't remember hearing about your store on there. Do they have you listed on their websites?"

"All of my money is not that, I have internet marketing and I count my website expenses as marketing too." Malika defended.

"This is what I mean by evaluating." Yonna pointed out. "I trust Maine if he says he doesn't hear you mentioned on the radio because he works for a record store. He knows what's being promoted and who's coming into town because that helps him sell the music. Outside of school, I volunteer at a community center that works with at-risk youth—all they listen to is 102Jamz. I wanna look at what you're paying and what you are being told you are getting because between the three of us, we listen to the station enough to say you may need to re-evaluate how you're spending your money there."

"Yeah. Maybe using the money being made in different avenues will increase the margin large enough that you'll see more of the increase in revenue." Maine suggested.

"That sounds nice." Malika got up as a customer came into the shop. "Maybe we can meet in a few days?"

"Sounds like a plan." Yonna and Maine got up and they each gave Malika a hug before they left. Farooq gave each of them a head nod.

When they got out of the shop, they walked back to campus. "I think I know where to start and we have it easy since we're marketing majors." Yonna talked about the case.

"I hope she didn't run into one of those fake brokers who created some fake invoices with the logos on it." Maine suggested. "I should call, but I don't want to get anyone at the station in trouble."

"I don't want her taken advantage of either," Yonna stressed.

"I don't either." Maine replied. "I'll get with Willie and see if he knows someone that can find out for us what's going on without getting too much attention to us. The way she talked, she believes she's paid for some form of advertising but I'm on that station all the time. I know the Burger King Cordell is at plays the local radio so I'll see if I can get him to listen for us two."

"Yeah—let's tackle the marketing expenses first then we can handle everything else."

It felt good to deal with Yonna and not have to argue with her about who did what. Maine made sure he walked with her side by side to avoid the temptation of watching her switch her ass. Sex with Yonna was good but he wasn't trying to go down that road again. They still had a project to do and just began patching up their situation from the unprotected sex scenario.

"Did Gemini tell you who was coming to the concert yet?" Yonna asked once they got closer to her apartment. Her unit was near the entry way of the complex.

"Not yet. I think ol' boy is keeping it a secret this time." Maine replied.

Gemini was a junior, Vice-President of External Affairs of the student government association. His job was to promote campus awareness activities and put together the festivities for Homecoming and TechFest. He was the assistant to Quaysean, the current SGA President who held the post the year before.

"Well, I hope we have some good acts cause I don't want to hear no one from Central or SU talking about our show." Yonna pulled out her keys and unlocked the door. "You can come in if you want to."

"Naw, I'm good. I'm about to do some homework before I got to go check in at Willie's tonight." Maine told her.

"Renee keeping you and 'Keem on a tight leash?" Yonna inquired as she reached down and pulled Maine closer by his pants.

"I don't have a leash, I'm grown." Maine answered as he reached for her hand and pulled it out of his pants. He hated she knew the right touch to make his dick hard.

"All I need is fifteen minutes of your time," Yonna pulled him inside. "Chelle ain't gonna be here for another few minutes. "I don't want you, I just want some dick."

Four magic words that always caused problems. *I want some dick.* Spoken like a command, Maine almost always felt obligated to obliged. "I don't have any condoms."

"I don't either." Yonna let him go. "Run get some from your house and come back. I know Marlon got a few you can have. Him and Bathsheba be fucking all the time."

Maine really wanted to hold out for Spence. The time was adding up and he needed some ass—Spence's raw ass that was just for him. And he wanted to suck some dick—he didn't get to do that the last time he had sex with 'Keem. Maine left to go retrieve the condoms from his room. He really didn't want to fuck Yonna, but he knew his dick was the bargaining chip that would keep the peace. He headed to his room and grabbed a few condoms from the fish bowl and ran back out of the house. As he was locking the door, he saw Spence pulling up with Vanessa and Sierra.

"Bruh, what you getting ready to get into?" Spence asked after he rolled down his window.

"We're about to party?" Sierra rolled down her window and smiled at him.

"I gotta take care of this issue with Yonna real quick, then I can meet y'all somewhere. Where y'all gonna be at?" Maine admitted to Spence that he was gonna go fuck Yonna without having to say it.

"We're gonna be at the girls' place. Think you can be there in an hour," Spence seemed like he was cool. Maine was trying to read his face but he couldn't grab him. "One of their homegirls is gonna be there and I don't wanna be the only dude."

Spence winked. Maine knew what that meant.

"Aight, let me hurry up." Maine put some pep in his step and made his way to Yonna's. He opened the door without knocking. He found Yonna laid in the middle of the couch, her hand down her pants moving at a furious pace.

"I'm glad you didn't stand me up." Yonna pulled her top off with the opposite hand then unclasped her bra from the front.

"I," Maine peeled his shirt and tossed it to the side. He dug out one of the condoms and tore it open with his mouth. "I wouldn't do that." His pants and underwear fell in one swoop. He stepped away from his clothes, only wearing the Reebox and black And1 ankle socks. Once he opened the wrapper, he flicked it on the floor and quickly unrolled the condom on this dick. He got on top of Yonna and quickly positioned himself for entry.

"Boy!" Yonna attempted to push him away. She nervously grinned while nodding her head at the open door. "You're not gonna close the door?"

"I don't give fuck." Maine lifted her legs and put them over his shoulder. "I'm not showing them nothing they haven't seen or don't want to take a peek at."

In one move, Maine comfortably slipped inside Yonna. She pulled his head closer and kissed him on the lips. Maine looked back and realized the door was opened wide and shook his head. He was already in there and he needed every second he could muster to get in there and get out. The fact they could get caught turned him on and what better way than to just give everyone a chance to look in.

Maine showed no mercy as he pounded Yonna with no mercy. He knew that if he could center the large vein on his dick near her clitoris, he'd made her cum multiple times. To do that, he lifted her ass off the couch and put more hunch in his back. This maximized the distance his dick went in and out of her pussy. Within seconds, he got the results he was looking for as Yonna flooded his nuts and the couch.

"Oh God, oh God, don't stop."

Maine continued pounding into Yonna. He knew he wasn't going to feel his nut come soon. Truthfully, he didn't want to. He knew Spence was bringing him in on a group them his girl and their girl. Maine flexed and pounded faster as Yonna continued to coo in his ear.

"I think I'm a bust." Maine lied as he squeezed his body tight. "Ooh—ooh-ooh-ahh-ahh-haha-haha-hahahaha." Maine forced his eyes to flutter.

"That's right, cum in me." Yonna encouraged.

Convinced that his act was working, Maine continued to pretend. "Shit! Fuuucckk!" He jerked in and out of her real fast. He twitched his body and pretended to spasm. Maine fluttered like he was diving in and after counting to ten in his head, he ended his act and fell on top of her. Yonna was so wet and had just had another orgasm. She was satisfied.

He looked out the door. Someone stood at a distance and watched. He got up and quickly headed to the bathroom to remove the condom. He rolled the condom into a paper towel and balled it in his hand real tight.

"I told you someone was watching." Yonna pointed to the door.

Maine grabbed his things, nodded he head and ran out the door. He didn't bother to put his clothes on. He grabbed his keys out of his pant and quickly unlocked the door. He covered his midsection with his clothes and put his seat belt on. He made sure none of the nosey ass neighbors were in the way and he bolted out of the driveway.

He successfully faked an orgasm with Yonna, he was satisfied.

26

Signs And Wonders

"Them girls wore us out!" Spence bragged as he licked the paper to finish rolling a joint. Wasn't five minutes since those thick juicy soup coolers were licking Vanessa to an orgasm while Sierra was riding on his dick. He looked sexy to Maine in his navy wife beater and matching navy NC Tech basketball shorts. His hair had been pulled and twisted and looked an unkempt mess.

"Hell yeah," Maine took the blunt and took a few puffs before passing it back. "I can't believe you faked an orgasm on ole girl. That shit makes me laugh just thinking about it."

"Hey, I had to get out of there," Maine was nonchalant about it. "I knew I was gonna have more fun with y'all anyway."

"You think she could tell." Spence inquired.

"Don't care," Maine leaned back in his chair. The air was crisp and the view from the porch was amazing. They watched as different people made their way to their apartments. Maine pulled out his phone and could see it was almost three in the morning. "Bruh, we gotta go to class in the morning. Homecoming is coming early this year and I want to be caught up so I can party, not be stuck in the dorms and shit."

"Well, can I get some of that before we lay it down?" Spence got up and dropped his short.

"I wanna see if you can lay on the rail." Maine suggested as he licked his hands and began to rub himself.

"I better not fall—besides, if I lay across on my back, I'll have nothing to hold on to." Spence pointed out.

Logistically, Maine hadn't thought it through. He saw someone do it in a porn and wanted to try it.

"See, that's why I like your freaky ass." Spence complimented him as he went to sit in Maine's lap. "You always down for anything."

Spence lined up Maine's tool and promptly took a seat. As Spence made his way up and down, the two of them exhaled and looked into each other's eyes. Spence slowly got into a rhythm and was glad that his ass was getting wet to help ease the ride. As they got adjusted, Maine slowly stood up and rocked Spence on his hips back and forth.

"Let's go inside," Spence barely got the words out between Maine thrusting inside him. "I wanna try something else."

Spence lifted off of Maine as he pulled out. Spence walked inside and Maine followed. Spence smiled as he watched Sierra cuddle Vanessa on his bed. He lifted up the sheets and covered them. "I want you to roll me into a ball and fuck me upside down."

"Are you serious?" Maine asked.

Spence got into position. His ass still looked muscular and the view was inviting. Maine crouched over him and entered Spence going downward. When Spence rolled over and folded into a ball, Maine squatted and dug deep inside Spence. He looked down and saw Spence licking the tip of his dick, something he never knew his boy could do. Spence had a grip on his dick and as Maine pushed Spence down further, Spence was sucking his own dick as Maine went deeper. Watching Spence self-suck stimulated Maine's mind and in no time, he was lining Spence's walls with his seed.

Maine stumbled away and got a good view of Spence swallowing his load. Spence slowly stretched himself out and then stuck out his tongue to show Maine he had some of the goods left. Maine helped Spence get up and Spence got on Sierra's side of the bed. "I can't believe you sucked your own dick."

"I can do a lot of amazing things." Spence laughed as he brought the sheet over his head. Maine faced Vanessa and stole looks at Spence.

He definitely was amazing.

***

"So we got Ginuwine, Aaliyah, Missy Elliot, Timbaland and Magoo and Playa coming for Homecoming?" Renee inquired as soon as Chelle walked into class. Chelle was Gemini's assistant and an attendant to Miss NC Tech.

"Yeah, he just announced it a few minutes ago on the radio." Chelle took her seat next to Yonna.

"I feel like we got a surprise on the way." 'Keem grinned as he leaned in and gave Renee a kiss.

"IF there is a surprise, I will be too," Chelle took out her book.

Maine was sluggish. He did not feel like being in Dr. Finley's class listening to another lecture. Spence looked worn out too and Maine had to admit, those girls put a hurting on them last night and when they woke up in the morning. Elgin slowly limped into the classroom. Spence lifted up his head and Elgin straightened up. Elgin walked to his desk next to Maine and slowly took a seat.

'Keem shook his head. "A damn shame what y'all doing to them boys."

Another student walked in the same way. Maine slid Elgin his notes and his homework assignment.

"I went to the doctor this morning," Elgin leaned in and whispered. "He told me my T-cell count was stabilizing and that the regimen I'm on is starting to be effective. Took me a minute to get used to everything."

"And what about your ass?" Maine dropped the hint that he knew what Elgin did last night.

"You need to be asking Spence that question." Elgin quipped as he moved back to his seat. "I caught y'all when I was sent on an assignment." Elgin answered the unasked question. Maine looked around and Dr. Finley hadn't arrived yet. Maine leaned forward. "Fortunately, it was just me and my boy. And you know we won't say nothing. He was riding your dick the way a jockey rides a horse."

Maine chuckled. He was busted. Spence turned around and grilled Elgin. Elgin slowly adjusted himself in the seat and put his face in his book. That was the risk of having sex outside, getting caught. Maine knew Spence was gonna be shitty toward him the rest of the day.

Dr. Finely walked in and he didn't look too well himself. Even though he didn't sniffle or cough, something wasn't right about him. He got through the lesson. Explained what depreciating expenses and bad debts were. He gave the class time to practice the new concept and ask him questions in the rare study session they had in class.

When class was over Elgin and another student huddled together quickly before going their separate ways. Spence looked at Maine and rolled his eyes before walking out.

"Damn boy," 'Keem snuck up behind Maine. He hated that shit.

"Not now 'Keem," Maine was tempted to follow after Spence but 'Keem grabbed his arm. Maine jerked his arm back and grilled 'Keem. 'Keem stepped in his face and closed the gap.

"Don't think just because you had your dick in me that I won't fuck your pretty face up homeboy!" 'Keem's gritted as his head touched Maine's. "Cross that line if you want to."

Maine wanted to push 'Keem so bad. See what he was made of. It had been a minute since Maine had been in a fight and he felt like he had something to prove. Pretty boys can be pretty vicious when provoked.

"Let's not settle this here," 'Keem backed away as he eyed a few of the students looking in their directions. "You know where I stay. Seem in fifteen minutes partner." 'Keem walked off and Maine shook his head.

Maine had a two hour break between his accounting and marketing classes. He caught Cordell coming out of the bathroom with his Burger King uniform on.

"Them boys getting it in." Maine knew Cordell was talking about Elgin and the other boy in their class. "I'm thinking about doing that shit next year. Get my money up."

"Oh, you decided which one you wanted to do?" Maine was surprised.

"You and I are gonna do the brown and gold next year. Be the two illest bruhs on campus."

Maine chuckled. He couldn't believe his boy read his mind. "If you say so. I got that money for the car."

"That's what's up. I think my dad gonna help me get the Jeep from my uncle. We got the money and I been at Burger King long enough to be able to bring the Jeep home. I just don't want to pay NC Tech another one hundred and fifty dollars for a parking sticker."

"They be raping us on them parking stickers." V cut in. "You need a ride to work." He offered sense he still had the keys.

"Yeah."

"Here," Maine handed Cordell the keys. "I gotta stop by 'Keem's before I got to work. I need to walk for a minute catch some air."

"You sure man?" Cordell took the keys. "I can pick you up when you get off."

"I'm good. I'm ab about to head over there now."

Maine and Cordell gave each other a pound. As Maine made his way to 'Keem's, he found the walk was worth it and did him some good. He was glad that 'Keem lived close to the side of campus his classes were on and the stadium. A few minutes later, he found himself knocking on the front door. His guard was slightly up because he didn't know what kind of mood 'Keem was gonna be in.

'Keem opened the door and looked Maine up and down. "You gonna let me in?" Maine asked.

"If I gotta beat your ass, I'd rather do it out here because I just cleaned up and you not about to tear up my shit."

"I'm a good boy, I promise." Maine put his hands up as if he were surrendering.

"Aight," 'Keem's voice went up an octave before stepping back to let Maine in. "Don't start no shit, won't be no shit."

Maine walked in and could smell Pinesol and bleach. "Renee here?" Maine looked around as he took a seat on the couch.

"Naw, it's just you and I," 'Keem closed the door and took a seat next to him. "So Elgin knows you and Spence are fucking around."

"Yeah man," Maine didn't see the use in denying the obvious. "He told me he knew a month ago but I never addressed it."

"Well, it's not like everybody know. Everyone know Spence fucking that fine ass white girl at UNCG. Most people think you and Yonna got something going on—especially since folks said y'all didn't even close the door yesterday while you were screwing her on the couch."

"We just fuck every now and then." Maine admitted.

"Nothing wrong with that." 'Keem gave him a pound. "You want some Blimpies? I got some extra turkey cold cuts you welcomed to."

"Sure," Maine accept the offer and within seconds, he had a six inch sub and some Sun chips in his hands.

"You and Spence gone be alright," 'Keem spoke with all the faith in the world. "Elgin coulda used a little more discretion with y'all's business than what he did. And speaking of your boy, he good right?"

"Elgin cool." Maine took a bite out of his sandwich and wished he had something to wash it down with. "You don't have no drinks in this motherfucker."

"I gotta get some more. I do have a carton of orange juice in the refrigerator." 'Keem offered. Maine got up and poured him and 'Keem a cup. "So did you tell the boy you loved him?" 'Keem kept the questions coming.

"No man, I'm not crazy." Maine answered, passing 'Keem his cup.

"You dicking Spence outside definitely puts you on the wild side, Maine." 'Keem confirmed.

"It was a spur of the moment thing." Maine defended.

"Y'all some freaky ass niggas. That's why I fuck with you." 'Keem downed his drink like was a shot and placed the cup on the table. "Just be cool with ol'boy. I can't tell you how to have whatever it is y'all got, but I don't want you to fuck up a good thing."

"I'll remember you said that." Maine stretched out on the couch.

"Don't you got a class you need to be getting to in an hour or so?" 'Keem asked.

"You kicking me out?" Maine was shocked. One minute they were at each other's throats and the next he received five-star hospitality.

"I'm just saying, you might want to make your way back if you plan on freshening up before class."

Maine looked at the time. He grabbed his bag and put it over his shoulders. "Good looking out."

Maine gave 'Keem a hug on his way out. He could feel 'Keem press into him. "I didn't forget about little man." 'Keem volunteered. "Take care of that business with Spence first, then holla at me."

Maine left and made his way back to the School of Business. He decided to use the idle time to get some work done and to come up with ideas for his next meeting with Salma and Malika. He also followed up on some of the internships for the different record labels he put in. Anything to keep his mind off of Spence.

27

Just 2 B Sure

Inside Elgin's living room was a montage to Kenya, the strong nation in East Africa and the Pan African flag. A large portrait of Marcus Garvey hung on the wall and greeted everyone when they came into Elgin' home. Cinnamon, lavender and myrrh fought viciously for the senses as each fragrance attempted to over-power the other.

"Damn bruh, if you lived with us we would've stepped into the motherland." Maine became drawn in by the two Maasai spears that crossed as they hung on the back door.

"My uncle gave my sister and I a lot of souvenirs when he returned to Kenya last year. I have the Maasai robe he earned hanging in my closet." Elgin folded his black blanket to the side and placed it at the end of the couch. "Go ahead and have a seat."

Any other time, Maine would've welcomed a trip to Elgin's. It would've been a break from being at his spot or Spence's.

"So we are waiting on Spence?" Maine asked. He knew he had to be at Willie's in an hour and didn't want to be late.

"He's on his way." Elgin confirmed. "I just spoke to him an hour ago."

No sooner had he spoke Spence walked in using his key. The two men looked at each other but didn't speak. "I'm here Elgin." Spence yelled as he put his key in his pocket.

Elgin came out of the kitchen with cans of Coke and a bottle of Grey Goose for the three of them. "Cool. Cool. So look, I called y'all here so we can squash the beef and clear the air between the three of us."

Maine and Spence looked at each other and then looked away.

"Alrighty then, I'll just put it on the table. I know the two of y'all are fucking. The particulars aren't my business but I knew the two of you had a fling well before me and my line brother caught y'all the other day." Elgin pour a little Grey Goose in his can. "And I've been on line for a minute. Maine, you are the only person outside of this frat other than my mom and my sister that know what I'm doing."

"I'm not gonna say nothing," Maine pour him some Grey Goose in his can.

"Man look, it's 1999. Dudes been fucking dudes since the beginning of time. Young been going through trials and tribulations for the right to call themselves men about that long too. I'm more worked about the computers going haywire, the bank messing up my money and Y2K than I am about what y'all doing with y'all's dicks. If anything, once people find out I'm HIV positive, they will assume *I'm the one* doing a dude with my dick."

"My girl and I are both bisexual." Spence leaned into the sofa. "We're both swingers and we're both freaks. We like what we like. What I do with another man ain't nobody's business. Speaking of business, Elgin, I assume your line brothers will be violating code and having a drink or two as well?"

"We gonna be fucked up tonight?!" Elgin yelled as he poured some more liquor in his can. In no time, he threw the can back.

Spence shook his head. "Our boy wild. You supposed to have that much alcohol with your meds?"

"I'm nineteen, I'm not supposed to have alcohol period." Elgin reminded them.

"Good point." Maine took the bottle off the table and put it next to him in his seat.

"And what makes you think you are taking that bottle home?" Spence extended his can for Maine to pour him some.

"I'm the oldest," Maine pointed out as he poured him two shots and concealed the bottle and put it back in the couch.

"I forgot you and Cordell some old ass niggas." Elgin propped his legs on the coffee table. "We gonna be real suspect having a meeting without Cordell being involved."

"Cordell doesn't know I get down." Maine admitted as he took another drink. "It's one of my few secrets I have from him. If he knew I messed with men and some of the men I messed with, it might start a fight."

"You fuck Corey?" Elgin asked.

"No." Maine didn't lie. He *didn't* fuck Corey but they did everything but penetration and Maine sure *did* fuck with his mind.

"I'm glad we not beefing." Elgin drank more of his concoction. "But the two of y'all gotta do a better job of hiding y'all's secrets. Little public spats ain't cute."

"You sure you don't get down?" Spence asked. "You know too much."

"No, I don't get down. But since I've been going to therapy for this HIV shit, I'm stuck in a room where I'm the only straight man and every gay man and black woman find it hard to believe I don't sleep with men. My counselor and this old ass white lady who got hers from a blood transfusion are the only people who believe I caught it being reckless with a female. The gay guys talk and use all this lingo and I'm always having to ask what they're saying. This drag queen acts as my translator every time I get lost so they can keep the conversations flowing." Elgin spoke of his meetings. "I have to admit, meeting others with this death sentence makes life bearable. Truthfully, I almost hate that I go to these meetings because I wonder when I'll lose the next participant. Two people who were there when I started going a month ago are dead now."

Maine felt guilty. In some twisted way, Elgin seemed to be paying for the sins of his actions—or at least the judgment most would give him if they really knew how he lived his life. He wasn't trying to be out by any means, but the fact that Elgin could read between the lines of what he and Spence didn't say meant he wasn't as discreet as he thought. Deep down, he didn't want to beef with Spence, but the two of them couldn't have a typical relationship. Maine couldn't publicly go from man to woman to two different men to another chick. Last time Maine saw anyone in the media that looked and acted like him was when he read an article in *The Source* about an underground gay hip hop scene. Those guys reminded him of him. And Busta Rhymes was looking sexy as shit on that cover, too.

He had to admit, he and Spence had been reckless and they acted like they were exclusive. Just this morning, they got it in at the parking deck of the public library down the street. They were supposed to be studying and but after spending another night with Vanessa and Sierra, they couldn't resist. And they almost got caught by the security guard—or maybe they did and the old man didn't say nothing because he enjoyed the show. If they weren't careful, they were bound to get caught. And Maine didn't want to think of the consequences if that happened.

28

Promises of Fun And Laughter

Homecoming was in full effect and Bernie Mac, Cedric the Entertainer, DL Hughley and Steve Harvey got Monday night jumping with *The Kings of Comedy Tour*. NC Tech was featured in an MTVJams Homecoming Special in which several of the popular students got to participate.

"Y'all need to be cooking?" Renee was chilling on Maine's couch. Today's study party was light because everyone was trying to get ready for the fashion show hosted by the schools two modeling troops.

"I am not spending no more money hosting parties this year." Cordell answered as he put out chips and dip. "My dad finally talked my uncle into giving me my Jeep for Christmas and he wants the rest of his money plus the other bullshit Liam got me into paid for in cash."

"What Jeep you got?" 'Keem asked as he wrote down some notes from the marketing class. "And where are Elgin and Spence. They hella late to this function."

"Bullshit, y'all know where Spence and Elgin are." Chelle got in the stance of a baseball player and pretended to hit a homerun.

"You think they gonna cross at Homecoming?" Renee asked as she looked over 'Keem's notes.

"Ain't nobody keeping up with them." Cordell lied as he took his seat next to Bathsheba on the couch.

"Y'all better not start fucking," Renee looked up at the two of them and resumed taking notes. "And where is Yonna at?"

"Probably the same place Spence and Elgin are—but hold up, how you gonna tell me I can't start fucking in my house?" Cordell asked Renee as he took the notes from her and started copying them.

"Because, we trying to get some work done so we can go see the fashion show. You know coronation for Miss NC Tech is tomorrow and then the Greeks step on Friday and we gotta be at the Homecoming parade, game and concert on Saturday. I wish they'd done the gospel show and church service on the Sunday before Homecoming instead of the Sunday afterward." Renee brought up as she added to her notes.

"Don't change the subject. Let me tell you something Renee. I ain't said shit about you and 'Keem fucking on my couch, or in my bathroom. And don't think I forgot about 'Keem eating your pussy on the table I eat my food at. You gotta lot of nerve. At least Bathsheba and I get busy in my bedroom." Cordell clapped back then looked at 'Keem, who pretended to focus on the television.

"'Keem, you gonna let him talk to me like that?" Renee nudged him on his shoulder.

"This is his house." 'Keem mumbled quietly.

"Well at least I don't be doing the nasty while everyone up and can see me." Renee defended herself as she smacked 'Keem on the back of the head. "Chelle, tell Maine the next time he wanna fuck Yonna on y'all couch to make sure to close the door. Everyone's tired of watching him strut around this yard area buckey naked. At least make some videos like Donte Longstocking—speaking of which, y'all see that video he did with that big girl from Winston-Salem State? I didn't think he liked big women."

"Renee—I didn't mean to leave the door open." Maine didn't bother trying to lie about it.

"Nigga please." Renee rolled her eyes. "You just want everyone to see that you got a big dick. And I'm not gonna lie, you gotta big one."

"What's that got to do with the marketing class we're supposed to be studying for?" Maine asked.

"Well, I see that you have the product and it's in the right place. I just think we need to figure out who we're gonna sell it at the right price. I mean, you already promoting everytime you walk outside to pick up the newspaper in only your boxers or when you running to your car naked or to the house naked and however you want to broadcast it. I'm just saying, you can give Donte a run for his money." Renee suggested, applying some of the concepts they were trying to learn to the conversation.

"I'm not selling sex." Maine defended as he looked over his notes.

"The hell you ain't." Renee went on. "You know you wear those grey or those white sweat pants so your junk can stand out."

'Keem and Maine looked at each other. "I think every man does that." 'Keem defended. "It's the best way to advertise without drawing attention to it. It ain't no different with y'all wearing tight shirts that reveal how big the tittles are."

"We do not wear shirts showing off our titties, do we Bathsheba and Chelle?"

Bathsheba shook her head no while Chelle verbalized it.

"Oh, don't lie for your girl Bathsheba." Cordell warned.

"I don't show off my titties unless I'm in the bed with you." Bathsheba answered as she and Cordell shared a kiss.

"Don't be kissing him like that, that's how it starts." Renee balled up a piece of paper and threw it at them.

"I think we need to take this to the bedroom." Cordell suggested as he picked up the balled paper and threw it back at Renee.

"See, there they go." Renee yelled as she pointed at them. "See what I'm saying?"

"Well, I don't want everyone watching me lay pipe." Cordell replied as he held Bathsheba's hand. "Need I remind you this is my and Maine's house. We can do what we please." As Cordell and Bathsheba almost made it to his room, he turned around. "But don't you and 'Keem do shit in my house since you had so much to say."

"Shit," 'Keem vented. "I was hoping to break in Maine's bed cause I know them springs ain't worn yet."

Maine looked at 'Keem and shook his head.

"I hope you a minute man Cordell because the fashion show will be starting in thirty minutes. We need to get going." Renee got up and started putting her book in her bag. Soon, 'Keem, Maine and Chelle followed suit.

Maine couldn't believe Cordell and Bathsheba were gonna dip on them like that and then be so obvious about it. In no time, 112 was cranked up just a tad and everyone rushed to get out of the house. No one wanted to hear what the two of them had planned.

A knock on the door distracted Maine. He couldn't believe Corey was on the other side of the door. "What's up man?" Maine opened the door and let him in.

"Nothing much man—I heard y'all was gonna have a cookout this weekend and I came to put my bid on some food." Corey came in and looked around. "Where's Cordell?"

"He's in the back room fucking Bathsheba." Renee blurted out.

"Always," Corey shook his head.

"Renee!" Maine scolded as he nodded his head at Corey.

"Aww snap—you must be Cordell's younger brother." Renee laughed as she extended her hand to shake. "Y'all don't look nothing a like." She looked him up and down. "He got a big one too just like his brother."

"You have to excuse her." 'Keem extended his hand.

"'KEEM! Star football player at NC Tech. I see you in the paper all the time." Corey shook 'Keem's hand.

"I do what I do." 'Keem bragged.

"I'm Chelle—" Corey looked her up and down and shook her hand.

"Back to school house party." Corey recalled where he saw her.

Maine remembered too. Chelle answered the door when Corey wanted a ride home. "We're about to head to the fashion show. You wanna come?" Maine offered.

Truth was, he wanted to spend a few minutes with Corey. They hardly saw each other. He figured they'd run into each other at homecoming, but not like this.

"I'm game. Is Cordell coming or not?" Corey looked back at Cordell's bedroom.

"I wouldn't worry about Cordell," Maine put his arm around Corey's shoulders and followed the rest of the crew outside. "Tonight, you're one of the cool kids." Maine locked up and then he and Corey followed everyone out of the house. "So what brings you by?"

"I really was hoping y'all were throwing a party so I could have a place to hang for a minute and get some free food. Other than y'all two, my roommate and his girl, I don't know too many people up here."

"Use this time to get to know people." Maine suggested. "You can make a lot of connections hooking up with alumni and being social. Don't tell me you been in your room looking at porn and on some chatline all the time."

Corey's silence spoke volumes. Life was worse than he thought —Corey really didn't have no friends. "Look, fuck with us for a little while, but don't stay out too late if you got classes. Teachers still take attendance during homecoming."

"I'm good." Corey promised.

And Maine said no more. He and Corey followed the flux of students who were making their way to the auditorium so they could see which modeling troop was gonna reign supreme this year.

29

Deeper

NC TECH'S GOT TALENT ended the festivities for the third day of Homecoming Weekend. Maine and Cordell chose not to do a rap routine this year, even though they were praised for their skills last years.

"I still say you should've gotten up on that stage." Alize sat back and watched this girl group attempt to remake TLC's "Creep." Poor thangs had already been boo'd once and if they got off-key again, the fake Homey The Clown was gonna run them off the stage. "I saw you and that short dude last year, you got a little flow."

"Please don't tell him nothing else about his flow," Spence advised as he leaned up to watch the girls. "He already got a big head."

Maine smacked his lips.

"I'm beginning to think y'all two don't like each other." Broadus was staring at some girl's booty as she walked down the aisle.

"We gotta special love/hate relationship." Maine admitted. "We're like brothers."

"Just ignore his punk ass," Spence advised.

"I like how we got center seats." Alize complimented. "We not too close but we far enough to see everything." The audience clapping for the girl group interrupted Alize's thought. "I'm glad they didn't get booed. They got a little talent but they need to practice before they get on someone elses' stage again."

"I appreciate not being in the lobby selling music again." Broadus commented.

"That's because your ass is lazy." Alize pointed out.

"Hey, we not gonna start that." Maine warned. "Willie was nice enough to allow us to watch the show while he and his wife manned the booth. And we're getting paid. We didn't get that our first year."

"Sho' didn't." Spence jumped in.

"That's because you not special like us." Alize bragged. Before Maine or Spence could respond. "Ooh, hush! They getting ready to announce the next singer."

"Aight y'all. Give it up one time for the G'Boro girls!" Elgin announced as he led the audience in another round of applause. Elgin played a role in them getting good seat for the show this year. Cordell couldn't get off from Burger King so they had someone record the show so he could watch it later. He still was a little salty that he and Maine got third place last year.

"Next up is a young lady some of y'all are familiar with. She did her thing last year and was a crowd favorite. Singing a rendition of Janet Jackson's 'Together Again' is Miss Yonna!!!" Elgin announced.

Oh shit! Maine thought. He didn't know Yonna was going to participate again this year. The year before, she done a version of Tamia's "So Into You."

The slow jam appeared and Yonna wasn't on stage, but her powerful soprano could be heard floating over the beats. She walked to the stage with a mic in her hand and she was dressed in all black. The big black hat looked like one the elders would've worn to church. She found a jacket that accentuated the black bra she wore under her sheer outfit. Her pants looked like they were sewn on her. Yonna was a performer, no one could deny that.

She found Maine and the crew sitting near the front and she winked at them.

"Oh shit, here she go." Spence could be heard mumbling.

As Yonna got to the bridge and the chorus of the song, she had made her way Maine. At the second verse, she kept her eyes on Maine, drawing oohs and aahs from the crowd.

"I bet y'all fucked," Alize shared as Yonna made her way to the stage.

"Girl, hush." Maine realized he should've denied but decided not to address Alize's antics. She was digging for information.

"I'd hit it too, shit. She do look good." Broadus commented.

"No one asked you if you'd hit it." Alize raised her voice.

Broadus started to say something slick before Spence put his arm across his chest. "I swear this is the last time I take y'all anywhere."

"He started it."

On stage, Yonna ended the show by grabbing a picture of Maine from his senior year on high school. Maine's senior picture with the standard tuxedo, shirt and bowtie that many of the high school students wore was appeared on the screen behind her, drawing large oohs and aahs and screaming from the crowd. Maine was shocked because he couldn't believe she'd got her hands on it. She held it close as she looked up and sang the last lines of the song. He was pissed because not only were Alize and Broadus showing their asses, Yonna was embarrassing the fuck out of him and he couldn't do nothing about it.

"Give it up for Miss Yonna!" Elgin was shocked. The audience screamed and yelled. The performance was good, Maine just wished he didn't get dragged into it. "Sorry bruh, I didn't know. Next up..." Elgin kept the show going introducing the next act.

"I can't keep no secrets." Maine shook his head.

"So was it good bruh?" Broadus asked.

"If he don't want to talk about it, he don't want to talk about it." Alize defended. "But it must've been because he still look shook."

"Yeah he do." Broadus commented.

Maine slouched in his chair. He couldn't decide what he was gonna do. Yonna really went to the left with this performance. They needed to talk. He tried to remember the last time the two of them were intimate. It had been a few weeks.

After three more acts performed, it was clear that Yonna was gonna win the show. She had the best performance, drew audience participation and embarrassed Maine. That was the winning formula. When Elgin handed her a trophy and coveted tickets to the step show and the Homecoming concert, she hugged him tight and was congratulated by the other participants.

"So what are you gonna do?" Spence asked as they got back to their spot outside the auditorium. Willie's had set up to promote the meet and greet for Ja Rule, who was still promoting his debut album, *Venni Vetti Vecci*. It was going to be a big weekend as he was making a special trip to come back to NC Tech after homecoming.

"I don't even know." Maine handed out the flyer.

"Ummpf," the solid looking thick girl walked up to Maine and touched his chest. "I want you to go deeper." Maine faked chuckled while the crowd laughed. She took the flyer and went off with her friends.

"What happened in there?" Willie asked, oblivious to the joke.

"Maine put a spell on some singer in there and she publicly claimed they were gonna be together again." Alize put it nicely. "Got her singing he need to go deeper." Spence, Broadus and Travis started cracked up laughed. "I'll never forget you." Alize kept singing as she mimicked Yonna's pose holding his senior pic at the end.

"I told the two of you to keep it in your pants and that some of these girls are crazy." Willie warned him as he shook his head. Truthfully, Willie warned them about that and drinking and a few other things that he and Spence threw out of the window. "Well you will figure it out."

Maine couldn't wait to get his hands on Yonna. They had a lot to talk about and now, he had to play off being the joke on homecoming. For the next ninety minutes, Maine had to endure different people singing their own renditions of Janet's song. He wanted to look for Yonna, but decided against it.

When they got together again, it was gonna be on some other shit.

30

Homecoming Coronation

Spence and Maine sat across from each other in Maine's apartment. They were waiting on Elgin to bring them their tuxedos, shirts and ties from the cleaners. Elgin was part of the Homecoming Court as well as the master of ceremonies. Spence represented the fraternity and Maine was an extra in a skit and planned on attending the reception afterward and wanted to look nice.

He tried calling *Miss Yonna* after his shift was over with at Willie's but was unsuccessful getting her on the phone. Meanwhile, he spent the day enduring being told to "go deeper" and "I'll never forget you." After being teased so bad, he broke his copy of Janet Jackson's "Together Again" CD Single in half. He bought it for the slow version of the song and the remix to "Got Til It's Gone," but Yonna ruined it for him.

"You aight man?" Spence reached out for his hand. Maine looked around and interlocked his hands with Spence's.

"I'm gonna be fine." Maine answered.

"Forget about her and focus on me." Spence whispered.

Spence reached across the table and puckered his lips. Maine chuckled to himself. Spence looked so cute with his Afro blown out and his razor thin goatee and beard. Maine reached across the table and gave him a kiss. He felt this thickness awakening.

"It's been a while." Spence admitted as he took his seat.

"Yeah it has." Maine got up and made no effort to hide his manhood.

"Come here." Spence motioned him with his finger. "Thanks for letting me use the shower man instead of having to go back to my place."

"All you had to do was clean the bathroom and you straight. Cordell and I keep that joker clean after each of us use it." Maine instructed as he stood before him.

"I know, that's why y'all's place smells like bleach half the time." Spence stood up and he reached out and touched his piece. Spence leaned up and met Maine for another kiss. Spence slipped both of his hands inside Maine's pants and rubbed his manhood as they continued to share lips and tongue. "I love you man."

Maine continued kissing him. He'd heard Spence's declaration of love for him. "I love you too," Maine repeated and meant it. Other than Cordell and Corey, he'd never told another man that he loved him. Their relationship was far from perfect and included a plethora of extra people, but to Maine, what he and Spence has was perfect.

Maine dropped to his knees and unzipped Spence's pants. "Oh shit!" Spence hissed as Maine effortlessly swallowed his man muscle. Maine took Spence all the way down to the base and held his position.

"Aye guys," they could hear Cordell announcing his presence.

Maine quickly sat in the chair next to Spence and Spence scooted under the table, doing his best to discreetly put away his risen sword.

"Sup Cordell." Maine got up and gave Cordell dap while he signaled for Spence to get himself ready.

"I'll be so glad when this coronation shit is over with." Maine leaned back and seen Cordell fixing the rest of his buttons on his peach-colored shirt. "Bathsheba got a role in the skit they're doing tonight and I get to be her date."

Earlier in the day, they had a small rehearsal for the movie theme and were surprised that Miss NC Tech departed from tradition and chose something less formal. Once all the pieces were put together, they knew they were going to be part of an amazing show.

"Spence and Maine, your suits were ready." Elgin brought their stuff in. His black slacks sagged a little, but were perfectly cuffed over a shiny pair of Johnson & Wales.

In a brief moment, Maine thought about what life would be like if he married Spence ten years in the future. He'd hoped that gay marriage would be legal and he could openly bisexual in a world that would give zero fucks what any man, woman or whatever identified themselves as. In his heart, he knew he wanted that moment with Corey—but he wasn't ready to fight Cordell. He wondered if Cordell overheard him and Spence tell each other they loved the other. Elgin helped Spence with his shirt and bowtie while Maine made sure Cordell was together. They stole a glance at one another.

***

It was show time at NC Tech's coronation and the men were in the locker room making last minute adjustments.

"Donte," Maine called out as he saw the young man edging his bald fade in the mirror. "I didn't know they let non-NC Tech students participate."

"Well, I'm here because my 'ex'" Donte defined in air quotes "is here with her best friend helping make last minute alterations to the coronation dress. That and Penny is my cousin."

"I did not know that." Maine looked a little harder to see the family resemblance. Donte was fine and Maine hated he was attracted to him. And he loved to watch him in the videos. He looked so different dressed up like he was ready to attend the early morning church service. "So the girl that designed the dress is in high school?" Maine was still amazed. He'd met so many people doing what he felt he should've been on point with in high school. Made him wonder what he did wrong.

"Miriam and Mary Designs is owned by Mary Braxton." Donte pointed out. "She's a senior at R. J. Reynolds High School in Winston-Salem. She's been doing fashion design since she was in middle school. I helped her incorporate last year."

"You gonna film a video after the show is over?" Maine asked.

"You funny." Donte smirked. "Me doing any kind of videos at NC Tech would cause a fight between me and Penny Shanita Speaks. I barely escaped the last time she tried to crack a Bud Light over my head."

Before they could engage in anymore conversation, Whitney Houston's "Jesus Loves Me" blasted over the speakers. The men rumbled quickly to get in line and get ready to perform.

"Welcome to the 1999 Coronation of Miss North Carolina Technical State University. I am your host, Elgin Montego Wilkerson. And yeah, I'm rested from hosting NC Tech's Got Talent Last Night." A few of the students clapped as Elgin started the show. "And I'll doing double duty by hosting the step show tomorrow and I'll be making sure the only Que on campus won't be stepping alone."

The Omega men started barking and the Delta's did their call.

"See this is what happens when you forget Miss NC Tech is a Delta."

The Delta's got louder with their call. It was soulful and sounded like a chorus welcoming Jesus back on earth.

"Okay, I'm not in charge of making sure all the Greeks are here so we're gonna keep it moving. On behalf of Miss NC Tech, The Class of 2000 and the Student Government Association, we want to welcome you to the concert you've all be waiting for. But first, I want to introduce my co-host for the evening. She is a sophomore accounting major representing Reidsville, North Carolina. Very much no-nonsense and not scared to put a man in check. One of the very few people I know to catch 'Keem and tackle him to the ground."

A few people laughed because 'Keem was known to be very fast on the football field.

"Give a warm welcome to Renee Miriam Saadiq."

As Renee made her way to the podium, Maine could see the crowd rising to their feet. She looked stunning in a simple white gown worthy to be part of the Vera Wang collection. Her headpiece was reminiscent of the ones Melvina Horne used to wear in some of the shows she did in the 50's and 60's.

"Thank you. We are going to get the show started. Singing Whitney Houston's hit songs, 'Run To You' and 'Didn't We Almost Have It All' as we introduce the queens and kings of our various academic societies is the winner of last year's NC Tech's Got Talent, Janelle Crown." Renee got the show started and they had the tedious task of introducing all the groups.

When Renee and Elgin got done, some of the extras acted out the scene where Whitney's character first met her new bodyguard. After the applause, Elgin continued. "Singing 'I Have Nothing' and 'Exhale' will be Janessa Singletary. The voice you hear after that singing 'I'm Every Woman' and 'I Believe in You and Me' will be Michelle and a surprise guest. Next up are the queens and kings of our social club."

Unlike the suits and ties the academic societies wore, the social clubs came in wearing a variety of fall fashions. The crowd was getting into *The Bodyguard*-themed show. Maine knew from an earlier conversation with Penny that it was her favorite movie and that it was dream for her to meet Whitney Houston in person. After the social clubs had fun and kept people dancing on their feet, R&B singer Monica surprised everyone by coming out and singing "I Wanna Dance With Somebody." Wasn't no homecoming like an NC Tech Homecoming because only this school would be able to pull off an impromptu concert in the middle of an HBCU coronation. Monica also blessed the crowd with her hit single, "The First Night."

"This is how you know you have the greatest homecoming on earth, Monica just drops by, sings two songs and bounces." Elgin still sounded in shock.

"We didn't even know she's coming. Elgin, what you doing?" Renee called out after looking around.

"Looking for Brandy," Elgin was serious as he started singing the words to "Sittin' Up In My Room."

"Boy you a mess." Renee laughed. "I'm glad you can sing though."

Elgin continued, singing "Someday I'm Coming Back" by Lisa Stanfield. Then he pretended to pay attention. "Singing 'I Will Always Love you' and 'I Have Nothing' as we introduce the queens and kings of our BGLO's and our class officers and the court is the winner of this year's NC Tech's Got Talent, *Miss Yonna.*"

Maine dreaded hearing Yonna's voice again. He knew he couldn't say anything because it was almost time for him to be an extra on his scene from *The Bodyguard*. He watched as Spence was introduced with female representative of his organization. He then caught a glimpse of Yonna's performance and headed back to the stage.

"You and that girl need to straighten it out." 'Keem told him as he walked up.

"I thought you were with the football players." Maine asked.

"I was. I escorted our queen and then I bounced. You know I had to come back and watch my queen do the rest of the show. Plus, I'm gonna be in the next skit with you." 'Keem announced.

Maine acted like he didn't care. When it was show time, they quickly went toward the end of the movie and played their roles. Fortunately for him, he didn't have anything to speak and as fast as they started, they found their parts over. Maine made his way around the gymnasium and back to the locker room. He could hear someone singing "My Love Is Your Love" but he didn't catch their name. He loosened his suit and looked for Spence. He nor some of the others could be found. Maine decided not to miss the rest of the show and returned to his spot where he could see the stage.

"Introducing the 1999 Miss North Carolina Technical State University, leading the performance of 'Queen of the Night' with *Miss Yonna,* Michelle, Janelle Crown and Janessa Singletary is Miss Penny Alicia Speaks."

The crowd stood up as Penny made her way to the stage. Dressed in a replica of the outfit Whitney wore when she performed the song in the movie, even Maine was impressed with how flawlessly Penny emulated Whitney's performance. After Penny performed, the reigning Miss NC Tech met her on stage and they replaced the silver headpiece with a sparkling crown like the one she had on her head. Penny made her closing remarks and then everyone was dismissed to the celebration they that was hosted in the Student Union.

"That was a show." 'Keem pointed out. Maine was so into watching Penny and the ladies perform that he'd forgotten that 'Keem was standing next to him. Maine started to address 'Keem's comment but Yonna caught his attention. She was in the middle of the crowd, accepting praise for her performance and making jokes about how she made a fool out of Maine last night.

Drunken with anger, Maine made his way to the crowd to confront Yonna.

31

HOMECOMING

"You love me baby?" Yonna belted out as if she were on stage in front of a full audience. In a sense, she was as they were still inside the gymnasium and only a small number of people made it to the ballroom in the Student Union where the reception.

Maine started to continued his trek forward but his cell phone vibrating stopped him in his tracks. He looked at the message.

SHE AIN'T WORTH IT, TURN AROUND.

Maine looked to see where Spence was. He thought Spence would've been in line but when he followed the directive, he didn't see him either.

He looked at Yonna and the small crowd gathering around her. Spence was right, she wasn't worth it. Maine didn't love Yonna, so it made no sense to give her the attention she craved. Maine decided to let it go and walk away, even as she continued to call his name. He picked up the pace and found himself in a light jog away from the Student Union, down Cooper Hall and Scott Hall and down the street headed toward the auditorium. It sucked for him that Spence was his ride.

A young man in a black hoodie rolled down the window to a white 1997 Honda Civic. "Get in."

Maine started to question the man. He didn't know him from a can of paint. He saw that another man was wearing the same thing sitting in the backseat behind the driver. Maine looked back and seen random student returning to their dorms and decided he didn't want to wait on Spence, nor did he want to run the few miles to his apartment. He knew 'Keem and Renee stayed for the reception so going to 'Keem's hideaway wasn't an option either.

"Thank you," Maine showed gratitude as he took a seat in the front passenger seat.

"Yes, he's in the car." He could hear someone in the backseat speak into the phone. A few short seconds later, the phone went into his pocket.

"We've been instructed to take you home." Maine thought he recognized the voice of the driver. It didn't sound like the boy in class that Maine suspected was pledging with Elgin.

Silence was the choice of music as Maine made his escape from campus and down the road to his house. A part of him wished he'd parked his car at Willie's. But he appreciated the ride and he prayed he didn't get the young men who obviously were on a mission in trouble or put them too far out the way. He doubted that Spence or Elgin would send them dressed alike, but a ride home was a ride home.

In no time, the Honda Civic was pulling into the parking space. His off-white 1989 Buick Regal was available to him should he decide to go back into town.

"Thank you." Maine told the guys.

The driver took off his hood. Maine smiled. The last time Maine saw the driver, he had a muscle bound freak crying uncle as he thrusted his thick unsheathed pipe in the man's back door. The driver had the man pinned down by the shoulders and continued slamming his dick in him while they were on the floor. Maine and the driver would later tag team an older gentleman who craved two sons to fill his holes. It was a sex party that Maine attended before school had let out for the summer last sprint. Maine had only the driver a few times since the party but never had the courage to get up.

The driver gave him the fist bump, put his hoodie back on and drove off.

Maine unlocked the door and was happy to hear that Cordell and Bathsheba weren't cooped up in Cordell's room getting busy. Peace and quiet was a welcome change from the noise and distractions Maine dealt with in the last few days. No more, "go deeper" and "I'll never forget you."

Wasting no time, Maine rushed to the bathroom, took off his clothes and tossed them on the ground. He ran to his room to get his toiletry basket and put it on the sink counter upon re-entering the bathroom. He pushed the stopper in the drain and ran warm water, squeezing out some of his liquid soap for some bubbles. As Maine stepped into the tub, he could hear the door banging.

"Maine open the door!" He heard Yonna command.

Maine had half a mind to walk out of the bathroom and answer the door naked as a jaybird, but then he remembered the attention it would bring. He had no desire to deal with Yonna or her bullshit so Maine opted to step into the tub. The sizzling water felt good around his skin and he did his best to make his six foot four frame comfortable.

"Stop playing and open this damn door!" Yonna yelled like she was his mama.

But she wasn't.

Maine wondered how his mom was doing. A part of him felt guilty for not checking on her. He knew they had a long way to go to patch up their relationship.

Maine loved being in the water and he felt calm as he tuned out Yonna and just relaxed.

***

Maine awoke to find himself under his cover in his bed. He didn't remember waking up and he pinched himself to see if he was dreaming. As he stepped out of the bed, he found himself wearing some gray boxer briefs and some matching ankle socks. He got out of bed and smelled eggs being scrambled with bell peppers and onions. Sausage could be heard sizzling on the pan and hash browns made the presence known.

"Cordell's cooking." Maine grabbed his toothbrush and went to the bathroom and quickly brushed his teeth. After taking care of his duties, he rummaged through his dresser drawers until he found a matching NC Tech T-shirt and jersey shorts. Maine's nose led him to the kitchen where he took a seat next to Bathsheba and Elgin.

"I knew once I'd started cooking you'd get your ass up." Cordell announced as he poured cheesy grits from a pan to a serving bowl. The rest of the food was on the table. "I told Yonna she couldn't come over and start no shit."

"You were knocked out in the shower." Elgin filled him in. "Renee and 'Keem were with us so she and Bathsheba dried you off and Renee picked out your underwear. 'Keem, Cordell and I put you in bed. Renee tucked you in and you started sucking your thumb."

"We got pictures," Bathsheba cut in before he could deny.

"Damn!" Maine exclaimed.

"It's all good." Cordell put the tea on the table and everyone sat down and held hands and blessed the food. "I'll be so glad when Homecoming's over with."

"Halloween is next Sunday too." Bathsheba pointed out.

"I'm gonna egg the fuck out of Corey." Cordell stood up and pretended to chuck eggs at his brother.

"You're so mean." Elgin pointed out as he stuffed his face with cheesy grits.

"Mean my ass. He shouldn't have followed me up here. You should've seen his punk ass at the coronation. He attached to Loser at the hip and his big ass side chick." Cordell complained. "Few times I see him on campus, I don't ever see him hanging with or chasing after some girl. It's always that nigga and his blowup doll."

"Cordell!" Maine was shocked and tried not to laugh.

"She is not a blowup doll." Bathsheba tried to defend her.

"I bet if her ass was here, we'd have no food to eat." Cordell kept on.

"What did Corey do this time?" Maine asked.

"Eat, shit and breathe." Cordell replied. "Moreso the shit part cause I heard he ain't doing too well in his classes. He stopped going to one completely and he has no hope of even getting an F in another class. Who the fuck fails Indoor Sports? All you gotta do is show up and dress up and the teacher will give you at least a C."

Maine couldn't defend that. He hadn't thought to look for Corey for a minute now since he and Spence turned their situationship up a notch and the steady stream of ass and pussy he was getting from 'Keem, Renee, Vanessa and Sierra. And with the business classes beginning to get challenging and taking up his time, he, Cordell, Elgin, Spence and 'Keem depended on each other too much to stay in line with the classes.

"So who y'all think gonna win the step show tonight?" Bathsheba asked. "I'm calling the Deltas and the Sigmas."

"I'm thinking the Deltas and the Alphas, them niggas always win." Cordell chimed in.

"I don't care, I just don't want nobody messing up their show." Maine added.

"Or getting hurt." Elgin added. "The AKAs would've won last year if that girl hadn't slipped and broke her heel while doing their stroll. I'm glad she's okay though."

"That show was hot." Bathsheba got excited. "I really want the AKAs to win but I know two of the girls on the Deltas step team.

"Y'all got y'alls tickets?" Elgin asked.

"Who they got hosting the show with you?" Cordell asked. "Man, I swear they got you all over Homecoming this year."

"You'll be happy, trust me." Elgin drank his tea.

Maine looked out the door and could see Yonna watching him. He knew the two of them were going to have to deal with each other sooner or later. It wasn't going to be now because Maine planned on getting a second helping of Cordell's cooking and he planned to go into Willie's early so he could help set up do inventory for the Homecoming concert at the Greensboro Coliseum and the Gospel show. Willie's helped manage the meet and greets and both events and supplied the music and some of the promotional material for the artists to sign.

Once he finished that plate, he hopped into the shower and put on a polo, khakis and his dress shoes. He had no intentions on going to classes—like most students he skipped this Friday. Maine had a busy day ahead of him and he looked forward to the show and the afterparty tomorrow.

32

Homecoming Step Show Champs!!!

The section where Spence's frat sat celebrated as they were announced the 1999 Homecoming Step Show champions. Their *Friday* themed step show incorporated skits from the critically acclaimed movie as well as music from the soundtrack. Add to that a well-executed step show and Spence & Company deserved to win.

Maine and Cordell waited until some of the visiting chapters and the AKAs finished celebrating their wins before they made their move to the crowd.

"Congratulations man." Maine gripped Spence. He took off his blue fitted cap and put it in the chair.

"Thanks man," Spence hugged Maine and gave Cordell some dap. He took the rubber bands off the ends of his cornrows and started undoing his hair. "I can't wait to rock my Afro again. I only braided it so I could pull off playing Smokey."

"Damn." Maine commented.

Spence and Maine walked away while Cordell stayed behind to celebrate with the rest of the brothers. "You handle that business with Yonna?"

Maine didn't want to be reminded. He gave her some dick and spent the night at her house instead of enjoying the only night he and Spence had off this week. Chelle came in the room when they woke up and of course, it was another round with the two of them. Maine would've rather spent the night with Spence, Vanessa and Sierra, but he knew that Spence would be enjoying the spoils after a hard-won victory. "It was aight."

Spence chuckled. "I thought with two sets of ass and titties, you'd be sitting like a king."

"Aye Spence, where y'all breaking off to?" One of Spence's bruhs who dressed like Deebo called out.

"Maine, you coming to the frat house to celebrate with us, right?" Another brother who resembled Mr. Jones called out.

"Yeah man, I'll be there." Maine called out.

"We gotta get the rest of the liquor from Cordell and Maine's." Spence added as he pulled his keys from his pocket. Spence and Maine bolted from the gymnasium to one of the reserve spots for participating fraternity members. Spence had Vanessa's car and took his seat in the driver's seat. Maine adjusted the seat so he could sit comfortably. "I'm happy the AKAs won this year. Deltas always win."

"I thought they were going to win with the cowgirl theme they had this year. And their show was flawless" Maine commented.

"True…but I knew when the AKAs came out as T-Boz, Left Eye and Chilli, they were going to win. All the T-Bozs' had pink and green tresses and bob-cut dyes. The Left Eyes' had green and pink condoms on those glasses and pink and green band aids. And all the Chilli's wore sexy outfits the way Chilli would've worn it. And plus—that intro to 'Ain't 2 Proud 2 Beg' & 'Hat 2 Da Back' was tight." Spence commented when they pulled off.

"Yeah, and they had three of the sorority women singing and rapping all the songs like they were the real TLC too." Maine was hyped. "And they pulled off that concert and step show feel. Overall, all the Greeks did good this year."

"Thanks man." Spence smiled as he made his way off campus and down the street. In a few minutes, Spence was pulling up to Maine's apartment. Maine pulled out his keys and as soon they got in the door good and Maine locked the top lock, they were all over each other. "We gotta make it quick." Spence fell on the couch quickly pulled his pants down, spit in his hand and rubbed his moist hole. When Maine nestled himself deep inside Spence, the two of them both gasped for air.

Maine and Spence moved like a well-oiled machine. Spence squeezed and jiggled his ass, matching Maine stroke by stroke. For his efforts, Maine grinded hard. Spence felt like a warmed up oven and was the perfect temperature to make him cum quick. Maine wanted to take his clothes off but he knew they couldn't. Spence whimpering under him turned him on and when Spence clinched his ass tighter, he knew his boy was gonna cum. "Ah shit, ah shit, ah shit." Spence gasped and after a few thrusts, Maine wasn't too far behind, letting himself go inside Spence.

As they quickly got up to get dressed, Maine found where Spence dropped his leche and quickly lapped it up like a well-trained dog. To his surprise, he felt Spence's tongue digging deep in his ass. "Damn!" Maine moaned as he continued to throw his ass back. Spence's hands felt good as they massaged and parted his round cakes.

Maine looked back and saw Spence standing behind him, munching and moving his face back and forth like the ass was corn on a cob. His left hand was stroking his piece and his right hand was stroking Maine's. Maine struggled to keep his eyes open as Spence's tongue continue to fuck him.

Soon, Spence's tongue was replaced by his fingers as he continued to jack his dick. Maine started to flick his harden left nipple, enjoying the sensation Spence was sending throughout his body.

"You ready for this dick?" Spence asked as he got in position to enter Maine. He was caught up in the way Spence moved his fingers in, out and deep. As he leaned forward on the couch, he felt Spence's weight on him. Spence grinded his big dick against Maine's basketball shaped ass cheeks. "This ass feels so good baby." Spence whispered as he tried to catch Maine's hole on the stroke. Maine kept grinding into him. Before Spence could get into position good, his dick betrayed him and started oozing his nut on Maine's cakes and inbetween his crack. "FUCK!!!" Spence was pissed. He waited for a minute to get balls deep inside Maine, was *this close* and missed the opportunity by coming too fast.

Maine looked back and could see the hurt and disappointment in Spence's eyes. His man looked like he was about to cry. Many made the attempt to enter Maine and at this moment in time, Spence was the closest. Truth was, if Spence had gotten the head in, he wouldn't have stopped him. Spence wasn't packing no Vienna sausage and Maine was a little unsure whether or not Spence would be able to get it in.

A key jiggled in the door and Spence and Maine quickly scrambled to pull up their pants and zip them up. Maine ran to the kitchen since they were supposed to be getting liquor and pulled out the bottles of Grey Goose, Hypnotiq and Hennessey from the shelves.

"Spence, I can't believe you got it smelling like badussy up in here!" Cordell yelled.

"No I don't," Spence defended himself.

"Go hop your ass in the shower. You can't go to the party smelling like that. Maine where you at?"

"In the kitchen," Maine felt bad about Cordell calling Spence out like that. He hoped Cordell didn't come in and smell Spence's body oil on him.

He heard the front door open and shut. The frat brothers that dressed like Craig and Pastor Clever were with him. *Fuck, fuck, fuck* for thinking they could get in a quickie without getting caught. And another *fuck* for almost allowing Spence to enter his virgin ass.

"Why y'all let that boy smell like he just got done tearing up some pussy?" Cordell asked as he opened the refrigerator door and pulled out a forty-ounce malt liquor.

"Why you drinking 40's like you from the West Coast?" The Pastor Clever looking brother asked.

"Yeah, only Cali niggas drink that shit." The Craig lookalike chimed.

"Well, I guess this is Long Beach/Inglewood motherfuckers!" Cordell yelled as he tipped his bottle back and guzzled several drinks without gasping for air.

"I can't wait to get y'all motherfuckers on line." The Pastor Clever looking brother snatched Cordell's drink from him, took a few sips and set the forty down.

"Yeah," the Craig look alike took his sip. "We calling y'all Lowrey and Burnett cause y'all swear y'all some bad boys."

"This motherfucker over here got girls singing about him stage, sorority chicks fighting over him and shit."

"Naw, we calling them Marlon and Shawn."

"Fuck you both," Maine threw both middle fingers in their direction. He heard the shower running. He wanted to get in there and finish with Spence, but he knew if he left the kitchen and disappeared for any length of time, it would look suspect.

He liked his boys, but now wasn't the time or the place to finish round two. Maine continued playing around with Cordell and the frat boys, reminiscing about the step show. All the while, he felt guilty for not giving into Spence, and wondered what might have been.

33

Homecoming & The Night After

Maine and Cordell watched the parade as it passed through Lindsey Street on the way to the stadium. They were still a little sluggish and drunk after partying and celebrating Spence's step show victory. People were still talking about *Friday* and how it was going to be on BET right before the concert. They also talked about the TLC and how NC Tech had better beat Hampton at the Homecoming game.

"Man, we should've brought some chairs." Cordell struggled to carry the funnel cake topped with strawberries and whipped cream in the palm of his hand.

"Shit who telling?" Maine replied as they leaned against the street sign.

They watched high schools near and far performed in one of the greatest homecoming parades on earth. Many of the alumni organizations and local businesses built festive floats and drove expensive cars while showcasing the queens of their respective organizations.

"We should've got on a float this year." Cordell stuffed a funnel cake in his mouth. He topped it off with a can of Miller Lite.

"I can see how you drink that nasty stuff." Maine shook his head while ignoring the rumblings in his stomach. He wanted to hold off on eating anything until they got to the plots. Spence's frat had already promised to feed them and Vanessa's sorority sisters had a plate with their name on it too. Plus, the American Marketing Association was having a tailgate at Homecoming that Maine needed to show face at.

"This was the last drink at the party." Cordell held up his can before taking another drink.

Maine believed him. The alumni brothers bought extra liquor and all the chicken and biscuits they could handle from Mrs. Winner's and Bojangles.

"Y'all should be throwing a party."

Maine turned to face Chelle, surprised to see her. "I thought you would've been on the homecoming float with Miss NC Tech."

"I am an assistant," Chelle moved closer to them. "I'm not to be seen or heard. And besides, everybody and they mama gonna be on that float. I need a little space."

"Where's *Miss Yonna*?" Maine really didn't want to know the answer to that question. He just thought he ask out of courtesy.

"Boy, bye. We know you don't give a fuck about her." Chelle swiped the can from Cordell real quick and took a swig before handing the drink back to him. The look of contempt in his eyes were deadly. Maine thought he'd get murked just by association.

"Why you say it like that?" Maine inquired.

"Because you just don't." Chelle quipped as she watched another organization parade by. "Look. I know you and I fuck around off and on and I'm not confused about that shit. To me, you're just occasional dick that I 'might' get pregnant by one day. I prefer women, but I do dudes because the women I be around like that shit."

"Well thank you," Maine was sarcastic. He didn't want to admit that Chelle's assessment of him stung a little. All he was to her was some piece a dick. Sounded like he was in her way. "To answer your question," Maine changed the subject because he wasn't in the mood to have words with Chelle. It was nine in the morning and they had a whole day of partying and celebrating and Maine had to vend with Willie's tonight to help move the merchandise. Aaliyah and Missy agreed to do a pre-concert signing at the Greensboro Coliseum two hours before the concert began. The meet and greet was a rarity but one of the reasons Maine loved Aaliyah and Missy, they always looked out for their fans. "I don't lead your girl on. She wants what she wants and I want what I want and sometimes, it's the same thing."

"Right now she's craving attention." Chelle called out as she pulled out five dollars to buy some packaged snacks and a can of Coca Cola from a local mobile vender.

"I thought you were giving that to her." Maine responded as he watched Cordell lean on some thick chick, making her laugh and giggle. A little further up the street, he saw Patrice leaning into Melvin. Maine looked to see if Corey was in the vicinity but was disappointed when he didn't catch him.

"She don't know what she want and you don't either." Chelle called him out.

"What makes you say that?" Maine asked.

"Don't nobody know what they want. Look, the whole purpose of being at North Carolina Technical is so that we can find ourselves, get an education and build a future. For some people, that means they are going to find the love of their life and for others, they are gonna live life. Me, I know what I like. And I wouldn't say I would marry a woman but I know a woman is the only one that can keep me satisfied. I mean, you do good—but long-term, it's not what I want."

"I can respect that." Maine answered. He wondered if he would end up choosing a man or a woman, or if he'd have the insatiable need to want and desire both. He always dreamed about having Aaliyah and Ginuwine at the same time an in a few hours, he would be within arm's reach of both. There would be men and women who'd drop their pants for him right now if they thought it would mean they'd get to trade places with Maine for a minute.

"Do me a favor?" Chelle requested as she took a sip of her soda. "When you let her down, let her down gently. I don't want to live with a broken heart."

Chelle walked away from Maine before he could reply. He looked for Cordell and he could see him talking to Melvin and Patrice. No sign of Corey, *fuck*. Maine saw a young man that bore a strong resemblance toLiam staring back at him. Smooth French Vanilla skin, sharp eyes and thick lips with the tallest high-top fade he'd ever seen. The long tattoo that extended to the top of his shoulder to the tip of his middle finger confirmed that he wasn'tLiam. Maine hated that he thought of Corey. Watching Spence and his frat put on a small step show in front of their float made him smile for a minute. Spence looked good leading his line brothers into two intricate steps before the parade moved forward. Their eyes glanced at one another. Spence quickly threw a black power fist in his direction and cracked a smile.

***

Lil Kim rocked the stage as she opened as the surprise guest at the Homecoming concert. Aaliyah sang background on their version of "Queen Bitch" then sang the hook as Lil Kim did a verse to "I Need You Tonight."

Maine sang along as Aaliyah opened her segment with "Are You That Somebody?" and had everyone on their feet as she sang and dance. She eased into "If Your Girl Only Knew" "Four Page Letter" with ease.

Ginuwine joined her on stage as they performed and danced to "One in a Million" and "Final Warning." Ginuwine continued rocking the show as he kept the audience moving with "Same Ol' G," "None of Your Friend's Business" and "She's Outta My Life." He ended his segment by performing his smash hit "Pony" as the audience sang along with him.

Aaliyah, Timbaland and Magoo, Missy and Playa joined Ginuwine on stage for the cult classics "Up Jumps Da Boogie" and "Luv 2 Luv U." Playa stayed on as they performed snippets of their songs "Don't Stop The Music" and "Cheers 2 U."

Missy Elliot would begin her segment with "Hit Em wit Da Hee" before she slowed it down with "The Rain" which Aaliyah, Ginuwine and Playa sang background on. Missy sped it up with "She's a Bitch" and "All N My Grill."

The lights went dim and folks got pissed cause Missy cut the show halfway in her verse, talking about she had to go cause an emergency. Then a band started jamming to some disco music. For a minute, everyone thought they were at the wrong concert when the band started playing a snipped of "Too Hot." Some of the older people in the audience nodded their heads and sang along as the band also transitioned into "Hollywood Swinging" and "Summer Madness." Kool & The Gang had already performed as part of the Alumni Foundation's Old School Jamz concert and some of the younger people didn't recognized some of the classic hits they were playing.

The lights came on and Kool & the Gang hit the high chords of their smash hit, "Ladies Night." Angela Martinez surprised everyone by coming out and doing her verse and soon, everyone came back out and supported Lil Kim, Missy Elliot, Left Eye and Da Brat as they rapped their version of "Ladies Night" while Kool & the Gang sang backup. It felt like a block party and when the song was over, Kool & the Gang kept the party jamming for fifteen extra minutes mixing disco with some of the popular samples the crowd recognized from the era's top rap songs.

Only a performance like that would happen at NC Tech's Homecoming and was one of the reasons they had the Greatest Homecoming On Earth.

***

Maine was worn out from partying and celebrating Homecoming Week. The party wasn't over because Halloween was next weekend and he knew he had to get on his A-game if he was going to finish the semester strong.

Despite his growing love for Spence, he knew they were competing to be co-manager of Willie's. Each day, the tasks they faced got challenging and the two of them showed individually and collectively they could handle the job. Chelle had given him a lot to think about as it related to Yonna, but he also started evaluating his feelings for Spence and Corey. As for the men go, he struggled to decipher his feelings for Spence and Corey. Spence wanted him and sexually, Spence was the best fit because they liked men and women. But Corey had a hold on him that he couldn't explain nor easily let go. 'Keem on the other hand was like Chelle—he didn't want Maine, he just wanted a man he could trust to lay it down every once and a while.

As for the women, they were committed. Vanessa was Spence's girl and her roommate allegedly had a man somewhere. Maine never met him as far as he knew, Spence's girlfriend had a girlfriend and their quad-situationship was just fine. Chelle and Yonna weren't an open couple but Maine wasn't a fool to believe they weren't messing around with each other and other women when he wasn't around. He doubted he was the only man too, but he didn't care. And Renee only messed with him sparingly—usually with 'Keem watching or participating in some way.

Maine laid in the bed, ignoring Cordell entertaining Bathsheba for the umpteenth time for the night. A part of him wanted to be like "fuck it" and invite Spence over because he wanted some more of him, but he knew if Cordell knew his secret it would mess up the friendship they had with each other and Elgin. He wondered who Corey was fucking for the night—he doubted that he wasn't getting his dick sucked.

He looked over and there was no one to lay in his warm bed with him. Maine didn't want to jack off and go back to sleep because it would be weird as fuck with Cordell smashing Bathsheba in the next room. He didn't want to get his laptop and pull up a porn or watch one of the bootleg movies he got off of Limewire.

Instead, Maine got up and put on the underwear he'd worn earlier today. He walked into the kitchen and grabbed the fish sandwich plate he'd got from Vanessa's sorority sisters' and warmed it up in the microwave. He grabbed a small, plastic, navy and yellow NC Tech cup with bulldog logo on it and pour some Hypnotic and Hennessy in the bottom fourth. He grabbed some ice and put it in the cup, swirling the cup for a minute until the microwave went off.

Maine headed back to his room and broke the one vow he made to himself—he ate and drank for comfort.

34

Hello Ween?

"I can't believe Willie let us have the week off." Maine walked with Spence and 'Keem from the mobile cafeteria. Each had a burger, fries and some kind of desert in their takeout trays along with a canned beverage.

"I think he just trying to figure out how he's gonna let you know that the job is mine." Spence was sure of himself. "I mean, I don't want you crying and shit when you find out I got the assistant manager gig."

"Nigga please," Maine shoved Spence off. "I know that Willie isn't stupid. You trying to go back to Def Jam next year so you can be up under Dru Hill and DMX. If I don't get any of the internships this year, Wille'd be a fool not to give the position to me."

"Dude, it's about multi-tasking and I clearly do that better than you." Spence bragged as they headed closer to the plots. Maine could see Cordell chilling with other guys from Spence's frat. "Wait until we get to 'Keem's."

"You not trying to do nothing for Halloween?" Maine asked as he opened his tray and took out a fry.

"I'm a grown ass man." Spence answered. "I dressed up as Smokey for the stepshow, that was enough. Besides, I don't really celebrate Halloween like that."

"And I don't either." 'Keem butted in. "Besides, I'm not giving Satan any more due. And besides that, they don't make outfits that fit me right and I'm not into making my own. Renee going out with some of her girls tonight and I'm not going to see her until we get to class tomorrow. I'm looking forward to the three of us hanging out."

Maine knew 'Keem meant what he said about hanging. After being sexually frustrated and not getting none in ten days, Maine was ready for some action. Getting Spence and 'Keem at the same time was icing on the cake.

First thing's first, they had to pay a visit to Spence's plot. Various frat brothers wore their colors as they dressed in many costumes. Several of the guys around campus walked around without shirts on, opting to show off the physiques they worked hard for or were born with. The big guys wore comedic shirts or dressed up as oversized characters. The women walking around NC Tech were no better. A good third of them were strippers or had outfits in which only a bikini top and some pants were needed. Most of the students were headed toward the plots or were on their way to some of the nearby houses to party for the last on campus holiday.

"About time you motherfuckers showed up?" One of Spence's frat brothers greeted Spence with their secret handshake and just gave open ended shakes to Spence and 'Keem.

"Yeah man." Spence responded after he claimed a seat on the bench. "I'm just gonna chill here for a minute until I go to Vanessa's. I gotta get her the car back and spend some time with her."

"Isn't UNCG having their homecoming this week?" Another brother asked.

"Yeah, it's this coming weekend," Spence confirmed. "Vanessa is representing for her sorority so I'll be over for their court."

"And one of our cheer squad girls is a queen of one of their academic societies and I'll be their escort." 'Keem volunteered.

"We're going to the stepshow on Friday." One of the brothers announced. "UNCG frat showed out big time for us so you know we gotta rep at their show."

"Man, you see these two jokers." Cordell pointed out two young men dressed in Batman and Superman hoodies in the crowd. Maine felt his heart fluttered. Corey was sexy as shit with the Batman mask concealing the top part of his face. His goatee was sharp and he looked like he was gaining more muscle weight. His black hoody and black slacks couldn't conceal what Maine wanted to see again. He noticed Melvin's figure started to fill out nicely in his royal blue hoodie with the Superman logo in the center. His light brown khakis cuffed perfectly in his matching red and blue Jordan's. "Batman and Robin, going to get some candy and shit." Cordell yelled.

Maine wanted to get at Corey and find out his plans for the night. It would've been cool if he could finally finish that threesome he didn't get a chance to fulfill with Liam. Spence and 'Keem bottomed, Corey and Maine topped. Everyone would've been easily matched. Plus, Maine had a feeling that 'Keem and Corey would hit it off.

"I'm Superman bitch," Melvin shouted back as they kept on walking.

"Ignore them," Corey replied without looking back, I can't stand the frat dudes at this school."

"Awe, hell naw, that motherfucker was talking about us," one of Spence's frat brothers jumped up. He was a little drunk and ready to go off for no reason.

"Man fall back," Maine got up and placed his body in front of Spence's brother, "they're freshman, they don't know better."

"Melvin always talking shit," Cordell vented. "And if he and Corey want to be grown, let them get their asses beat."

"Carter, chill," Spence commanded, having Maine's back. "Gary, please make sure this nigga don't do nothing stupid to get our chapter snatched."

"Man, I'm good." Carter took his seat on the other park bench. "Why you gotta be so uptight?" The brothers were passing around a cup and offered Maine and 'Keem a sip. Both took the cup and partook in the libations. The vodka and gin mixture sat nice and only prepared the three of them for the night they planned on having.

"You should've hit that nigga in his mouth." Cordell encouraged. "He's my brother, I wouldn't have said shit."

Maine shook his head. He low-key hated the disdain Cordell showed Corey, yet he felt guilty for when he treated Corey the same.

"Aye man, let's go study for our Management Information Systems class." Spence stood up and gripped a few of his brothers on his way off the plot. "We gotta do that performance exam with Dr. Anthony and you know he don't play."

"Uugghh!" 'Keem slouched his shoulders. "Not another performance exam."

"Yeah man, we gotta get some practice in." Spence suggested. "I'll make sure I'm on top of everything and that you getting exactly what you need to pass this course."

Maine liked the slick code he slid in. 'Keem smiled as he caught the message. "Aight man. I'm glad you on top of this class man, I need all the help I could get."

Maine and shook hands with the rest of the brothers and the three of them made their way off the plot. Luckily for them, Vanessa's car was waiting on them to take wheels for their grand escape. Maine couldn't wait to get to 'Keem's so he could release some tension and spend his Halloween enjoying the tricks and treats Spence and 'Keem were going to bless him with.

35

New Edition

Maine, Spence and 'Keem laid back on 'Keem's king-sized beds. All of them were spent after a session of Spence and Maine tag teaming 'Keem's ass.

"Damn, I love y'all two." 'Keem sat up and grabbed the bottle of Seagram's gin on the dresser. He took a shot straight from the bottle and put it back. "Y'all know how to make a nigga feel good."

"I aim to please," Maine laid back with his hands behind his head.

Spence hugged Maine and played with his dick. "Yeah man— that ass is fire."

Maine didn't know how to take the remark. He enjoyed watching Spence twist a man almost his height like he was a pretzel. Watching Spence's dick go in and out of 'Keem was better than any flick on the net.

"Yours is too." 'Keem pointed out. Spence had taken 'Keem on his side earlier and then Spence laid on his stomach as 'Keem had dug him on his bed. "What's it gonna take take for me to go bareback with y'all?"

"Well," Maine sat up. "Spence and I are almost exclusive, except when we fuck you. I know Spence's not doing any other man besides you and he knows you're the only other dude I smash besides him. I know his girls are clean. He knows the women I messed with are clean."

"Say no more." 'Keem walked to his dresser and pulled out a small green index card from the Guilford County Department of Health. He passed the card to Maine, showing his negative HIV and STD status from the previous month. "So what's good?"

"The other piece Maine left out is that he's my nigga." Spence eyed 'Keem. "We do more than take classes, work together and fuck. We chill. We make time for each other. We share small simple moments that makes the two of us worth it."

'Keem sat back on the bed. "So do the three of us hang out together or do we do a combination of the two of us getting to know each other at a time?"

"How does Renee feel about you trying to raw dawg with us?" Maine asked. "She and I were real good about using condoms when we hooked up. And I've never seen the two of you not wear a condom."

Maine saw the look of frustration in 'Keem's eyes. "We ain't talked about it. She knows I want kids and she know I want them with her. We talked about making babies after we got married and I got in the NFL, but we ain't go no further than that. Obviously, she and I won't be wearing condoms when we conceive—at least that's the plan. She's scared of me catching HIV and ruining my career."

"Look, I'll tell you what," Spence moved over and rubbed 'Keem's back. 'Keem rolled his head from side to side. "You talk with Renee—then we'll talk with Renee after we decided we fuck with each other like that to lay it on the line. If we need two, the three of us can meet with Renee, Vanessa and Sierra and all of us can hash it out like grownups. Shit, maybe afterward, we can do a big ass orgy."

"West Coast Productions style?" 'Keem grinned.

"Something like that." Spence kissed 'Keem's neck as he fondled his nipples. 'Keem let out gasp of ecstasy and on cue, Maine was between 'Keem's legs, swallowing him like a champ. Spence and Maine eye each other mischievously as they knew they were in for treat.

Another round of great sex had begun.

***

"Overall, the class did very well." Dr. Finley walked around and handed everyone their test back. Maine stared at the red eighty-nine on his paper. He struggled with some of the concepts but he needed to get a ninety-four on the exam in order to ensure he'd keep an A going into the final. He saw Elgin fold up what looked like a sixty-nine.

"Bruh," Elgin turned around. "You and Cordell doing another study party? I'll host it this time if y'all can get everyone together."

"Shit," another student could be heard mumbling. Maine tried to see what Cordell got on his paper but he'd already put it away.

"Yeah, you know we hosting another party. I would like to go to Borders or Barnes & Noble just to get away from the campus atmosphere." Maine admitted.

"You ain't lying." Elgin answered.

"What the fuck y'all get?" 'Keem whispered. Maine could tell it wasn't good. What happen to *overall, the class did very well?*

"Eighty-nine." Maine whispered.

"About twenty points below that." Elgin pouted as he slouched in his chair. Spence looked at him and Elgin quickly sat back up.

"That was hot." 'Keem licked his lips. Maine knew he was talking about how the two of them went from suck each other's dicks to eating each other's asses before Spence rubbed his tip on 'Keem's hole. "I got a seven six. I think you got the highest grade in the class Maine."

For the next hour, Dr. Finley calmly and slowly explained every problem and at least two ways to come up with the solution. Listening to Dr. Finley made him feel like his mistakes were stupid or childish. Everyone in the class took notes and highlighted sections of the book they thought they missed.

After class was over, Cordell caught up with Maine and showed him his score. Eighty-eight. Maine wondered how they were the only two who seemingly did so well.

"I got a sixty-seven," Maine overheard Spence tell Elgin and the other guy they knew was pledging with him. "We fuckin' up."

Sixty-seven, Maine wondered. That didn't sound like Spence at all.

"Okay, I got a ninety-two, we got some work to do." Janessa complained as she walked up to them. "Homecoming did us in for real."

"Sounds like you got the highest grade in the class." Cordell sounded jealous. "Bathsheba won't even show me her paper."

"Can we do this party at your place or Elgin's on Thursday?" Janessa suggested.

"I think there's a probate on Thursday." Cordell mentioned.

Maine had almost forgotten about it. Spence dropped a hint for him and 'Keem to be ready for some surprises by the end of the week. He was happy for Elgin and that being on line for the frat would be over with soon. The frat were dropping big hints over homecoming weekend that Cordell and Maine needed to get ready, but Maine wasn't sure if it was his time or not. He had a lot of issues with Spence on his mind that he needed to work through.

"Aww hell for real?" Janessa asked. "I thought NC Tech only allowed Greeks to have lines in the spring?"

Maine shook his head. He knew firsthand folks did what they wanted to do. And it wasn't that uncommon for NC Tech to make an "exception."

"Okay. Well we'll figure out a date. But we need one soon. I'll catch you later. My next class starts in five minutes." Janessa started to sprint away.

"Aye, let's go to the house real quick." Cordell suggested as he pulled out the keys to the car.

"I'm cool with that." Maine followed.

Soon, Cordell and Maine were pulling up to their apartment. They cracked jokes and rapped along with DMX, Timbaland and Magoo and Busta Rhymes. "So check this out, I gotta go with Bathsheba to the clinic tomorrow."

"What she pregnant?" Maine asked.

"She might be." Cordell admitted.

Damn. Another one bites the dust. "She miss her period or something?"

"Told me she missed it about a month ago." Cordell's voice was low. "I don't know what the fuck I'm gonna do. I still need to get the Jeep from Uncle Roy. I'm not ready to be no father man."

"Look, if she pregnant, just have her move in with us. We'll figure some shit out like we helped Elgin through his situation. You not the first nigga to get a girl pregnant in college and I'm sure you won't be the last. Hear my mom tell it, I was conceived in one of the dorm rooms on Spellman's campus." Maine tried to inject comedy but Cordell wasn't laughing.

"I don't want to hear dad's mouth about this shit either. He gonna complain about how he sent me and Corey with a box of condoms each." Cordell pointed out.

Maine remembered because he been ran out of the condoms Cordell and Corey's dad sent him to NC Tech with, too. He didn't think Cordell knew so he didn't tell him. Otis lowkey stepped into the father role the last few years with Maine, getting him right here and there as he stepped into manhood.

"Things are different now. NC Tech got a daycare, you working mad hours at Burger King, I think you live there half the time. Bathsheba might be a little prissy, but she seems responsible. She can cook." Maine pointed out as Cordell shook his head. "And you can still pledge or whatever."

"Yeah. I'll cross that bridge when we get there." Cordell went to the cabinet and poured him a drink. He offered Maine a shot but he declined. "I'll know by Thursday what the deal is. If she not pregnant, we gotta be extra careful."

"Yeah—fuck her every other day, not every day." Maine suggested.

"I don't fuck her every day." Cordell denied.

"The hell you don't," Maine cut in. "If you not in your room knocking on the wall, y'all just as loud when you take a shower together. And I know you not wearing a condom when the water is running."

"I fell into that same trap you fell in." Cordell answered. "Now I see why you acted the way you acted."

Maine reflected on the time he entered Yonna without protection—and the fact that he and Spence didn't wear any. Changed the sex game completely.

"Well look. We know it's gonna be what it's gonna be. If she pregnant, I got your back. If she not, we still good. Just fuck her every third day." Maine suggested.

"Nigga fuck you." Cordell vented. "You be sure to close the damn doors while you smashing Yonna in every room but the bedroom and put on some clothes when you walk outside."

Maine laughed. He wasn't worried about Cordell and trusted his boy would do the right thing no matter the outcome. He was anxious to find out if Cordell and Bathsheba were expecting. That mean that Corey would be an uncle and he would be a godfather. He'd get to see Corey more frequently. But Cordell would be somebody's daddy. He knew his boy would make a good father.

The two men headed back to class and Maine thought about Cordell's pending situation. He almost wished he had that drama with Yonna instead of the HIV scare. But he didn't want no kids with Yonna either. And 'Keem wanted to take the rubbers off.

Cordell's situation had him second guessing everything.

36

Party All The Time

"Yo' make my Whopper like the Rodeo Cheeseburger with light barbeque sauce. King size my combo and I'm with my study party." Maine ordered his sandwich his way.

Cordell's manager was cool as shit for letting him host the study party at Burger King while he was on the shift. He knew he couldn't get the time off and he needed help so he'd be able to work and study. Maine handed the cashier a twenty-dollar bill while staring at a fine young girl who walked in. She looked a little was about five foot three, one hundred fifty pounds and thick in all the right places.

"You need to keep the line moving." Yonna butted into his day dream. The cashier gave him his change once Yonna got his attention. Yonna looked in the direction Maine was lusting in and rolled her eyes. "You've had better."

"Jealous are we?" He questioned as he moved down to the end of the line, waiting on his food.

"Let me get the fish sandwich combo with onion rings instead of fries for here." Yonna ordered. "Hell no," she directed toward Maine. "Why be jealous of her when I got better at home?"

Maine cracked a smile. He didn't want to tell Yonna that Chelle doesn't light a candle to the new girl. He also wasn't in the mood to start no shirt with Yonna nor was he gonna disrespect Cordell at his job.

Maine and Yonna grabbed their trays and headed to the table. Maine really didn't want to share a table with Yonna but he had little choice. Spence had Elgin and another classmate huddled and they bounced after a few minutes. 'Keem had football practice and he was in and out already too, promising to come back if folks were still there. Janessa was working with some students in another class and Renee hadn't gotten back in yet. Bathsheba was at home sick and Maine knew that Cordell was stressing the exams and the idea of being a father.

Yonna took her seat and opened her book to the chapter they had reviewed the day before. Yonna had an eighty on that last exam and she admitted that she had hoped for a higher grade, too. As she and Maine worked through the problem, he wondered what life would be like with just her. Would they still have drama? They worked well together and had great sex, but outside of class and the bedroom, all they did was tit for tat. Maine knew he didn't want to spend the rest of his life like that.

Spence and Yonna. Until now, Maine never put much thought into the comparison. Both were smart—both were sexy, and that's where their similarities he was attracted to ended. Yonna was bossy and felt like the world revolved around her. Spence was slightly conceited and very much the alpha male. Yonna liked to argue, but Spence would roll his eyes and ball his fist. They both matched him on the freak scale, it wasn't too many places he didn't have either Spence or Yonna screaming his name. Both were bisexual—but Spence had the advantage of being a man and being able to understand Maine, even when they were mad at one another.

"I see Renee and 'Keem finally decided to show up." Yonna nudged Maine to look their way.

'Keem faced him then turned away. Maine didn't know what that was about. Renee never glanced at his direction once. He wondered if they had the conversation and how that turned out? Maine and Spence were firm on their position.

"That's cool. Our final is almost a month away and I'm ready for it to be over." Maine brought the conversation back on subject.

"Over, we have 102 next semester and at the rate we're headed, we'll have to find another spot to study." Yonna pointed out.

"We can take over Olive Garden or Red Lobster next time." Maine joked.

"Yeah right."

"I finally get a break in this joker." Cordell sat beside them with a double cheeseburger made with a croissant, fries and an apple pie.

"What the hell?" Maine asked.

"Don't get mad I'm trying off the menu items," Cordell bragged. "One day soon, we'll be serving breakfast twenty-four/ seven. I told the managers that was the best way to make money." Maine had to admit, the meal looked appetizing. Cordell looked at Maine's book while he kept his eyes on the front.

"I'm going to get something else, you want anything?" Yonna offered.

"I'm good."

Yonna got up and Maine looked through her accounting book. He saw Cordell look around then gaze at him. "She was seven weeks."

Maine leaned his head forward and tilted his head in Cordell's direct. *"Was?"* He couldn't believe it.

"I wondered if laying all that pipe killed the baby." Cordell whispered.

"I'm sorry to hear that." Maine told him.

"I wasn't ready to be a father." Cordell looked around and faced Maine. "Bathsheba's not taking it too well. She's blaming everything from smoking to drinking to studying too hard to spending too much time in my bed and not enough time in hers. She still had periods, we didn't even know she was pregnant." Cordell took a bite out of his sandwich.

"I heard that was common." Maine admitted. "Women have had periods up to their sixth or seventh month."

Yonna made her way back to the table and Maine noticed Elgin walking into the restaurant. He walked up, gave the cashier an order and then walked to their table.

"Nice of you to join us," Yonna called Elgin out.

"I had an emergency," Elgin answered. "I'll need to copy your notes and spend some time with you so I can get right for this test."

"We good man." Maine told him. "I hope your family's well."

"Thank you."

Elgin headed to the front where he carried out a few bags. "That boy ain't had no sleep." Yonna shook her head.

A part of Maine worried about Elgin. He pulled out his phone and checked his messages. Spence sent him a message with a bunch of sixty-nines. Maine smiled and put his phone up. He wished Spence was around but he wasn't worried about him.

The three of them studied for another twenty minutes before Cordell had to get back in the kitchen. The "study party" at Burger King was good and different. With only a month left for finals, Maine knew everyone was going to have to put in some work to get the results they wanted. And he was ready to do what he needed to do to pass the class.

37

Frat Frat Frat, Incorporated

The November night was cold as Maine and the rest of the campus watched Spence and the frat lead eight young men to the student union for their probate. They wore black Kangol hats, sunglasses, black jumpsuit with black boots. It was obvious their heads were shaven clean. Thousands of students and family members cheer as the line got closer.

"Forward, forward, we are moving forward.

Forward, forward, ain't no looking back

Forward, forward we are moving forward.

Forward, forward, where my brothers are at."

As the young man chanted, they moved tightly instep. Left foot front, right foot back. Every step one took the other had his back. Once they got to the center of the student union, they were instructed to stop. Their dean was tall and regal looking. His caramel-colored skin shined bright against his white line jacket. Spring 97 on the sleeve and the line name "Cyclops" was legible from where Maine stood.

"About face!" Their dean shouted.

Maine was glad he got to the show early. Cordell had to go to work and Maine hated that their video camera wasn't working. He had a good spot next to some of the visiting brothers. He noticed a young man with slick, sea sickening waves on top of dark chocolate colored skin. He was slender, but well built.

"You know one of the guys?" His voice was deep, yet raspy. Something about him seemed familiar. His leather Atlanta Braves jacket was the right color.

"One of my boys is on line." Maine answered.

"My younger brother is the ace. I'm Troy," he extended his hand.

"Maine."

"Greetings to the students, faculty and staff of North Carolina Technical State University!" The line greeted the campus. The response was a loud eruption of praise and cheering.

"I-85 was a mess getting up here." Troy told him.

"Oh, shit. You from the A?" Maine asked.

"Born and raised." Troy answered.

"Small world. Me too." Maine replied.

"Nice."

"Brother, A Prayer for You—line speak." The line leader stepped out with his fist crossed touching at his chest.

"If the coldest night and the brightest moon should ever part.
Brother oh brother where for thou art
I will find you, clothe you, help you find a new start.
Brother dear brother, alone you aren't.
For God has sent me to be by your side.
I got your back, day or night.

If the warmest day and the reddest sun should fade away.
Brother oh brother, I am here for you today.
An answer to the prayer to the Lord you say.
Brother dear brother, I'm here to guide the way.
For love is real and brotherhood deep, will not fade.
I am the warmest of blankets, the coolest of shade.
Good brother I am here, an answer to your prayer.
Brother, A Prayer for You!" The line spoke in unison.

Maine noticed Troy spitting the poem, too. "Our dad is a brother. I learned the poem before I learned to talk."

"Legacy?" Maine wondered.

"Fifth generation," Troy confirmed. "My great grandfather pledged under the founders."

Maine nodded his head. He couldn't see Troy as a frat boy. His tats were numerous and the tongue ring was hard to hide.

The line spit organizational history, greeted the sororities, dissed the rival frats and greeted the visiting chapters. Each brother was greeted to a tune of a popular song on the radio. Dr. Finely, their advisor, was greeted to the tune of "Superman Lover." He danced and did the greeting with him. It was good seeing Dr. Finely in a different light.

"I'm coming to NC Tech next year after I finish my active duty. Family tradition." Troy continued their conversation.

"What branch you serve?" Maine inquired. Troy didn't look like he could be enlisted, especially with his hair.

"I'm in the Air Force. It's been fun but it's time for me to buckle down and have a different experience. Need to be around some people. But I know where I know you from." Troy caught his interest.

"Know me?" Maine wondered what he was talking about.

"You're the starer. I used to wait on you to come inside, but Edward got to you first." Troy told him. In the back of Maine's mind, he wondered if he'd seen Troy at Wicked Park, but he didn't want to call him out on it. "I'm on my *don't ask, don't tell* so don't worry about me."

"Introducing the Fall 1999 Line of Our Great Chapter, the Eight Signs of Revelations." The dean stood at the front of the line.

He removed the Ace's glasses and he was nearly a spitting image of Troy. Their father was easily found and he hugged his son. Their genes were strong. "Chauncey Wilford, junior, biology representing the ATL. 4-0-4 stand up!" Chauncey broke away and encouraged the crowd to get hype. "They call me Sight One Seen because I'm the first one to see trouble and I make sure my line is never in the midst of it."

Chauncey ran to a spot and got in position. A few other Aces from previous lincs and other chapters got in his face and hyped him up. Maine saw the smile on Troy's face. As they looked on, he recognized the second dude as being the driver of the car who took him home. "Tyrone Erick Badu, senior, hospitality management major from Danville, VA." Tyrone stepped forward and threw two fingers up, two fingers down. "They call me Two Be Warned because my brother sees the signs, I make sure everyone is ready for battle.

The line leader was the tre. "Benjamin Andre, sophomore, accounting major from Winston-Salem." All the guys from

Winston-Salem yelled "TRE-Four", the city earned nickname and also the code for one of the hardest jails in the state. "They call me TREumphiant Victory because I make sure God is with us and that the victory is won."

The number four and number five were the other two guys who were in the car with Maine. He learned they were fraternal twins from Greensboro, North Carolina. Donald Perkins, the darker skinned one signed his information while Donatello Perkins, lighter skinned one told everyone what he was saying. They called him "TasteFOUR Sound" because while his hearing may be weak, he could sense trouble by reading other people's lips. Donatella was called "QUINTessential Element" because he master fall five senses and was dependable for having his brothers' backs.

Elgin was unmasked and stood before the crowd. The cheers went up for him and Maine smiled and nodded his head. "Elgin Jermaine Sanders, sophomore, political science and accounting double major from Winston-Salem." More "TRE-Fours!" were yelled. "They call me SIXsense because I use all the tools given to me to help my friends and to keep us out of harm's way."

Maine recognized the next guy unmasked but he'd forgotten his name. "DayQuan Timothy Jermaine Lennox, senior, transportation and logistics major from Charlotte, North Carolina." A lot of people cheered. "That's right, your Student Government Association Attorney General is finally a brother. They call me SEPT-Tim-BURR because any information you plant within me, I'll use my fertile ground to nourish it and protect those around me."

"Hey!" the brothers started yelling and rocking the last brother waiting to be unmasked. "Hey!" Spence gave the tail of the line a hug and then pulled back. "Hey!" The dean shook his hand and whispered in his ear. "Hey!" One of the brothers raised a football helmet in the air. "Hey!" Another raised a high school football jersey. "Hey!" Another brother raised a Carolina Panthers jersey. "Hey!" All the new brothers unzipped their jumpsuits to reveal wearing NC Tech football jerseys. The whole school and the brothers yelled "hey!" one last time and to everyone's surprise, 'Keem stood up and threw the fraternal hand sign in the air.

"My birthname is Dawid Aakil Hakeem Allah—prince of the wise and intelligent rulers under Allah. Y'all know me as 'Keem, your star wide receiver for the NC Tech Bulldogs. Junior, business education major representing Matthews, North Carolina. They call me InfinEIGHT Wisdom because Judgement Day is coming and every secret stays with my circle and I spew information to help, not hinder those in my path."

The new brothers of the fraternity got in formation and did a quick step show. Maine was shocked because while he knew Elgin was online, he had no idea that 'Keem was, too. After the end of the show, the new brothers of the fraternity got back in line and they chanted and marched throughout campus to the fraternity plots. Once they arrived, the each took off their boots and marched across the sand before joining the other brothers on the plot.

Maine was proud of Elgin and 'Keem. He knew some of the other brothers on the line but he figured in due time, he'd meet all of them. Elgin broke and 'Keem broke free from the brothers and each approached Maine and gave him a hug. Maine felt bad that he only had a small gift for Elgin but in the back of his mind, he knew what he'd get for 'Keem.

38

This Is How It Works

"I'm gonna start charging y'all every time I have to pull buffalo wings out of the oven." Cordell complained as he laid the hot baking sheet full of meat on the table.

The brothers of the fraternity hosted a private party for the new line with close friends and family. It was the weekend before they let out for Thanksgiving and a lot had changed. Maine noticed that 'Keem was still crunk since the probate.

"Cordell, we appreciate you," Benjamin told him as he stacked his plate with half of the wings.

"And you're gonna take half of them?!" Cordell shouted as he pointed to the nearly empty tray.

'Keem shook his head. "I tried to warn you he was a stingy one."

"Hold up LB," Benjamin defended himself. "How many study parties did I missed out on because I was handling business?"

Everyone got quiet. Troy, Chauncey and their father walked in and grabbed the rest. "You got any more food?" Mr. Wilford asked.

'Keem got up and offered the elder his seat. "We can make a store run real quick." He offered. "Food Lion down the street and I got my MVP card."

"Get your line brothers to pitch in." Spence ordered from his spot in the kitchen near the stove.

Mr. Wilford pulled out his wallet. "Young brother, everyone can pitch in." He pulled out a fifty-dollar bill and passed it to 'Keem. Soon, everyone pulled out money, including Spence. Mr. Wilford took a bite of wing on his plate. "Yeah, stop at Church's too, so that this young man doesn't have to do all of the cooking. Get some biscuits and fried okra."

"Dad, you know—" Troy started to reprimand his father. Mr. Wilford put his finger up. "I am sixty-five years old. I was made in this chapter in the Fall 1955. I am among brothers, family and friends—one day I hope you son, will cross this chapter. I'm going to enjoy wings, sweet biscuits from Church's and fried okra and if I take a bite and Jesus calls me home, make sure they do a church service inviting lost souls to become save and not a sad ass funeral for me."

"Yes sir!" More than one person answered as they handed 'Keem the money.

'Keem nodded his head to Maine and the two of them stepped out of the apartment. "And bring me some Crown Royal and a bottle of Coke." Mr. Wilford ordered.

Maine grabbed the keys hanging next to the door and he and 'Keem made the trek to Food Lion.

"You are full of surprises." Maine told 'Keem as he drove done Cone Boulevard.

"Come on bruh," 'Keem defended himself. "Everyone can't know my business."

"I get that." Maine answered as they pulled into the Food Lion parking lot. "I thought sleeping with your frat brothers was taboo."

"It is," 'Keem admitted as he grabbed a shopping cart from the parking lot. "I had every intention of keeping my situation under wraps. I pursued you, not Spence."

Maine knew that was true. He tagged Spence along so they could experience 'Keem together. He had no intention of messing around with more than one guy in the same frat. Well, technically, 'Keem wasn't frat—hell, he didn't even know 'Keem was interested.

Maine and 'Keem ran through Food Lion, getting plenty of wings, chips and Coca Colas. He also bought a stack of Solo cups so he and Cordell wouldn't have to wash a whole lot of dishes. 'Keem made a phone call and arranged for someone to bring him a bottle of Crown Royal in the parking lot.

Once they were out of Food Lion, they caught one of the older members of the football team leaning against Maine's car. They exchanged grips then the man was on his way.

"So how does you being frat affect your relationship with Spence?" Maine asked as he started the car and made his way back to his apartment.

"That's really a bridge Spence and I are crossing together—maybe if you make it on this side, we'll be there to help you." 'Keem replied. Maine rolled his eyes. He did not like 'Keem's answer and hated when 'Keem got slick with the mouth. "You and I have one type of relationship for now and Spence and I have something completely separate. The three of us do our thing when we do our thing. I try not to get everything mixed up because I know where I stand with each of you."

Maine didn't bother bringing up the topic for the rest of the drive to his place. He knew he and 'Keem were going to have to work some other shit out but the party wasn't the time or the place.

40

World AIDS Day

Donald and Donatello greeted members of the student body in McNair Auditorium. They each handed out a program commemorating December 1 as World AIDS Day. The brothers of the fraternity escorted various students to their seats. Maine, Cordell, Corey, Melvin and Patrice had seats right behind the chapter. They looked around and could see students and faculty standing.

"Greetings and welcome to our fraternity's World AIDS Day Awareness Program." Benjamin greeted the audience as he walked to the podium. A large red ribbon was placed under his fraternity pin on the left side of his black suit. His black bowtie was hand tied and his white shirt and slacks recently pressed. "We want to thank the students of North Carolina Technical State University, Bennett College, Gilbert State University, The University of North Carolina – Greensboro, Guilford College, Greensboro College and the students of Guilford Technical Community College and neighboring community college as they supported our initiative. We, along with all of the collegiate chapters and alumni of the National Pan Hellenic Councils of Greensboro and Guilford County, North Carolina sponsored in various HIV and STD testing and education seminars throughout the county."

Applause could be heard around the room. Maine looked around again and the standing room was tight.

Chauncey walked to the stage. He looked around and smiled. "Are you here?"

Maine spotted Troy and Mr. Wilford. They were dressed in identical suits and bowties.

"Everyone knows my voice." Elgin spoke into the microphone. The lights went out and the audience gasped. Maine could feel people rumbling and moving around him. One light beamed on the center of the stage. "I wanna take y'all through what my life has been like over the last two months."

"Like many of you, when I enrolled into North Carolina Technical State University, I took a physical. I participated in wellness checks, blood donations, anything advocating for men's health. I'm not at risk for prostate cancer, but I go and take elders and young men just so they can get checked up. I'm not a carrier for sickle cell anemia, but I organize events and charity functions to raise awareness for the disease. I'm not a broadcast journalism or radio communications major, but the reason I've probably been trusted to host many events for student here is because y'all have trusted me to keep it real and to advocate and stand up for what I believe in."

Another light came on and the stage was still empty. Maine looked around for Elgin. He could hear him but he couldn't see him.

"If you asked me at the beginning of the summer if I wrapped it up every time I had sex, I would've lied and passed out condoms like I was giving out lifesaving water. At the end of the event, my brothers and I will be handing out condoms so make sure you get two—I know some of you need more than that, but two a person is the best we can do for now."

There was a chuckle in the audience.

"I wasn't sure I was going to do this." Elgin's voice stumbled. Maine stood up and looked for him. He hated not knowing where Elgin was and hoped he wasn't about to witness a horrendous event. Even though he knew Elgin's mental state was improved and that Elgin was taking his meds—he didn't like the idea that Elgin could potentially have a slip up in front of hundreds of students and peers. "I'm glad the university allowed this to be broadcasted simultaneously on our news feed and on our campus radio station."

"I turn twenty in two months and I always viewed the future as mine for the taking." Elgin continued. "I got into the best frat in the world, and with the exception of my last accounting exam, I've passed the majority of the tests given by my professors."

Applause could be heard again.

"I take care of my body—no, wait—that's a lie. If I take my shirt off and strip down to my boxer briefs, I'm willing to bet good money I'd have most of the women sweating."

The women ooed and aahed. Maine knew Elgin was telling the truth because even he did a double take sometimes. Another light came on. Elgin still wasn't on the stage.

"Yeah, I like the attention. Behind closed doors, I like being naked and being the center of attention. When I was a little boy, I was always told I was ugly. My teeth were crooked. I had big ears and big lips and a big nose. I wasn't light skin. And to add insult to injury, I hate wearing my glasses. My mom was the only one to tell me I was beautiful—but don't nobody want to hear that from their mom. I wanted to hear that from the other girls. Once I hit puberty, my teeth straightened with the help of some braces. I grew into my ears, lips and nose. My skin cleared up beautifully.

"As I got older, I finally heard what I wanted to hear. 'I was beautiful.' Fine enough to be placed on the most desired with. Athletic enough to have an excuse to walk around shirtless during football and track seasons. And I learned that I had something between my legs that almost guaranteed that I not only would be told I was beautiful everyday, but that women would want to do a beautiful dance with me.

"And that's what sex was—a beautiful dance. A chance to guarantee that I wouldn't be alone. Sex became a drug and I had to have it, constantly. I fiend for it worse than a heroin addict or a person fixed on crack. Because I was beautiful, I thought I was invincible. Because I was beautiful, I thought I'd remain healthy.

"As I gained more notoriety, more women pursued me. As I gained more confidence, I got more reckless in my pursuit. First time I had sex without a condom—my God! I see how Adam and Eve fell the way they did. It's like that first high and all you want to do is chase it again and again. I see how people lie, steal and cheat for the hit so they can get one last high. Like any other addict, I wanted to get high like the first time. And I got high all the time, praying one day, I'd hit it high like my first time.

"One of my friends got an STD scare and a group of us went to get tested." Elgin got to the familiar part of the story. "I'm a nineteen-year-old, heterosexual black male, and I thought the worst thing that could happen to me was catching gonorrhea. I wish that's what I'd caught because all I'd need was a penicillin pill to make it go away. The first HIV test said inconclusive, and we thought the herpes I'd contracted was the reason why I tested that way. Two additional tests confirmed my worst fears. I'm Elgin Jermaine Sanders, nineteen-year-old, sophomore, political science and accounting major from Winston-Salem, North Carolina and I tested positive for HIV before my twentieth birthday."

One could hear a pen drop. All the lights came on and all of Elgin's line brothers were lined up on the stage in height order. They looked up to the sky as they faced forward. Elgin still couldn't be seen.

"I looked good at my probate show a little more than a week ago. When I got the first HIV positive test, my line brothers and my big brothers cried. My chapter advisor made sure I wanted to continue my process. And still see his uggmug three times a week in our accounting class."

A few of the brothers chuckled. Some of the audience was still in shock. Elgin just told the world he was HIV positive and Maine still couldn't see him. He looked all over the crowd and couldn't find him nowhere. His line brothers still held their spot in the middle of the stage with other chapter brothers standing at various spots on the stage and around the auditorium.

"My best friends Cordell, Maine, Spence along with Cordell's brother Corey and his roommate Melvin made sure I didn't try to kill myself the first month and some change after I was diagnosed. They made sure I went to my classes and that I got my sleep and that took the twenty-three pills I now take to keep my life in check. Melvin's girlfriend, Patrice, helped me call as many women as I could remember to tell them my status and urge them to get checked."

The door to the auditorium opened and Elgin walked in, gripping his microphone. Everyone in the audience stood up.

"I thought I was going to be HIV positive, alone." Elgin walked down the steps close to the stage. "Ryan White did it alone.

Numerous gay and bisexual men become alone—at least that's what they share with me when we do group therapy. Women who become positive through the men they slept with wonder if they will remain, alone. I don't like to be alone."

Elgin walked on the stage and his brothers parted to open his space in the line. Elgin took his place and he continued talking to the audience. "I'm not alone. I come out today to reveal my status because I need help not doing this on my own. As far as I know and from the women who reported their status to me—I've not infected anyone. If I did, I know no sorry in the world may fix what I've done. I don't know if the woman who infected me did it on purpose or if the truth is, she doesn't know. Either way, I don't blame you because just like you let me enter you without a condom, I was the one who chose not to wear one. I forgive myself for being reckless, irresponsible and a horrible role model for my classmates and those coming after me.

"I decided to share my story with you not for fame—or even to confirm or dispel rumors. This is a warning. Be careful with your life—you only get one. And once it's gone, it's gone. Beauty is vain —don't be—or else this song will become about you."

The lights went off for a brief second and when they came back on, only 'Keem was at the podium. "My brother didn't have to share his story, but I'm glad he did. No man or woman walking this earth is without sin. We have no room to judge one another. Immediately following our program, we will hand everyone two condoms and information pamphlets on HIV and other sexually transmitted diseases. For those of you who got tested, if you're negative, continue to protect yourself. If you're positive, begin your new life by checking on yourself and being around people of good mindset. And like the people from Charter say—if you don't get help here, please get help somewhere. Thank you."

The new line came back on the stage and they walked single file out of the auditorium with the chapter brothers following behind them. Everyone else filed out of the auditorium and Maine could see that some people were still in shock. He was proud of Elgin for telling his truth. Outside of the auditorium, Elgin and a preacher were in the center of the group and all the brothers had their hands on his shoulder and many brothers reached their hands to touch the shoulders of other brothers. Some of the students recognized the prayer circle, also extended their hands, teaching each other in agreement. Maine and Cordell also joined.

"Father God, we come to You now asking that You not only watch over Elgin and heal his mind, body and spirit, but You continue the work You've set out to do through this young man. Continue to use him for your benefit. HIV is not the beginning or ending of life, yet it is a cornerstone that when used affectively can promote life and educate those around it. We ask that you continue to bless Your son, all the students and the families of and the families affected by the people under the sound of my voice. And of these things through your son Jesus Christ we pray, Amen."

A resounding Amen could be heard throughout the building. When Maine looked up, he found that the circle had extended out of the building as evidenced by the cold draft coming in. Maine made his way to Elgin. The two men looked at one another and gave each other a hug.

41

And The Winner Is...

"I'm glad y'all two could make it." Willie announced as Maine and Spence walked into the store.

Maine almost didn't answer the phone when Willie called after class. He knew it was important as it was rare for Willie to call him. Spence told him he'd gotten the same call with the same instructions.

Maine knew the time was coming when he would find out if he or Spence was going to be the new assistant manager of Willie's. He really wanted the spot, especially since he'd been rejected by Sony and A&M Records for their internships. Spence knew he was going back to New York and back to Def Jam.

"Seems like y'all had a rough semester." Willie continued as Maine and Spence stepped to the register. "I know the accounting class was no joke and personally, y'all be dealing with some issues, especially with the national mandatory suspension of membership intake your frat is going through Spence."

The fraternity put a two year moratorium on making new undergraduate brothers due to the settlement of a hazing lawsuit. That was the reason for the "unusual" fall line at NC Tech and at many schools across the country. Most of the students were finding out the news shortly after the fraternity hosted its World AIDS Day Awareness Program. For Maine, if he wanted to pledge the fraternity, he would have to wait until the Spring 2002, his senior year.

"I've decided to make both of you assistant managers of Willie's.

"Spence, you deserve it because of your ability to use your connections to help secure artist and bring talent. Also, your ability to bring Travis out of his shell is what's needed if we are going to continue to groom the future.

"Maine, your plans have come out flawless. You pay attention to the market and upcoming trends represent the forward-thinking this company will need if we are to make it into the twenty first century.

"The reason I'm doing two assistant managers instead of one is because the two of you can work together. I can give you a task and one person doesn't undercut the other to get it done. In business, you will learn to treat people the way you want to be treated. And to watch the bridges you burn. I have seen presidents and vice presidents become entry level employees overnight. In turn, I've watch people rise to power and supervise people who've hired them. Continue to build bridges with each other and make Willie's strong."

"Thank you." Maine was appreciative. His hard work paid off. In spite of everything going on with school and his outside drama, he was moving up in the world. And his boy Spence was moving up with him.

"Yeah man, we did it." Spence gave Maine dap.

"The high school students won't be in for later but I know the two of you have finals y'all need to study for. I'm going to give both from now until next Wednesday off so you can study and pass your exams. Let me know your holiday schedule so we can make adjustments." Willie told them.

Maine seemed relieved. He could stay in the apartment for a minute and work at Willie's during the summer break. He knew he couldn't stay with Eric, Cordell and Corey the whole winter break. He knew Cordell was only going home for a few days before and the day after Christmas, but planned to be back on campus and ready to work at Burger King.

"I'm glad we both got it." Spence admitted as they clocked out and walked out of Willie's. "I'm appreciative."

"You and me both." Maine told Spence as he headed to his car. The week off was a bonus because Maine knew he needed all the time to study he could get.

"Follow me to my spot so we can celebrate." Spence suggested as he turned the engine on Vanessa's car.

Maine smiled.

***

Maine and Spence gasped for air as they laid across Spence's bed. Two rounds of sex had the two of them spent and neither one wanting to get out of the bed.

"What are y'all doing for the study party tonight?" Spence rubbed his hand on Maine's chest. Maine loved the way Spence felt when he grinded on him, when he sucked him, when he touched him. As Spence's hand made its way lower to his abs and to the fuzz he started growing again at the base of his dick, he inhaled deeply.

"I really don't want to go." Maine admitted. "But we gotta pass Dr. Finely's class and I'm on thin ice with all the other professors. I'm passing my classes but they are still tripping over the nude pics that were taken of me earlier this year."

"And you fucking Yonna with the door open at her apartment." Spence added.

"I'm a grown ass man. Folks know they want to watch me put it down." Maine answer cockily.

"I'd film us getting down if I knew you and I would be the only ones to see it." Spence admitted.

Maine smiled. A part of him wanted to watch him lay some pipe as well. He knew what others said the view was like, but he wanted to see it for himself. "Maybe we'll call Donte and have him film it."

Spence shook his head no. "You on some other shit. But for real, I'm glad we worked everything out and learned to work together."

"Speaking of working together, how is it now that 'Keem is your frat brother?" Maine never had the chance to ask Spence and when he and 'Keem spoke about their unusual situation, he was evasive.

"On one hand, 'Keem isn't just my frat brother, he's my chapter brother. He ain't the first but if I can help it, he'll be the last. Between the two of you, I get what I need. We've talked, and I mean sat down, stated our grievances about one another and then got down to business. I like the fact that he doesn't prefer to top. I'm fully verse so that works for me. Don't get me wrong, what he lacks in size he definitely makes up for in stroke. But on the real, when 'Keem and I get down, we get down. Frat goes out the fucking window. When you and I get down, we get down. I don't think about Willie, Cordell, Elgin or any other of them motherfuckers. I want to bust as many nutts as possible. When it's the three of us, we get it cracking. And I like that." Spence sat up. A light knock could be heard from the door. "I'll get rid of whoever."

Spence slipped into some navy NC Tech sweats that barely covered the crack of his ass and walked to the door. Maine didn't trip. He pulled the covers up on the bed and concealed his nude body.

"Aye bruh, you going to the study party at Maine and Cordell's tonight?" Tyrone asked.

Maine sat up and looked around. He couldn't find his clothes. Tyrone's voice made his dick hard as he remembered how Tyrone was pipping some of the dudes at the sex party he last attended. He didn't think about Tyrone until he gave him that ride from the coronation and now, he had to see the joker on a more frequent basis. He wondered if Spence knew Tyrone got down.

He wondered if 'Keem knew.

"Of course I'm gonna be there." Spence confirmed. "I'll get you a ride in about an hour or so—but bruh, I'm in the middle of handling some business."

"My bad bruh." Tyrone could be heard saying. "Tell Vanessa I said what's up."

"I ain't telling her shit. Later Badu." Spence closed the door and shook his head. "He used to *always* catch me when I'm laying pipe to Vanessa." Spence pretended like Vanessa was standing in front of him and he was hitting it from the back. "Mid-stroke and this nigga banging on the door and shit."

Maine laughed.

"You know he and Mushroom have the same major. I can have him look out for Corey and shit. Make sure that boy don't flunk out." Spence offered as he slipped off his jersey pants.

"That's what's up. I'm sure Corey would appreciate that." Maine offered as he peeled the sheets back.

"You know he was with Elgin when we got caught on the porch." Spence mentioned.

"Oh word?" Maine replied. *So he knows?* Maine thought himself. Tyrone knows that he and Spence were fucking. He wasn't too concerned because he knew Tyrone wasn't going to out himself or Maine—wasn't worth the risk to keep his business down low.

"Yeah man." Spence crawled on the bed and straddled Maine. He moved his ass up and down, seducing Maine to an erection. "Can you fuck me one more time before we get out of here? We not gonna see each other in two days and I need this to last."

Maine sat up and started kissing on Spence's nipples. Spence continued bouncing his ass up and down Maine's dick. When Maine was fully aroused, Spence adjusted himself. He sat on the head and moved around for a while, then slowly slid down, letting Maine penetrate his walls.

"Fuck." Spence whispered.

And that's exactly what Maine intended on doing.

42

Come To Class, Wash Yo' Ass!!!

"**Hey Maine, next time we have a party we're charging these** motherfuckers." Cordell vented as he gathered the trash to get ready to take to the dumpster. Cordell and Maine spent the last hour cleaning up their place before they called it in for the night. "Niggas done left their drinks all over the place. And I'm kicking whoever ass it was that left this open condom wrapper in the middle of the cushions."

Maine saw the red Durex wrapper and shook his head. Maine knew Cordell's dick was as big as his and they had no business wearing anything other than Magnum or other large condoms. Maine and Cordell had been a little lax with how their friends used their place but seeing the wrapper had him thinking about changing the rules.

"Well we know how to throw parties." Maine tried to keep the conversation positive. "Why don't we start a promotions company? We can plan the parties, meet up with people who own the venues, secure the DJs and the acts."

"Maine," Cordell rolled his eyes, "you know how many people have promotions company at NC Tech? It's like a new one starts every week. If we're gonna start a business, we need to start something no one has done before."

Cordell was right. A promotions company was easy to start and every time you turn around, they were being passed a flyer or a flyer was on their windshield for some party or event a new promotions company was sponsoring. Several of their classmates had their own record labels, or clothing lines, or consulting businesses. Some of the older students had janitorial services, or catering firms.

"I'll tell you what would be cool," Maine suggested, "I've always wanted to go to a barbershop and have my haircut by a stripper."

"What the fuck Maine?!" Cordell couldn't believe his ears. "We already agreed on the luxury barbershop. We said we'd have a minibar with a DJ and guest hosts and events for the shop."

"We go back to the A." Maine started.

"Oh hell no!" Cordell shot him down before he could complete his thought. "The reason I'm going to NC Tech is to get the fuck out of the A. I don't want to start no business in Atlanta. There's too many black folks there already. I want to go somewhere where I know I can make some money with the population we have."

"Alright, what about Charlotte?" Maine wasn't giving up on his idea.

"Okay, so we are going to have a barbershop/gentlemen's club. Charlotte doesn't have the population to support the idea and the minute we try to do something like that in the A, someone with money will copy our idea and then what?" Cordell asked.

"Either way, we start with the idea and set the bar high. We give people an experience every time they come to our apartment to party. We apply that same skill set to the new venture." Maine continued to press his ideas. "Our strippers will go to the best barber schools, have an interest in sports, be able to talk."

"Nah, I can deal with the strippers cutting hair, but they got to be good, Maine. One wack haircut and we lose our business like that." Maine noticed Cordell coming around. "Fades gotta be done right and they gotta make sure they can do basic shit. How about this, the girls who cut hair can wear Hooters-like outfits with the baby tees and the daisy dukes? But only one stripper dancing. That way, the girls cutting hair can focus on doing that and the girls stripping can make that dough. And if a dude want a private dance and haircut, we have a VIP Room for that."

"And we gotta serve good drinks." Maine added.

"So what are we gonna call this barbershop/strip club?" Cordell wanted to know. "We still haven't come up with a name for the last joint."

"I haven't thought that far ahead." Maine admitted.

The knock on the door interrupted their conversation. Cordell looked outside and shook his head. He opened. "You didn't ask if you could stay the night." Maine looked outside to see Corey carrying his backpack and his suitcase. "And don't tell me you got put out."

"I flunked all my classes." Corey barely admitted above a whisper. "The university gave me forty-eight hours to vacate the premises."

"All the classes?" Maine wanted to make sure he heard Corey right.

"Naw, naw, naw, motherfucker. You fucking failed Indoor Sports?!" Cordell asked. Corey affirmed with a head shake. "Bruh, that's the easiest class. Come to class, wash your ass, get a 'C'. And I know that's on the syllabus because I kept mine. I couldn't believe they put it on there."

"Man…" Corey started with an excuse. Maine could see Melvin and Patrice outside waiting to see if Maine and Cordell were going to let him in.

"Man, my ass. You fucking failed Indoor Sports! What else did you fail?" Cordell shook his head but didn't open the door for Corey to come in and park.

"Math 101." Corey started to list.

"Who was the teacher?" Cordell inquired.

"Dr. Parent." Corey mumbled.

"Ah hell naw," Maine shook his head.

"Nigga—Dr. Parent is the easiest teacher to have. All you have to do is show up and wear blue and white at least once a week and turn in all the assignments, even if you don't finish. What the hell?" Cordell was pissed. He looked back at Maine then look at Corey. "I swear to God. Simple instructions on how to get C's and you messing them up. What other class you have?"

"I had Biology with Dr. Alibaba and World History with Mr. Keing." Corey answered.

"And that's it?" Cordell quizzed.

"I had English with Dr. Bessant but I dropped that before midterm."

Cordell rubbed his head. "So let me get this straight—you dropped an easy class before midterm. You had thirteen credit hours and you managed to fail *every* class?" Cordell slapped his right hand into his left. "You got to be the dumbest motherfucker on earth! You had no business failing Math 101 because the school pays the math tutors to be available twenty-four/seven. And I know if you had taken advantage, you would've heard a few students tell you to show up, where blue and white and attempt half the problems. Dr. Parent loves her sorority so they also would've told you to write in blue, tell her you hope her sorority wins the step show, slip and say 'blue-tiful' at least once in the semester and ask her for help. She rents out the auditorium in Martina so she can lead a weekly study hall. Dr. Alibaba hard as fuck so I can see failing that class. But Mr. Keing, I can't give you a pass on that because he's been using the same test with the same questions and answers for the last fifteen years. The exams are passed down generation to generation. You must not have made any friends."

Corey rolled his eyes. "Look man, I'm not going back to Atlanta and telling our father I'm flunking out. If I can't stay with you, let me know so I can get on the street somewhere."

Cordell reached out, grabbed Corey by his loosely fitted NC Tech basketball jersey and drug him inside. "Get in here motherfucker."

"Call me that again." Corey bucked at Cordell. His face turning red. Maine quickly jumped between them before a fight could escalate.

"Hold the fuck up!" Cordell pushed Maine out of the way and got in Corey's face. "You coming to *our* house asking for a place to stay because *your* dumbass didn't handle business and you telling *me* what *I can* and *can't* say." Cordell quickly punched Corey twice in the face and lifted him up and flung his body against the wall. "You're in my domain now and I run the fucking show. I told your fucking ass not to follow me here and look at what you do."

Cordell dropped Corey and stepped away. "Swing at me and see what happens." Cordell threatened as he got in Corey's face.

"Come on Cordell…" Maine tried to intervene. He didn't want to see Corey get his ass whooped.

"Maine shut the fuck up, before I whoop your ass!" Cordell grilled Maine then put his attention back on Corey. "You even got my best friend trying to defend your lame ass. That's your fucking problem. You came to NC Tech and thought all the bullshit ass stunts you pulled on Mom and Dad were gonna fly here, but guess what, it didn't work.

"You know why I'm hard on your ass? In the same semester you quit one class and flunked out of the rest, I took six, three-hour courses. I know after I take my last exam tomorrow, I'm gonna have four A's, a B and a C on my report and I'll be on the Dean's List again. I put in thirty-five to fifty hours a week at Burger King every week and I made time to party, fuck my girl everyday, fuck a few bitches on the side, help run a student organization and I got my work done.

"You didn't hold down no job. Was part of no clubs or sports teams or the band. Took classes that aren't even a third as hard as mine and you *still failed*. You should've gotten *straight A's*. One of my A's is in statistics, so don't give me your classes was hard. You failed because you was too fucking lazy to get help, study for an exam and do some work. I know you didn't do the work in Dr. Parent's class because you could've wrote one plus one equals two and she would've let you redo the homework assignment. And I know she told you to do that because she tells everyone to do that.

"So tell me nigga, what did you *really* do at NC Tech? Or who?"

Maine was pissed at Cordell for pushing him and threatening to fight. Yet, he couldn't say shit because in his heart, he knew Cordell was right. He wanted to know who Corey had been fucking. He also wanted to know how Corey fell through the cracks. A part of him felt guilty because he spent a large part of the semester looking for Corey so they could fuck and rekindle their fling. It was his opportunity to show Corey he really cared about him and Maine failed.

"Come to class, wash your ass, get a 'C'. I'm not understanding what was so hard about that. All you had to do was show up and take a bath to get a fucking C. I'm serious as fuck right now, what did you do at NC Tech? Watch Melvin fuck Patrice all semester?! Did they fail their classes?"

"No." Corey mumbled.

"No, you didn't watch them fuck all semester or no they didn't fail their classes?"

"No to both." Corey answered.

Cordell eased away. "Go have a seat."

Corey looked like he wanted to cry. His face was still red and he knew Corey was pouting.

"This is how this is going down." Cordell stood over Corey. "Our lease is up in June—after that you gotta find your own place to stay. You *will* get a job—I got a job, Maine got a job, your mother fucking ass will have a job, too. You *will* find your own transportation. When Uncle Roy gives me my Jeep, I better not catch your ass near it. Greensboro Transportation Authority got bus passes or you can see Melvin for a ride or it's plenty of places around here hiring that you can walk to. It might be in your best interest to get *two jobs* because you'll need a security deposit and first and last month's rent wherever you move. You can't fuck no bitches in here unless you buy new furniture and I better not hear you when or if you do. When you use the bathroom, you clean that joker every time because Maine and I clean it every time we use it. You will buy food and you will cook at least two meals a week—Maine and I rotate cooking duties.

"I'm not going to make you go to school, but you will get a job. I'm dead ass serious. And I better not see you at Burger King. In fact, I'm calling all the managers to let them know not to hire your ass. I don't even want to see you sitting in the restaurant breathing air. For once, I will have it my way and you will not step foot in a Burger King—do I make myself clear?"

Corey looked up. "Yes sir."

"You got three weeks to get a job or I'm putting your ass out. If the apartment manager finds out you're here and puts you out—that's on you. We're splitting all the bills three ways—on the first of the month, you better have one third of the rent, one third of the power, one third of the water, one third of the cable and internet. You're responsible for your own phone—we don't have a landline. You don't have five days after the first. January 1st, February 1st, March 1st, April 1st, May 1st, June 1st, bitch, you betta have my money.

"And I'm not telling Dad you flunked out. And he better not say shit to me about it or I'm whooping your ass again. I make myself clear?!"

"Loud and clear."

Cordell looked at Maine. "You feeling froggy, do we need to jump outside?"

Maine put his hands up and shook his head. "We good."

Cordell rolled his eyes at Maine, then walked to his room and slammed the door. The tears fell from Corey's face. Corey knew he fucked up. Maine cleaned the rest of the house and then walked to Yonna's and Chelle's. He knew if he stayed in the house with Cordell any longer, the two of them were gonna have some problems.

43

Almost Counts

Chelle and Yonna allowed Maine to take a shower and chill.
For the first time in a hot minute, the three of them *did not* have
sex the minute the opportunity struck. Chelle was done with her
finals so she went to sleep so she could get up and go to work
early in the morning. Yonna and Maine studied for their Money
and Banking final they would have at noon.

It was three in the morning and after quizzing each other on
definitions, concepts and mathematical problems, Yonna and
Maine called it a night. He didn't want to walk back to his
apartment but his motivation was Corey.

Corey was sleeping on the couch and Cordell most likely was
entertaining Bathsheba in his room. Truthfully, Maine could use a
few hours a sleep, but the opportunity to touch, feel, be with
Corey was worth a few moments of discomfort.

Maine was still pissed at Cordell and he knew the two of them
would settle their difference some point after finals. He pulled out
the key and unlocked the door.

Look at him, Maine thought to himself. *He looks like an angel,
resting comfortably on the couch.*

Maine carefully hung his keys on the key hook by the door and
slipped out of his shoes. He walked past Corey and put his head
next to his. *He doesn't snore.* Maine smiled. He liked that.

He walked back to his room but looked down the hall to
Cordell's room. He saw the door open and Bathsheba stepping
outside in nothing on but her nightgown. Cordell was sprawled
out on the bed with nothing on.

"Just getting in?" Bathsheba asked as she headed to the bathroom.

"Yeah." Maine smiled.

Bathsheba looked at him for a moment before she went inside. Maine knew that as long Bathsheba was in the room, Cordell wasn't coming out until it was time to get breakfast.

Maine headed to his room and changed out of his clothes and put on an old NC Tech t-shirt and some jersey pants. He waited until he heard Bathsheba go into Cordell's room and stayed in there for a whole hour. Cordell wouldn't have to be at work until eleven and he didn't know what Bathsheba needed to do, but it would require her getting up and leaving the apartment before ten.

Maine headed out of the room and checked on Corey. He walked to the couch and kneeled before Corey. "Wake up Mushroom."

Maine shook him gently. Corey tossed and turned to the other side. Maine was happy to notice that Corey wasn't wearing a shirt and only had on some boxers. Corey's fruit extended out of the loom and by habit, he reached down and touched it.

"Wake up Mushroom." Maine whispered as he looked at back at the hallway. He made sure to pay extra attention to any sudden sounds.

Corey turned back around. He opened one eye and then the other. "What time is it?"

"Four in the morning." Maine answered as Corey sat up. He rubbed his eyes and stretched then kicked back on the couch. Corey reached for a blanket to conceal his member but Maine pulled it away.

"Really?" Corey questioned.

"I wanna finish something." Maine put his hand around Corey's member and stroked it. "Just watch the door."

Maine went for it. It felt so good having Corey back in his mouth. He missed it. Maine could feel Corey's breathing become labored. Slowly, Corey's hips thrusted upward. Maine loved the way Corey's mushroom tip hit the back of his throat. Maine stopped for a minute and looked up. He took off his shirt and his pants and crouched over Corey and began to praise him. Corey's hand crept across his back, giving him strong massages on the way down. As Maine continued finishing the head he'd started months ago, he felt Corey's finger slip down to the small of his back, down deeper, parting his ass. Maine sucked harder. He came up and licked the tip.

Corey's precum tasted so good. He heard Corey spit and he felt Corey's wet fingers penetrate his hole. Maine continued to suck, not minding that Corey was invading his territory.

It made him suck harder.

Maine moved his ass to Corey's finger flicking and was pleased that his skills had improved tremendously since the last time they went down that road. "Fuck!" Maine whispered as he enjoyed having three fingers in his ass.

"Let's switch positions." Corey suggested as he stood up and dropped his boxers.

Maine sat on the opposite end and Corey kneeled in his lap. Maine licked his fingers and slowly slid his index finger in Corey's hole. He heard Corey hiss and moan as he looked back to make sure Bathsheba and Cordell stayed put. Corey went to town and Maine found Corey would accommodate a second finger and slipped it in. Corey was nice and warm, like a well baked chocolate chip cookie. *I wish he'd bottom.* Maine thought to himself as he stretched out. His eyes rolled back as Corey continued fulfilling his need.

"Have you bottomed yet?" Maine asked Corey.

"Nah, you?" Corey threw the question back to Maine. "You trying to?"

"Hell naw." Maine answered as Corey stood up. He saw Corey lean over the couch and Maine took the time to stretch. He opened his legs. "Lay on top of me."

Corey complied. His hard dick on top of Maine's. He leaned in to kiss Maine's lips and the two of them became entangled in their new tongue dance. Maine wrapped his legs around Corey and he could feel the power in Corey's thrusting as Corey grinded his hips into his. Maine felt Corey's hardened nipples rub against his and between that and the way Corey's balls rubbed against his on the stroke caused him to moan. He held on to Corey, knowing the frottage was a close to fucking as the two were going to get, for now.

"Turn around." Corey commanded as he sat up.

Maine obeyed. "You better not try to enter me."

Corey laid on top of Maine and pulled his hair. "I won't."

Feeling Corey's dick grind into his ass made Maine's dick hardened. He liked that shit. Corey kissed and bit his neck as Maine rotated between throwing his ass back to Corey and pretending the couch was his bitch. "I'm about to cum." Corey whispered in his ear.

"Bust in my mouth." Maine begged as he leaned his head back.

Maine turned on his back and within seconds, he had Corey's exploding member in his mouth. His nut tasted as sweet as before. "You come yet?" Corey asked. Maine looked him in the eye, shook his head no and continued to swallow. Corey backed away. "It's your turn."

Maine stood up and looked down the hall. Cordell and Bathsheba were nowhere in sight. Maine looked at Corey's plump ass sitting in the air. He stuck his tongue out, parted Corey's cheeks with his hands and went to work. Feeling Corey push his ass back while getting penetrated with Maine's tongue was a turn on for him. He wished Corey would give it up so he could really be inside Corey. He knew Corey would feel good inside.

I bet a threesome with me, him and Spence would be hot. Maine thought as he laid on top of Corey, rubbed his dick between his cheeks and pretended he was a twelve year old boy scared of pussy. Corey gasped and bit the couch as Maine continued dropping his strokes while pinching and flicking Corey's nipples. Maine felt his balls tighten. "Where you want it?"

"On my back." Corey whispered.

He couldn't believe Corey said that. No sooner than he had a chance to process what Corey said, Maine let himself go and his man juices hit the small of Corey's back and on his broad shoulders. When he was done freeing himself, Maine licked his concoction off his back and gave Corey a kiss, passing their fluids back and forth as their tongues danced in the ocean of their mouths.

When they broke away from the kiss, he watched as Corey made a weird face, swallowed, then licked his lips. Maine quickly put on his pants and t-shirt and Corey reached on the floor for his boxers. When they were dressed, they sat next to each other on the couch.

"That was hot as hell." Corey admitted as he stole a look down the hall. Maine looked too. They'd gotten away with murder for they knew Cordell would kill them both if he'd walked out of the room.

"Yeah man." Maine admitted. "I gotta get you and Spence together. Tomorrow, I'll help you with the job search and we'll figure some shit out."

Corey nodded his head. Maine got up and looked at Corey again, wondering if the day would come when he'd have a chance to crack the seal open. "Good night Mushroom."

"Good night." Corey smirked and laid back down on the couch.

Maine walked to his room and then looked back at Corey. It felt like what happened minutes ago was a dream. He looked at Cordell's room then headed inside his. Maine took his clothes off and hopped on top of the bed, too lazy to get under the covers. Maybe next time, they'd play around in his bed.

44

We Not Gonna Make It

It took Maine ninety minutes to complete his Money and Banking exam. He rushed home, hoping to catch Cordell before he went off to work so they could settle their differences. Instead, he was treated to walking in on Corey enjoying a two-piece meal from Mrs. Winner's. The grease from the drumstick Corey just bit into highlighted the thickness of his lips, making Maine's dick jump.

"You catch Cordell?" Maine asked. He hoped that Cordell and Corey didn't get into it while he was gone.

"Yeah." Corey put the drumstick down. "Bathsheba surprised me and cooked breakfast this morning. He and I talked. I can admit, he's right about me not staying on top of my shit and getting a job. There's no way in hell Dad is gonna let me live down flunking college. My mom's probably tossing in her grave right now.

"How was your exam?"

"Good. I left feeling like I did what I needed to do to secure a solid B in the class. An A would be asking for too much, but I'm good with that." Maine answered as he took a seat next to Corey. "I've been trying to catch up with you all semester—I wish you'd answered the phone more times than what you did."

"Why?" Corey looked at Maine. "So you can get some ass?"

"Yeah, I wanted some ass. Been plotting on it all semester." Maine answered honestly. Corey cracked a smile. "On the real, if I had known you were struggling with classes, I would've gotten you some help. Contrary to popular belief, I'm not an asshole."

"You've shown me otherwise." Corey wiped his fingers on the napkin laid on his side. "Cordell said he thought the Taco Bell on

Summit was hiring, but there's someone who works there I'd rather not see."

"A job is a job—in your case, you don't have too many options." Maine kept it real with him. "Cordell meant what he said about wanting his money on the first. Right now, stores are still hiring seasonal and you probably can get a job or two at the mall. One of the managers at Aerostyle is Spence's frat brother. Elgin is cool with him so I'll have him call him first before you fill out an application."

"Thank you, man." Corey finished with his food and threw the disposables in the trash.

"It's the least I can do." Maine told him as he dug into his pocket and pulled out his phone. "Go jump in the shower. Use my room to change in if necessary. Wear something you know Aerostyle can sell. Try to hurry up so we can get there in an hour. Four Seasons is usually slow around this time so we can get in and out.

He watched as Corey did as he was told. Maine was tempted to get in the shower with Corey but he vowed to get his hormones in check. Corey needed this job and he didn't need any distractions. He walked to his room and pulled out clothes for him to change into and got his shower caddy together. Maine planned on staying fresh and clean because he never knew who he was going to run into.

Once Corey was out, Maine ran into the bathroom and quickly cleansed his body. When he came out, he found Corey wearing a green and orange pin-stripped button up shirt with a green turtleneck underneath. His black slacks fit loosely on his frame and the cuff rested perfectly on his butter-colored Lugz. Maine grabbed his keys and followed Corey out of the door.

"I'm going to take you the way the bus route takes you." Maine told him as they put on their seatbelts. "I can help you get a bus pass. Willie gets the hookup so I don't mind getting you one."

"Didn't you have to go to work today?" Corey wondered.

"Spence needed to have Saturday and Sunday off so I switched with him." Maine answered.

"So what's your situation with Spence? I saw that y'all weren't wearing a condom." Corey inquired.

"Me, Spence, Cordell and Elgin got tested at the same time. That's when we found out Elgin's status." Maine started off. "Spence and I only bareback with each other—and we might do it with another mutual partner we have. That's still being decided."

"Is Spence your boyfriend?" Corey got straight to the point.

"No. We're friends with the best benefits package available." Maine smirked as he thought about his and Spence's situation. "We talk and keep each other in the loop."

"Does Spence know you and I bumped and grinded last night?" Corey asked.

"No, but he will. He'll probably want to bump and grind with you, too." Maine suggested as they pulled into the mall. "The manager's name is Lincoln. He's a jerk, but if you can make it work with him, you'll basically get to make your own hours, work as much as you want and the discount on their clothes is sweet. They have other ways for you to make money, but you'll have to figure that out once you get started."

Maine and Corey got out of the car. Maine headed toward the food court. "You not gonna come with me?" Corey wondered.

"Nah man." Maine shook his head. "You gotta get these jobs yourself. Lincoln don't like me or Cordell and he and Spence got some kind of beef I don't know about."

"Okay. You said Elgin called him already?" Corey checked before separating from Maine.

"Yeah. Put Elgin down as a reference and use your old school address. And tell him you're willing to work any shift. Managers love to hear that shit."

Maine watched as Corey headed to the store. He really hoped that Lincoln would give him a chance and hire him. He knew Corey had no job skills but he also knew that Aerostyle and Lincoln needed help. Maine hoped that by sending Corey to fill out the application, he and Lincoln would be able to help each other.

While he waited on Corey, Maine grabbed two slices of S'barro pizza and a cup of water. He wished his phone had games on it he could play instead of having to face the thousands of shoppers coming in and out of the food court. He looked at some of the ladies and while he thought they were cute, he wasn't going to

WHAT'S BEST FOR YOU 249

make a move. Meeting guys at the mall wasn't really his thing but he didn't mind taking a peek every now and then.

"I got the job." Corey told him when found Maine at the food court. "I start tomorrow and Lincoln gave me forty hours this week."

"That's what's up." Maine congratulated him.

"I only get minimum wage, but I guess that's cool. I gotta start somewhere. Who knows, I may like the job—I already like some of the clothes and know I fit the image they're looking for to sell." Corey was excited.

Maine was happy for him. Getting the job at Aerostyle would be a great asset if Corey stayed with them until July. It was on Corey to decide if he was going to be successful and Maine hoped that he made the right decision.

45

End of Semester

Three A's, three B's. Not a bad way for Maine to end the semester. He logged off his NC Tech account after making sure his Spring semester classes were set.

Maine wanted to sell his books, but he decided to take Willie's advice and keep the books from this semester. Willie had told him and Spence they would become the foundation and reference guides for anything they would need to know if business.

Maine walked out of his room and seen Corey rushing out the door. Aerostyle wasted little time in hiring him and he wished Corey the best of luck when it came to dealing with Lincoln. Cordell was sitting on the couch watching BET.

"You check your grades?" Maine started the conversation. He and Cordell hadn't spoken since Corey moved in.

"I'm straight on that." Cordell answered without looking at him. "I already know what I got and my Spring semester is good, too."

"Look man," Maine sat on the loveseat so he could face Cordell. "I see what you were saying about Corey needing to grow up. I saw some things yesterday I ended up checking him on."

"I'm good now. I said what I needed to say." Cordell looked at Maine. "I just don't want you or anyone else babying him because I can't toughen him up if we keep bailing him out. By the way, thanks for helping him get that job at Aerostyle. I meant what I said about him having my money on the first."

"Yeah. We can't have no freeloaders." Maine co-signed. "And I told him he needed to keep that job until he found something else —I actually suggested he needed to get a second job."

"Knowing Lincoln's punk ass, he'll try to be possessive over Corey's time. Aerostyle always needs help so Corey will be gone fifty to sixty hours a week." Cordell smiled.

"Think he'll go back to school?" Maine wondered.

"Don't know, don't care." Cordell flipped the television off. "My job as the older brother is to help make Corey a man. It's a big world out there and I'm doing my job to make sure he doesn't turn into a bitch. Corey can't expect a handout or for Dad to bail him out every time he turns around."

Maine agreed with that. He looked at the time and knew he had about an hour before he had to get ready for Willie's. "I can't wait to get my Jeep man—this walking and catching the bus shit is for the birds."

"So what are you gonna do when you get it?"

"I'm gonna see what work needs to be done. It's the end of the year so I may upgrade to a newer car, but in reality, I need to keep the Jeep at least another year. That way I can trade it in in July and save a few thousand so I can make a large down payment or outright payoff what I do get." Cordell planned.

"That's what's up. I'm gonna keep the Buick." Maine answered as he felt his phone buzz.

Come see me tonight. 'Keem texted him.

Cool. Maine responded. He knew Spence was going out of town with his family so he'd only see Spence a few days before he came back for Spring semester. Chelle and Yonna, like most of the students on campus, went home for the holidays. Maine didn't chill with the locals like that and he did like 'Keem.

Maine got ready to go to work. The holidays were coming fast and the store stayed busy with people buying CDs and tapes as stocking stuffers and last minute present ideas.

***

'Keem opened the door to his loft. Maine enjoyed the look of his dark chocolate body.

"Why aren't you going home?" Maine asked as he stepped inside. The smoky fragrance of lavender, chamomile and myrrh teased Maine's nose. He loved that about 'Keem's home, it was always so fresh and so clean. Maine could tell that the bathroom was recently clean and the dishes drying in the dish rack.

"My family went to Sudan for the holidays." 'Keem answered as he followed Maine inside.

"How did I know you were going to answer the door naked?" Maine took off his shirt and got comfortable on the couch.

"Don't act like you didn't know I'm a nudist." 'Keem took a seat on the love seat. "Renee went to be with her family in the Trinidad. I stayed behind to condition for wrestling and to make sure I was ready for the outdoor track and field team. I want to do throw the javelin and shot put this year."

"So you're not going to be around family at all for Christmas?" Maine couldn't believe it. He only planned on spending a few hours to get the rest of his things from his moms, but he'd spend the bulk of the time with Cordell and Corey before he came back to work.

"I told you my family is Muslim." 'Keep replied. "Christmas doesn't mean to me what it means to you."

Maine hadn't been in church all semester. He only planned on going if Cordell and Corey went. "I'll be up here most of the holiday too. I'm the assistant manager at Willie's so I have to work."

"Congratulations on that." 'Keem got up and walked to the kitchen. "You want anything to drink?"

"I'm good." Maine looked as 'Keem brought out the alcohol. "I'll take a shot with you." He offered so 'Keem wouldn't drink alone.

Maine loved looking at 'Keem. His movements were fluid and flawless. 'Keem handed Maine a shot and he threw it back fast. "Damn Maine. You could have at least waited until I sat down and had a shot with me."

'Keem poured him another shot and this time, they took the shot together. "You spend any time with Spence away from the frat?"

"Yeah, we were just together last night." 'Keem admitted. Maine chuckled to himself. He was sure Spence and 'Keem got it in before he left. "It's a delicate balance we're learning to master together. We even talked about mixing it up with Renee and Vanessa. I'm sure Renee will go for it."

Maine loved to be a fly on the wall for that hookup. "I guess I better get me a girlfriend."

"You better claim Sierra." 'Keem suggested. "We said that before. You still messing with Yonna and Chelle?"

"Kinda—moreso Yonna. I was gonna let her go but I hadn't gotten around to that." Maine told him.

'Keem poured another glass. "So you still gonna go deeper, huh?"

"Y'all gonna stop bringing up Homecoming. That was two months ago." Maine put his glass down.

"I'm just fucking with you. I really want you to give me my Christmas gift." 'Keem licked his lips.

Maine knew what he wanted. "Spence give it to you already?"

"Last night."

Maine believed him. Spence didn't mention it but he respected Spence's ability to be discrete. And he knew the only reason 'Keem told him was because he was still trying to build that trust.

"So how do you want it?" Maine got up and unbuttoned his pants.

"I wanna ride it." 'Keem got up.

Maine followed 'Keem to the bed and when they got to the foot, they shared a deep, passionate kiss. He could feel his nature rising and 'Keem reached down and grabbed. 'Keem stroked his and Maine reached down to stroke 'Keem. "Did y'all flip?" Maine was more upset about not being able to watch then the fact that they did it.

"Yeah—but you know I don't care to top. I was just enjoying being taken care of." 'Keem pushed Maine on the bed and straddled him. 'Keem leaned forward and kissed Maine again as Maine cupped his ass.

Maine scooted up on the bed until his head almost reached the headboard. 'Keem grabbed some Astroglide out of the nightstand and poured some on Maine's throbbing dick. "The strawberry one smells better."

Maine watched as 'Keem rubbed some on hole and then mounted him again. He couldn't believe he was about to take that trip, again. 'Keem lifted up and grabbed Maine's lubed member and rubbed his mushroom tip at his opening. Maine knew once he got inside 'Keem, there was no turning back. Maine's tip broke through 'Keem's entryway and they both gasped for air. 'Keem twisted his body and moved his ass in a circle, the palms of his hands resting on Maine's chest. 'Keem worked his way down Maine's thick dick until his ass kissed Maine's nuts.

"Shit!" They both stared at each other as 'Keem slowly rocked on him up and down. 'Keem felt good inside and Maine didn't ease up on the thrusting either. After a while, he rolled 'Keem on his back, put 'Keem's legs on his shoulders and dug in there. 'Keem's sphincter had a better grip on Maine and the tightness caused them both to rock fast and moan.

"I'm gonna cum!" Maine yelled.

"I'm cumming," 'Keem yelled. Maine looked down and could see 'Keem's leche pour on his pecs and abs like icing on a cake. Maine thrusted and released himself deep inside 'Keem.

Maine and 'Keem kissed for a moment and Maine rolled over, closed his eyes and went to sleep. The ass was that good.

Post Credits

March 2018

The pounding in Maine head increased as he slowly opened his eyes. *How the hell did I end up on the floor,* he wondered as he slowly stood up and shook his head. He looked at his naked body. The brand on his left peck, which was his undergraduate chapter's favorite fraternal symbol, still looked nice and sharp. His muscle tone was more define then it was in undergrad. The V-cut was perfect. His crotch was perfectly shaved.

It had taken him a year to lose all the extra weight he'd gained from taking care of his uncle and working a job that literally tried to kill him. He stood up and he looked down. The stretch marks served as a reminder of his weight loss. Maine looked in the mirror and couldn't believe he had a shiny bald head. His goatee had a nice mix of silver and black hair. He smiled and his pearly white teeth shined. Colgate paid him well to show off their work. In the mirror also saw 'Keem turn over.

"Really motherfucker, you kicked me out the bed?" Maine struggled to keep his composure. He didn't want 'Keem to see him mad, but he knew this argument was gonna happen and he wanted to get it over.

"No bitch," 'Keem sat up, "I kicked *Corey* out the bed. I told you about calling me that shit. My name is..."

"Dawid Aakil Hakeem Allah, the sensitive bitch motherfucker." Maine cut him off.

'Keem jumped out of bed. "You really want to start with me motherfucker!" 'Keem got in Maine's face. "It's not even seven in the morning and you in my house trying to fuck with me. Last time we threw these fists, it didn't end well for you pretty boy. For a moment, I forgot I love you and beat you to a pulp."

Maine tried to block the incident from his mind. It was a birthday he'd never forget. Their fight played a role in him fleeing Charlotte and moving to Asheville to look after his uncle. That, and getting scammed out in a business deal that went south.

"I fuckin' hate you!" He gritted through clinched teeth.

"I hate you, too, nigga." 'Keem stepped in Maine's space and kissed him. Their dicks touched. The feeling turned him on, but Maine was so mad. Once again, 'Keem took him there.

"Man move!" Maine shoved 'Keem and tried to move around. 'Keem pushed him back. "I'm trying to get my son!"

"Oh! So you gonna get your son from Cordell's, but you gonna leave my boys behind? You a selfish and crooked motherfucker. I knew I shouldn't have let my wife have a baby with your punk ass!"

Maine rolled his eyes at 'Keem. He couldn't say shit because he remembered he begged 'Keem to let Renee carry his seed. Maine loved 'Keem and Renee's unconventional marriage and that he was a part of it. "I will get David and Aakil when I pick up Damon." Maine told him as he walked through the walk-in closet to get to the private shower 'Keem and Renee had in their room. He turned the water on and looked at 'Keem out of the side of his. "Look man, I'm not trying to fight with you. I didn't appreciate waking up on the floor when I know you were wrapped in my arms last night."

'Keem stepped into the walk-in closet and grabbed a set of towels. "I wanted to make love to you this morning. Enjoy our vacation before I go to Spartanburg to handle business. I'm trying to make sure the Carolina Panthers win a super bowl before I retire next season. I already got two rings with the Steelers, I want to get one with Cam."

Maine knew that was the goal. 'Keem wanted three rings and he remembered the celebrations 'Keem and Renee threw when the black and yellow came through.

'Keem grabbed Maine from behind after he set up the tub with a gracious amount of lavender soap and bubbles. He was still a little sore from being on the floor for God knows how long, and he felt like his head hit the nightstand or the wall. He could feel the Remy in his stomach and knew that he and 'Keem had too much to drink last night.

Maine leaned back and kissed 'Keem. "You know I could never hate you." Maine admitted as he took a step into the tub. It was nice and steamy and had room for the both of them.

'Keem stepped inside and as he sat down, he leaned his back into Maine's chest. "If I hated you, I would've left you at that group home."

The last thing Maine wanted to be reminded of was his stint at People Helping People In Need, Inc. Working for the group home and with racist white people was the worst experience in his life. If it weren't for his friends and his brothers, he wouldn't have made it through.

"I know babe. We been doing this thing for almost twenty years. That's longer than most marriages gay or straight last." 'Keem laid his head back and enjoyed Maine rubbing on his chest.

Over the years' Maine and 'Keem developed a boomerang type of love. They loved hard and fucked hard for a while, then one would piss the other off and they'd have a big fight, usually with words. Then somehow, they'd get back together—half the time with Renee's help because she didn't let too many men get to close to her 'Keem. Maine loved Renee too as she helped him keep his bisexuality intact. Out of respect for her, Maine stopped messing with women she didn't approve of after she gave birth to his son seven years ago. To this day, he only barebacked with Spence and 'Keem.

He felt bad for how things ended with him and Spence. He called Spence by Corey's name, too. They'd hook up a few times but it wasn't the same. Spence went on to manage a music publishing company that owned the rights to songs written by S'More and Tristan Tunz, another one of Maine's exes. They only speak at fraternity functions and the occasional Christmas card.

"Tomorrow, I go renew my license so I can continue cutting at Cut Up if I have to." Maine reminded 'Keem as they continued to soak in the tub.

"You gotta keep that up. And don't forget to make sure you have the bartending stuff taken care of. It's about to get busy this summer. With Cordell managing the straight shops and you managing the gay ones, both of you need to stay on top of the business.

"On the real, I'm proud of Cordell. It's been five years since he's been clean and I think it would be cool if we throw him a celebration party." 'Keem suggested. He washed his body and soon left Maine in the tub by himself.

"Let me know what you want to do and I'm on board." Maine promised as he emptied the water and stepped out of the tub. He grabbed 'Keem's vetiver and hemp lotion and rubbed it all over his body. He also applied the body oil to enhance the scent.

"I think we can get the undergrad chapter to do a program and some of the other alumni brothers to help sponsor some drug recovery programs in honor of Cordell. I like that he helps others recover and fight drug addiction." 'Keen suggested as he slipped his black slacks over his jock strap. He wasn't surprised that 'Keem almost went commando. That was his style.

Maine grabbed his button up shirt and blue slacks from his section of the closet. Having three young men for the next few hours was going to be exciting. He planned on taking the boys to Chuck-E-Cheese while he set up appointments for potential video shoots and upscale events at the seven locations.

"Aye 'Keem," Maine called out. "When was the last time you checked on Elijah to see how he's doing?"

He remembered 'Keem's friends from Florida A&M. He knew 'Keem checked in to make sure the boy was okay and that he didn't want for anything. He knew Ian and 'Keem stayed in touch over the years and was surprised when Elijah reached out to him a few years ago to find out more information about his father, Chaz. They both were surprised that the boy found out about his father's sexual connection to 'Keem, but they respected him for asking the source instead of whatever information the boy got his hands on.

"He's coming into his own." 'Keem answered. "When he graduates, I'll send him the money I put aside for him so he can go to school, start a business or just enjoy life."

One of the reasons Maine respected 'Keem. He liked that 'Keem always looked out for his friends and fought to lift them up. One of the attributes Maine fell in love with about 'Keem. As he got dressed and grabbed the keys to his fully loaded silver 2014 Hyundai Sonata, he prayed he and 'Keem could keep it going for as long as possible. At the moment, Maine had young men he had to look after and take care of and he was doing to make sure they grew up to be like 'Keem. The most of important thing in the world was to make sure that everything done was about them.

Maine October Winston will return…

Style & Grayce by Isaiah David Paul & Cedric Quincy
GABB** by Jaz Punchard

And THE AVENGERS will win the war against Thanos!!!

I can't help it, I'm a fan.

Acknowledgments

First, God, thank you for keeping me sane. 2016-19 have been some tough years but with you, I made it. I look forward to your next assignment. I pray I pass with flying colors.

My family and friends for helping me make it through another book. It's been so many now. Thank you for accepting the CQ joints like you do all the others.

To the readers who supported this novel when it was called TOUCH ME, TEASE ME and was one of the premiere fan fiction novels in 2016. Y'all helped me make it through one of the craziest times in my life.

Tyson Anthony, man, you have taken everyone on a memorable journey with ABOUT HIM. When you told everyone that you looked forward to seeing what we'd come up with as we waited for season two...I boldly claimed Vincent. I thought I'd do some short stories about Vincent's semester at NC Tech with Damien—didn't know I'd do a full-length novel. Thank you for the challenge. I got to explore my own collegiate journey and relive a life I never thought I'd see again.

Henderson Maddox, thank you for bringing ABOUT HIM to film. This has been one of the best literature-to-motion picture adaptations I've ever seen. You and the team definitely broke the internet. Alvin Agarrat, you've been a big supporter and a bigger friend in our short time together. Thank you for listening to my visions and continuing to encourage me to make them come true. Kimberly Jones...our fearless mother. I have intentions to make myself more visible at as many literary events as possible. Can't wait to see your work in print.

Gary Lavard, my muse. Watching you play Vincent has been fun to say the least. You work just as hard, if not harder on your film career as I do on the books. As always, wishing you the best.

Rico Pruitt, Lando King, Sherrod Willis, Alex Jante and Rahim King Brazil, thank you for lending me personal pictures to support my promotion of this fan fiction piece and forwarding the postings as I made them. Brandon Karson, Darone Okolie and Tripp Ali, y'all played pivotal roles for making ABOUT HIM what it is today. And Tripp, thank you for the cover, greatly appreciated. Thank you for making the story your passion and for bringing our favorite characters to life.

Jaxon Grant, thank you for allowing me to pay homage to your novels in this piece. Between your help and motivation, I got it done. I hope I did Chaz and Ian justice as well.

Carter J. Banks, brother what can I say? I can't wait for THE MAN BEHIND THE MAN 3 to come out. I know your fans are going to love it. Keep moving forward.

D. Rashad Battle, Jai A. Smallz, Lore, James L. Gibson, Keith King Jordan, Quintarrius Shakir, Warren, Deryl Ali, y'all have been an inspiration. Poe, we gotta get up again in Durham or something. Mondell Pope, you need to send me the rough draft of the book coming out in July and the book you're working on now —thank you labelmate.

JD Morrison, going through this novel again without you has been very difficult. Thank you for taking this project seriously and holding me accountable. May you enjoy your rest. Your insight helped me with my presentation. Chrishawnna Perry and Crystal Satterfield, thank you for helping me make sure I represented "NC Tech" to the fullest and for reminding me how it went down when we were at T.

Lee Hayes, James Earl Hardy and Stanley Bennett Clay—thank you for paving the way for this generation of LGBTQ authors and for reminding me that representing the "B" and the "Q" (even though I'm really Pan, but who cares) is nothing to be ashamed of. I do what I do. Author Skyy, and Fabiola Joseph for making room for me. When I come out with my "L" book, I hope y'all enjoy it.

Travis Hunter, for always making sure I'm where I need to be and polished at all times.

Liam Caldwell, I believe you were the first to go from novel to webseries in this genre. Thank you. Corey Knott and Wesley Henderson, thank you for keeping me in check and helping me sharpen the iron. Can't wait to see what y'all come up with. Rico Milan, bruh, I have not forgotten, I want it. Ra'Mone Marquis—can't wait to see The Uglies. I have a feeling I fit in.

King Brooks, I promise to do a better job of taking care of myself this year.

If I didn't name you, please don't take it personal. Pray for me.

Cedric Quincy

Follow Me on Twitter: @cedricquincy
Follow Me on Instagram: @cedric_quincy

Like My Facebook Page: Cedric Quincy Facebook Page

Email Me: cedricquincy@gmail.com

About the Author

Cedric Quincy is a private family man with an ex-wife and a few children who understand that he lives on the wild side. Now settling down, he stays on the down low in an effort to protect his family from his shenanigans. He writes erotica and speculative fiction.

A controversial literary figure known under a more popular name; he is a well-respected faith fiction, young adult author and controversial columnist where he has written and contributed to over a hundred books.